CW01666515

A TIME FOR CHANGE

D.S. WEST

This edition first published in paperback by
Michael Terence Publishing in 2022
www.mtp.agency

ISBN 9781800944725

Michael Terence
Publishing

This novel is dedicated to all people suffering from any form of cancer. I have been battling incurable cancer, called multiple myeloma, for six years and took to writing to help me cope.

I hope anyone reading this book will enjoy it as much as I had writing the story.

Also, I would like to thank my family and close friends for their kind patience and support.

I

In June of 2022, four people with a passion for metal detecting live in different parts of the UK, and their paths are about to cross for the second time. Their first encounter was at the yearly metal detectorists convention in Manchester three months ago. They all sat at the same table, and there was plenty to choose from as other tables were empty, but they were all drawn together on table ten. Introductions were made, and all shook hands. All agreed they had not met before but felt it was the right place to be; they relayed stories of how they took up this hobby that interested them all. They all talked the night away as though they had known each other for a lifetime. Then, as they parted company, names and phone contacts were exchanged for future events, promising to keep in touch, which rarely happens in this hectic world. Yet, that simple hand gesture has set something in motion that none of them knew would change the lives of others and themselves.

John Downs, forty years of age, a maths teacher in a local comprehensive school, happily married. Jane, his partner of twenty years, gave birth to twins Susan and Stuart. Now reaching the age that most parents hate, they have to make life choices that will dictate how their lives will pan out in the future. Both hope they have given them the tools to choose wisely; they are puzzled by John's fixation on metal detecting; it is so dull and nerdy. But the nerdy father had given them a good education in maths and other subjects that would certainly help them through their next steps to university. So instead, John had developed a weekend obsession with finding objects in the local vicinity of Ingleby Barwick.

It started when he found a roman coin in a field where building works had disturbed the ground. Even he was surprised by how excited he got, and this started his obsession, finding the odd trinket of historical nature but nothing of great value.

Denise Nichol was a housewife who took early retirement from the local banking services at the ripe old age of fifty. She became disillusioned with the severity of the banking system, she wanted to help struggling people in the community, but her hands were tied by the system. Her husband Don worked away offshore on a gas platform, working a rota of two weeks on and three weeks off. Many neighbours were jealous of his time off, often calling him a lucky so and so, to his face, not realising he hated it intensely; only the time off and his colleagues made the job worthwhile. Two near misses on the helicopter sealed his fate, and he left long before some of his colleagues; in hindsight, financially, the wrong decision, this was just another one of the many bad decisions in his life. While he was away, Denise needed something to fill her weekends; after all, your friends only needed to see you now and then, and contact by phone was an easy option. She needed to get out, but what could entice her? Denise took up her hobby after watching an excitable woman on the internet gesticulating the virtues of metal detecting. She was sure she must have had a glass of wine or two; the lady's enthusiasm sucked Denise into her new hobby.

It was like a classic sales pitch, which you cannot say no to when pushed into a corner.

Where could she buy her first metal detector to follow her passion for her newfound hobby?

Then, fate steps in, and she receives a message that she does not want to hear, her Uncle William is gravely ill, and he is desperate to speak to her. Denise rushed to the hospital, she did not know William was sick, and his rapid decline only served to fuel her anxiety.

On her arrival, he asked everyone to leave the room quickly so that he could speak to Denise in private. Since childhood, William had been her go-to man when she had a problem, her favourite uncle who would do anything for her. Denise and her uncle had been close, helping her grow into the woman she is now, but even she did not know about his metal-detecting hobby.

William told her after everyone had left that he had bequeathed his metal detector to her. Then, telling her, before he went to the afterlife, 'You will find something that will change your life; I have seen it, don't be afraid,' his eyes closed, and his grip loosened on Denise's hand as he slipped away with almost a smile on his face, Denise sobs uncontrollably.

Living in the centre of Leeds, she had never considered such an item before and started to think, was it fate she was there to hear his remark? After all, a metal detector was mentioned on two separate occasions; it is fate; indeed, she must pursue it now. It was an emotional time, so she took the bull by the horns and took up metal detecting. Over the year, she had found odd items, one of which is now showcased in the local museum, a small roman dagger, her proudest moment to date.

At thirty years of age, Peter Howes is a long-time university student at Portsmouth studying philosophy.

Supplementing his income by working at the local fast-food chain, hoping any degree will help him climb the ladder to success.

But unfortunately, too many students mistake him for one of the teachers; he had been on campus far too long; even though he laughed, maybe it was time to move on. But, standing at 1.8mteres tall and a regular at the gym, he is well-toned as the mirror could vouch for; constantly looking at his abs, vanity can be a curse to many men, but Peter loved it.

He decided to take up detecting because of Julie, who was at the next desk to him in the classroom; she had taken it up a year ago with some success, showing her findings to Peter. He was thinking maybe a couple of weekends to keep her company, but you never know where it might lead. As with all detectorists, the first find is the best. It stimulated Peter's interest; he was hooked.

After a couple of months, his relationship petered away, but his interest only grew; the odd find had increased his fiscal income, so the desire to find objects became money-driven, not historical. Nevertheless, Peter had sold several items, and his savings showed some signs of this success.

Joanne Hope is from the small village of Danby in the North Yorkshire Moors. She would only admit to being thirty-five but, in essence, had just pushed past forty.

As a result, her birthday cards are taken down swiftly after one day. Joanne loved to walk in the moors and watch nature at its best, and she was a country girl at heart. While on one of her many walks, she found an old metal pot and, to her disbelief, found out it was over two hundred years old.

An idea was born to buy her first metal detector, and she has not looked back since; even her husband, Kevin, is envious of the joy she finds from her new hobby.

Positive and assured in her work as an HR Manager for the local police force, she took up this unusual hobby to help wind down from the constant pressures of work, which sometimes can be a thankless task. Joanne's partner works as a sales manager in a car dealership, often cursing that 65% of customers always try it on to get a cheaper deal.

They tell him they can get a better deal down the road, and he tells them to go to the other dealer in annoyance. But come back when you have read the fine print; you will find our deal is far superior. Working most weekends, he has accepted that Joanne needs some time to wind down, and it is only one day anyway. Joanne, like the rest, found very little, but the fresh air alone was enough to keep her going. All were regular contributors to the local metal detectorist clubs.

It was where people could banter about their finds and even be surprised by some of the monetary values discussed in their discoveries.

2

On the third of June, there was an unusual storm, especially for the time of year, so the Met office gave it the name Storm Chase; typically, it was usually a women's name many people were baffled by the chosen name. Winds over seventy miles an hour with significant lightning strikes across the dark sky, illuminating vast areas of land. In Haltwhistle, a small town in Northumberland, locals were quite concerned as they had not witnessed anything like it before. Locals are proud to say that the lightning strikes seemed to be centred around the town, which coincides with Haltwhistle being the centre of the United Kingdom. Unfortunately, many people are oblivious to the significance of this event, but in four areas of the UK, four people will have a restless night with visions of the past, or are they only dreams?

In the days to come, with these memories in their heads, each one will be drawn to a field on the outskirts of Haltwhistle. The field has not been used for farming or building due to a covenant on the land; the locals inform anyone who enquires 'that it is cursed.

The field is exactly one square mile, from corner to corner; it has not been touched for hundreds of years, yet the ground is not overgrown. Locals are amazed, but as time passes, people forget, as it is located down a disused lane. The four detectorists cannot get the visions from their minds, then pictures of the field start to come, and they feel compelled to find it, but how, where could it be? Three nights pass before it becomes clear, a vision of the UK, a line from one corner to the other, and they dissect the centre of the UK.

Unknown to them, something is about to start beyond their wildest dreams.

Can they cope?

What are the meanings of these dreams/visions?

Can they decipher what they see?

3

By the weekend, the desire to discover what is happening is getting stronger, should they go off on a whimsical journey. But, of course, it could be dangerous; good grief, they all think as if they are one, they are only looking at a field.

Joanne, always pragmatic, decides to use the internet to see if she can find any details of the area where the cross has been located; it gives coordinates. She searches around the area to find a farmhouse, and a postcode is found nearby, unusually not for the farmhouse. Surely a farmer must own the land; Joanne decides to contact the local land registry as she will need permission from the owners before going on the land. The following day Joanne receives a call from the land registry; this adds more mystery to her task. She is informed that the records pre-date 1862, when the registry was formed. But a covenant has a fixed date that a sealed document can be opened on the third of June 2050. Perplexed, she goes back on the internet; she scrolls over the farmhouse; the detail is sufficient enough to see that it is extremely old. Her thoughts are. 'Why does no one know about it.'

Peter, the furthest away, used his university contacts and talked to the history professor Luke Warme at Durham University, often cursing his parent's sense of humour for his name choice. The university is only 48 miles from Haltwhistle, so he knows it well. However, Luke informs him it is a local legend; nobody is allowed on the land, and getting permission to walk on it will be challenging.

Peter thanked him; this only made him more determined to try; his desire to find out was now more compelling.

He books a hotel for Friday evening; he is going come hell or high water; Peter must go, and he has no idea why. So, Peter sets off early on Friday morning; he has over three hundred miles to go; it will take around eight hours if he stops regularly. Hence, the added worry of his father's old Ford Escort 1600, which had seen much better days and ceased to function due to poor maintenance on many occasions. Worse, he had not replaced the eight-track cassette still in the car. He thought that by the time he got to the Northeast, he would become proficient in sixties music. He crosses his heart as he starts the engine, thinking, 'I hope the gods are with me today, even though he was a devout atheist. Strange how we call on a celestial being when we need help; maybe if I give it a good blast on the motorway, he thinks, it will help the engine.' But, instead, it gently purrs away the best it has ever sounded; that celestial being must have listened, his confidence growing by the minute.

Denise had decided that if she drove to Haltwhistle, there should be enough local knowledge; it would be easy to find, forever the pragmatist. So John had been in touch with the local detectorists club to see if they knew anything of this field, precisely one square mile in measurement. He was slightly taken aback by the reply that it was local knowledge and cursed. But, never to back down from a challenge, John has decided to go on Saturday. All four made separate arrangements; it was unknown that three would arrive at 10 am on Saturday.

Each questioned why the desire to travel such a distance was something they had not done before.

Joanne had worked for the police for several years and used her contacts to get a contact number for the farm that nobody knew about, 'there is no farm there, she was informed.' Returning to her computer and refreshing her internet, she can see the farm in all its glory.

She will arrive early to ask for that valuable permission to walk on the land. The non-existent farmhouse intrigued Joanne, now more determined to get to the bottom of her little mystery; Saturday came. And she left her home at 7. 00 am, leaving a note for her husband. Then, putting everything into her mini clubman estate car the night before, two flasks later, she is on her way.

Peter is now accustomed to his father's sixties music, singing away at the top of his voice on odd occasions, motorists passing by, smiling, all-knowing what he is doing. He stops at the motorway services to freshen up and get fresh coffee, to keep himself going. By the time he gets to the final motorway services before he reaches his hotel, he is singing the sixties songs out loud. OAPs wondered how the young man could remember songs from their era. Peter books into his cheap hotel, noticeable by the lack of facilities, 'well you get what you pay for,' he thinks it is only for one night, thank goodness. He will have a couple of drinks at the bar and retire for the evening; it has been a long journey, especially by yourself. Peter smiled when he saw the bar, two seats, and it was full, 'oh, if I had only gone to a two-star hotel.' Sitting down at the bar, he ordered a drink, pleasantly surprised by the barmaid, who mentioned, 'you must be in room 6; I know that room well.'

Peter will be happy he came to that one-star hotel, even though it will only be for one night, but he will remember that night for all the right reasons.

Joanne is driving along the moors roads, her mind excited by the unknown; before long, she has reached motorway traffic, quiet for the time of day, and she points her mini clubman towards Durham.

John kisses his wife goodbye; she is still half asleep; a night out with the girls will do that to you, looking for the headache pills as John disappears.

John turns out of Ingleby Barwick onto the A19, heading for the A1; it won't be long before he gets to his destination.

Denise has packed her picnic hamper, putting in more than usual; she does not know why it seemed the right thing to do in her mind. As she drives up the M1 towards Durham, her mind is getting flashbacks of her meeting with John, Joanne, and Peter for no apparent reason. Unknown to her, the others are getting the same flashbacks, all cursing they had not been in touch; they will ring when they get back home. The sky is a beautiful clear blue, and the sun is shining, with no wind; what a great day to go detecting, they thought in unison.

4

Joanne turned off the A69 and toward Haltwhistle via B6322, not realising she had passed the small lane she needed to go down. Arriving in Haltwhistle at 9. am, much earlier than she had anticipated, Joanne had decided to park up and gather her thoughts and have that obligatory caffeine boost of strong coffee to make sure she was awake. Settling her nerves, Joanne was thankful she had printed an ariel view of the area; she could see the farmhouse at the top of the lane, the field looking fresh, the green grass exceptional in colour. Joanne did not realise that she was lucky indeed for this snapshot because, shortly, this farmhouse would disappear till the next millennium, if required. Looking at the picture, she could see the small lane; she was annoyed having driven past it. With a deep intake of breath, Joanne started the car and turned the car around, and headed toward the A69 and the small lane. Ten minutes later, she found the lane with no signs of being used for several years. She stopped her heart racing. Joanne stepped out of the car, looking down the lane to see if she could drive the car down it. Walking fifty to sixty metres up the lane, Joanne assessed that the car would go down the lane quite easily; as she turned around to return to the car, she gazed at the field. It was immaculate, looking over the one-metre-high hedge, staring in amazement; this could not be right. The hairs on the back of her neck raised; this only added to the situation's intensity. Joanne got back into her car and slowly drove down the lane; she came to a dead-end; looking to her left, she could see the farmhouse, and her jaw dropped.

Joanne felt as though she was in times long gone; the farmhouse looked like a moment lost in time; her first thoughts were, 'good grief, it must be two hundred years old; no one can live there, surely.'

Thirty metres from the lane end, old farm tools and wooden barrels were strewn across the ground, even an old hand cart with a pitchfork stuck in the hay, as though somebody had walked away and left everything. No farm machinery, she expected to hear hens clucking as she smiled. Yet, as she got out of the car, a sense of calm overcame her, always curious but unafraid.

Behind the house was a forest, the trees tightly packed, having grown to excess, which she had not noticed in her picture, wondering why the forestry commission had not managed it properly. The sun cast shadows across the trees, falling short of the farmhouse. Walking toward the house, a wisp of wind moves the leaves on the trees. As she gets closer to the house, the cart suddenly falls forward onto its handle, and the hay and fork fall to the ground; it startled her for a moment but did not deter Joanne's curiosity. Although Joanne was only two metres from the front door, she heard the sound of the door latch, and the door opened; she was still not afraid.

Nobody came out, but a friendly voice called her in, 'Please come in; I do not know your name,' this was the first time she felt nervous; she hesitated, 'my name is Joanne.'

'Do not be afraid; please come in.' she hesitates for a moment. On entering, the visibility was poor, but she could see what she perceived as an old gentleman, but there was something different about him; she could not put her finger on it due to the dim light.

The sound of what she perceived to be a man's voice was gentle and soothing, and he beckoned her to sit down in a chair from years gone by; inside the house, it was an antique dealer's heaven.

Joanne thought, 'this is eerie! Why am I not scared.'

'I would offer you a drink, but we do not have time.'

Then, Joanne noticed the man did not speak, but she could hear his voice in her head. It was the only time a sense of panic came to the fore.

'Do not be afraid, as I only have a short time to tell you why you are here.'

Joanne relaxed; she noticed his clothes were not modern, but she could not place the era, dressed in a fully buttoned-up white shirt. With a leather waistcoat, breeches, and leather boots, making a mental note for later, she was mesmerised by the man's eyes, more prominent than normal, but no whites of the eyes but a solid light grey. His facial appearance was slightly elongated but smooth, which puzzled her, as in her mind, he seemed old, his nose smaller than most, in many ways childlike, and a small mouth, but it did not move; seated in a rocking chair. Yet he seemed to command the room without saying anything. Even now, it did not worry her that he was not human

'What do you mean a short time.'

'I can only tell one of the four; the rest will hear what I am saying to you.'

'What others.'

'They will be here shortly; you know them; they are not strangers; you have met them all before; your meeting has started this essential task.'

'Who are you? I do not understand.'

'My name is Asku; I do not belong to your world yet; my race helped create what is in front of me.'

'What?' still, she did not panic, her curiosity getting the better of her; she had no fear, such was the calmness of the voice in her head.

As Asku said, Peter, Denise, and John could hear the conversation in their heads, yet they all felt the calmness that Joanne was feeling.

They were still driving but only a short distance away; they all pulled over to comprehend what was happening; they should have been frightened but were not; such was the strength in Asku's voice. They all listened intently, with each thinking they were the only ones involved until he mentioned others, but who were they?

'I have so many questions to ask.'

'Many will be answered on your journey.'

'What journey? I have to be home to make dinner tonight.'

'Do not worry; you will be home tonight.'

'I do not understand; what do you mean.'

I will start at the beginning, but please do not interrupt; look at the wall to your left.'

At this instruction, a light shone on the wall, but Joanne could not see where it originated from, for what seemed a long time was only twenty minutes.

Asku explained the origin of his species and what the people say on this planet; now, we conducted a social experiment on a disused planet. When we saw the amount of water on the plant, we knew it would sustain a lifeform but did not know how it would mutate into the lifeform now before me. Joanne was compelled to speak but could not; she could not open her mouth; Asku raised his hand to his mouth.

Joanne took this to mean she should keep quiet till he finished. She did not comprehend he had only four fingers, slightly longer than most people.

The others wanted to scream questions in the air that no one could hear; they also could see the images in their heads and yet did not panic.

Asku carries on; we came 200 000 years ago, the planet was going through many changes, it was dangerous and an uninviting world; many of my kind told us to leave it alone. No one can survive in that environment; strangely, you are reaching that same scenario now by the many decisions your leaders have taken.

We sedated two Homosapiens, as you have named them, one male and one female, and placed a genetic marker in them, which is only visible to my kind, it was placed to see how it would evolve. We have visited several times in various forms, we can manipulate what you see, but we were not allowed to interfere as your species evolved. Sometimes we came as orbs or a light form, and your leaders still try to hide it from you even now. On many occasions that we have visited, some of our crafts have crashed, and we have lost several of our species. I must find one of these to get home, and I must get to one of them from one of your bodies; my conscious self will transfer into that craft; it will be a journey nobody else will experience. You will return as though nothing has happened, and the world will change. It was the only time a sense of panic came to everyone, and Asku calmed their thoughts. I will explain further; only your subconscious will be used; your body form will remain here.

You will be in your ancestor's bodies; minutes, days, and even weeks will pass in your minds, but you will return to this day when your task is completed.

I cannot make you do something you do not want to; my voice will only be guidance. Since our first visit, we did not realise how your mutation has a belligerence for war, with no feelings for other beings. In many ways, this is why your planet lives in isolation, and many species would have made first contact but are afraid of your barbaric nature. But this planet is dying now, and we as a collective can alter that; that is why you are all here today. The four listen intently to Asku, but human nature is scepticism; will they all believe what he says? Could they cause more harm than good?

They may cause problems that will cause the human race untold misery. Nevertheless, it is a risk that Asku must take; another millennium and this planet will be dead; they must help. So Asku tells them, 'The field outside is a perfect square; there is a gap precisely in the middle; another opening is directly opposite. You must split into two at these gaps and work towards the corners so that you all reach them simultaneously. And by using the detection instruments, that you have all brought with you here today. You must do this as the instruments will generate a protective shield around the field for your safety. All are starting to get nervous, yet again, the calmness of Asku's voice; their nerves are quickly forgotten. Asku carries on; once you all reach each corner; your machines will detect something; I must insist you all do this simultaneously to get maximum protection around the field. In their heads, all participants agree they will do this, not knowing why and yet it feels like the right thing to do in their minds.

Joanne is mesmerised by Asku; another five minutes pass, and she can hear the sound of other vehicles coming up the lane.

5

Asku tells Joanne, 'It is time to go now; I wish you all well in your journey of discovery.'

Joanne wants to ask countless questions, but she does not have time with the arrival of the others. She thanks him, but he does not reply, not wanting to leave, the others beeping their car horns for attention. Finally, Joanne is forced to step outside into the farmyard; she hears the door latch close, turns around, and wonders what has just happened. As she walked past the cart, that wisp of wind returned, and the cart returned to its original position. Not surprised now by anything that happens after recent events. She calmly walked toward the friends she had met three months ago and recognised them all; they shook hands; a slight tingling was now felt between them, and they all looked at each other with an air of excitement about what was about to become of them all. Each is trying to speak at the same time; Joanne holds her arm up, and if by some silent command, they all stop at once. They all looked at her, waiting for instructions to proceed. Standing by the field, looking in awe at how immaculate it was, Peter was the first to speak, 'surely this must be that Astroturf stuff I have heard about.' Oblivious to the fact the word Astro was so significant to this whole scenario. The rest grinned, knowing what it meant to them, and then John spoke, 'are we all okay with this? It is strange, but what an adventure it will be,' with an air of bravado.

Denise says, 'We will not remember anything about it, though.' Joanne tells everyone to write it down on their phones as a reminder, do not send it to anyone; they will think we are mad.'

Short notes were taken, and their phones were put into their car gloveboxes if something were to happen to them. All except Joanne, she wrote things down with pen and paper. John comments how very old school but still quaint to see; Joanne smiles and blushes, not knowing what to say. Joanne and Denise went to the nearest opening and waited until John and Peter reached the other opening. As soon as they entered the field, they could hear each other's thoughts without having to speak; not frightened by this, they carried on preparing for their task.

Their task was about to start, but they did not know what that task was. Then all remembered that Asku had told them he would be their guiding thoughts. With excitement and trepidation, each individual switched on their instruments and carried out rudimental checks to ensure they would not pick up any false readings. Then placing the instruments close to the ground instantly, a light generates from underneath them. The light joined across the opening in the middle. They could feel it vibrate as they gradually began to walk slowly toward their now designated corner; moving forward, step by step, swinging the instrument left to right, the light carried on till they reached each corner. As soon as they reached the corners, the light went entirely around the field; they all turned and looked at each other in amazement. Then, they looked up to the sky in unison for some reason. Looking up into the clear blue sky, they could see a planet similar to Earth but much larger; no one on Earth could see it other than these chosen four. Unknown to them, the house had disappeared from view as soon as they operated their detectors; this would never be seen again.

Asku had said his kind would return in the following millennium. But unfortunately, Asku died in a crash over Roswell, New Mexico, several years ago.

Unknown to many people, the remains were transferred to an area many miles away, designated as Area 51 in Nevada, USA.

What Joanne had seen was a hologram of the past. When all four shook hands, this sent a signal that set this life-changing task into motion. Asku and another alien called Xylens were in the craft that crashed. Unfortunately for Xylens, he survived and is a prisoner at an undisclosed black site in the USA. The crash instigated a safety protocol for storing the hologram on their home planet.

That handshake signalled its release for Joanne and the others to hear many years later.

Having reached their corners as expected, the four detectors sounded simultaneous; all started digging into the ground, finding a metal box each. They carefully brushed away the soil and saw a box with strange symbols; it was about 250mm x 250mm square. Lifting the boxes, surprised by how light they were, they all placed the boxes on the ground, expecting them to be heavy, but they were light as a feather. They looked all over the boxes, and there were no signs of an opening that they could see. There were no hinges, no physical lid to open; thinking it was a solid piece of metal. Their curiosity is a virtue long gone now, and they must know what is inside. The condition of the boxes would suggest that this whole thing could be a hoax; it was as though they had been made yesterday and not placed in the ground hundreds of years ago.

They have come this far now, and there is no point turning back; how do they open the boxes?

Are they supposed to open them?

Why was Asku so vague?

What shall they do?

An inner voice in Joanne's head said they must all put their hands over the symbols together; this thought transfers to the others, and they place their hands simultaneously on the boxes. As they make contact with the top of the box, it dissolves into all the sides; they should have been shocked but are now so intrigued they carry on. Inside is what looks like a gold amulet with symbols similar to the box's exterior. While they are on their knees, they do not notice that a mist is suddenly coming down; there is no temperature change, so they do not look up to the skies; the mist will remain until they return; it only covers the field and none of the surrounding area. All have an overwhelming thought to place the amulet on their wrists and take it out of the box; the sensation of touching it is different from a metal artefact. The desire to put the amulet on gets stronger after this contact; they all place the amulet over their wrists at the same time. To their astonishment, it dissolves into their skin as soon as they put them onto their wrists. They should panic; common sense tells them to scream what has just happened. still un-nerved, they try to turn to each other but cannot. Instead, they can hear Peter's voice in their heads, 'good grief, what next, everyone.' At this point in time, they all now have a stronger genetic marker than Asku; this will help in their task to come. To their amazement, the box lids reappear; they return the boxes to the hiding places they had been for hundreds of years and cover them up.

Unfortunately, due to Asku's death, their subconscious will not be dictated by him, unaware that their decisions will be their own; this could create utter turmoil in their new world.

Could there be an outside influence that will help them?

6

Three months ago, after that now famous handshake between the chosen four, somewhere in the Nevada desert, in a black site that does not exist. A dormant alien starts to stir from an unconscious state; there is excitement from his capturers. Men and women in white overcoats run desperately between different monitors, lights flashing and alarms ringing on various machines as they pick up vital signals from its brain. Phone calls to superiors and the chain of command are long in this facility, and more urgent calls to higher authority in the Pentagon go through to the highest level. People with substantial gold braids and pips on their jackets demand respect, only answering to the president.

Xylens's body was brought to the facility in 1947; his brain showed no signs of life, but they did not register him as dead. Instead, there were signs of one heart slowly beating, and the second heart was lifeless, or so they assumed. Then, the brutality of the human race, they dissected Asku's body, learning how his body worked, for questionable research purposes. Finally, finding out what to drip feed into the body to keep him or her in a comatose state, their species had moved on, and their reproduction system was different from humans. The irony is that Asku and Xylens were here to help the human race and warn humans about the catastrophe they are blindly racing towards. They had tried to warn the world's leaders several years ago. Still, humans have a trait for greed and material things. Any new invention that created a cleaner environment was hidden from the populist, as financial gain always beats common sense.

In addition, many world leaders denied the existence of an outside force. As always, a military force was always a deterrent; again, the tendency to fight rather than talk was always the preferred option. Then piece by piece, they meticulously transferred the damaged craft back to Nevada; over several years, they had reversed-engineered certain technologies, which have moved the electronic world forward far too fast. Again, many large corporations benefited gratefully; once again, fortunes were made from someone else's demise.

Engineers had found that the craft used an energy source far cleaner than we have on Earth but refused to let it be known, beaten down by global industrialists, who could see that their fortunes would diminish and the hold on financial markets would be gone. Questionable ethics rising for the power of money, people killed that would affect their bottom line

This ignorance of power and money has brought the planet to its knees, destroying the ozone layer, which Asku and Xylens had come to warn the human race about many years ago. But unfortunately, that accident may cause the destruction of the planet because they could not tell anyone in time, and it could be too late now unless Xylens can get free. Asku and Xylens were chosen to give the inhabitants of this planet their last chance after their elders held an extraordinary meeting to select if the Earth should die. They had watched how a minority few had changed this Earth over the years, all strong people with no fear for the consequences they left behind. The majority, led by the minority, is far too familiar and afraid to question rather than right the wrongs of their predecessors, anything for the quiet life.

Many people have died through various conflicts, or was this the natural order to reduce the Earth's inhabitants and increase the human race's longevity? It was a last-ditch effort; they did not want to influence how the Earth moved forward, but a dying planet was the last thing they wanted to see; they must interfere for the survival of this species, called humans. Interacting with installing their genetic marker has become a continuous monitoring situation, similar to that of a mother watching her children. The accident, like most incidents, was purely pilot error, a misjudgement of the terrain, travelling too fast to avoid detection, the crash killing Asku and leaving Xylens unconscious. The army arrived quickly to calm the local residents, but enough of them saw debris to confirm their suspicions.

Rumours abounded from Roswell, was there only one craft? Indeed, there was more, and many aliens died that day; such is the mindset of the human race to spread ridiculous rumours

Xylens sensed the handshake, and his second heart slowly started to beat, but not detectable by the monitors. He does not know how long he has been a captive; when he finally sees the outside world, even he or she will be surprised at how much it has changed through their inadvertent technologies. Advancements are so subtle that in many years, people will be listened to discreetly through household electronic equipment; if you create the desire, they will buy without fail. It is so simple, and once the desire is made and accessible at a low cost, you can monitor your audience without them knowing. An advancement that Xylens and his fellow beings would disapprove of; even on their planet, they have freedom of choice and live happily, or do they?

Xylen's brain is in turmoil, as this scenario was only a brief gesture on the way to Earth. Not in their wildest thoughts did they contemplate that anything would happen to them. They had visited several times without any issues, and it was only the urgency of their mission to save humanity that they returned. Over the decades, their genetic maker was getting weaker, and fate indeed brought Xylens back to life, later rather than sooner, hoping it would not be too late.

7

The mist has thickened; Joanne, Peter, Denise, and John are now frozen in time., in a suspended state. However, their bodies are all kneeling, and they look at peace as though they are praying; this took place instantly; they covered the soil over the boxes. The mist will remain till their task is complete so no prying eyes can see their bodies and interfere if they are disturbed; any chance the Earth has of survival will be gone.

At this point, the local constabulary passed the lane end, and the two police officers noticed the four cars parked. Aware this lane has not been used for several years, other than by local ramblers, their curiosity is aroused, and they turn around to investigate. There have been reports of wanton destruction by mindless youths with nothing to do, thinking the world owes them everything. Tentivately they enter the lane, surprised by the wall of mist, thinking it could be a weather phenomenon; after all, the weather has been strange lately, particularly in this area. Both remember the sudden intense thunderstorms of late, local weather forecasters taken by surprise, as they did not see them coming; even modern instrumentation had not picked them up. The four vehicles look abandoned; they take the registration numbers and request the owner's names from the DVLA database. Even more surprised by the random addresses, three within a seventy-mile radius, and more curious is the old Ford Escort from Portsmouth, surprised it got here, by the current state, looking like a wreck.

So many people would have willingly scrapped the car long ago; what are they doing here?

Finally, after further enquires, the home phone numbers for John, Denise, and Joanne are found.

The senior officer rang the various phone numbers to be

informed that John, Denise, and Joanne were metal detectorists and would return home that evening.

It was confirmed by Joanne's insight, who had placed a card inside her car, reading (Metal detectorists searching with owners permission). The officer's phone calls had unwittingly caused panic in these three households as their partners thought their spouses were detecting alone. Within minutes of the revelation that their partners were not alone, the mobile phone in three cars started to ring, and frantic messages were left; there would be several calls throughout the rest of the day, all unanswered. All the partners wished they had taken more care in listening to where they had gone; was it Durham or Northumberland?

Good grief, where did they go?

Ridiculous questions are asked in their minds, mainly about non-existent affairs; the mind can play cruel tricks on the recipients after the police ring your house. Officers Goode and Daye strangely have an air of self-satisfaction when they hear the phones ring and are surprised the detectorists did not take them.

Nevertheless, the two officers are happy with the situation and decide they will check the lane tomorrow as a matter of due diligence, hoping they are all safe. As they turn, officer Goode is mesmerised by the mist; looking down the lane; he can see the mist only exists within the field boundaries; his curiosity could destroy everything.

He moves forward to the opening in the centre of the hedge, and then officer Daye shouts to him; he has received an urgent call to a severe multi-car collision ten miles away; they must go immediately.

Once again, an act of fate has come into play and given the planet a chance at survival. As the police vehicle reaches the entrance to the lane, they turn left, sirens sounding as they head toward the motorway. The opening closed inexplicably as the officers got into their vehicle; the undergrowth had grown into the hedge and stopped any access into the field. Once the energy field had been energised, a safety mechanism was built-in, only closing if someone tried to enter the field. Furthermore, it would only open if someone had the same genetic marker as the others.

Six ramblers scurry toward the lane entrance one hundred meters from the lane, wondering why the police car left so quickly. Excited to see the police in action for once, they remarked between themselves. Three couples have reached the age of fulfilment and the urge to wander the highways and byways of the countryside. They wanted to fill their lungs with questionable fresh air. There was so much air-born pollution now due to the industrial revolution, unforeseen when the human race found a machine that would make life easier. For the past five years, they have used this lane as the halfway point of their ramble, only walking this route twice a year as part of their planned itinerary. Dressed in standard walking attire, strong boots and obligatory woollen socks rolled up just above the boot. Denim jeans, suitable jumpers, and ski sticks seem popular these days; wild boars will obviously attack them in the countryside, and the ski sticks will help fend them off.

Wet weather attire in their backpacks, the British weather can be unpredictable as they constantly mutter about it. As they walk half-mile up the lane toward the square mile field, comments about its pristine condition are always part of the conversation until they notice the blanket mist over the field, an air of hesitation from them, and hairs on the back of their necks rise. Then, the talks about the weather suddenly stop as they stand in awe at the sight before them. A solid blanket of mist or is it fog stretched as far as they could see, but it was within the field's boundaries.

Everyone reached for their phones, set them to camera mode, and took pictures; by the time these intrepid walkers get home, these pictures will have faded away. So many questions will be asked in the evening to come. Phone calls to each other, what happened. Did they all imagine it?

The clouds break their formation while looking at the field, and the sun shines, feeling the heat on their necks.

They all turn around in unison as though hypnotised, and without a word, they carry on walking; it will take another two miles before the group utters another word to each other. So the conversation continues as though nothing has happened, and all look at each other curious that the last thirty minutes passed by quickly, as if in auto-mode. And why are they there and not at the square mile field, memories are vague of that day, but one of the group has written something in their diary. Will they remember to look?

8

Xylens is aware that the chosen four are in a suspended state; the genetic marker has gotten stronger now. Millions of people have this encoded marker, but these four are in the same country and have bonded to form a strange alliance. It could have happened elsewhere as they took precautions to have similar pickup points in most landmasses worldwide. Instead, many have been destroyed as the Earth's population grew larger, and many, unfortunately, in areas that became landfill sites, the boxes will be lost for aeons to come. It has taken many years for this one chance at survival.

When Asku and Xylens were given their vital task, there were always questions to ask. Could it be their interference to experiment by introducing their genetic marker that created this hostile human race, which has self-hatred of itself? As each minute passes, Xylens awareness gets sharper, and he drifts inside the heads of his captures, looking for the one with the strongest marker; this will be his way to freedom. Unfortunately, the chosen four do not realise their essential role in getting him free; he can summon the other four genetic markers for inner strength and speed his healing process. It will help him shapeshift into another human, but the recipient must be within fifty meters. The odds that someone in the room will have a marker is slim, and he has nothing to lose, but patience is a virtue he has learnt now, at the moment. One such individual has just driven through security and is parking his car in his designated spot, his secure ID ready as he walks towards the facility.

Raul Rodriquez has been at the facility for twenty years, a renowned physicist of high regard, with many letters after his name, his reputation beyond reproach. Even his neighbours do not know where Raul works, avoiding most people, so they do not ask; his life seems to be getting more lonely

Raul scans his ID on the entry post, and the doors open automatically; he walks forward to yet another security position, placing his bag on the conveyor to be scanned by the x-ray machine.

'Hello, Dr Rodriquez; I think it will be a quiet evening tonight,' Raul nods and smiles; it has been the same ritual with Bob on security for ten years. But Raul must still show his ID, and Bob knows that Dr Rodriquez looks down on him as a lowly security guard, not knowing he is a decorated soldier who now wants a quieter life.

Raul takes a deep sigh; familiarity breeds contempt as he had done the same routine for years, and complacency is always around the corner. He heads to the large hall where Xylens has been kept. After de-contamination and scanning his card yet again, there will be three more security doors to go through. As Raul enters the main hall, the monitors come to life only momentarily, as unbelievably, Raul is the marker he needs. Scientists rush to the monitors to see a spike for a milli-second, not knowing what it means. Xylens can sense Raul walking closer; he must not elevate his vitals, or they will see it all too clearly. And then, one of Raul's colleagues calls him to the office; the signal becomes weaker as the office is two hundred meters outside the main hall.

While other scientists congregate around a large table, they compare notes, occasionally looking over at Xylens, who has become part of the backdrop and is rarely looked at until Raul's entrance to the hall.

Looking at each other, they throw around theories about Xylens lifeform, trying to determine where it is from, what solar system, etcetera. These same questions for years to the point of boredom; their technological advances have not helped; if they only asked the right question, answers would come quickly.

Two hours pass, and some scientists from the large table are called to the main office as Raul enters the hall. Unfortunately, these individuals will be redundant by the end of the day. The government has delivered another financial blow, and funds have been cut back again for the fourth year. Several security guards appear from nowhere to escort their sacked colleagues out of the building. The rest look aghast at the system's brutality; some with ashen faces rush to the toilet to throw up; saved for another day, Raul waves to the rest of his colleagues still sitting at the table. Not one to usually approach Xylens, he is strangely drawn to him. Unfortunately, there is a barrier twenty meters away from Xylens. No one can pass this barrier unless they have level one access, Raul's being level two, but tomorrow he will be raised to level one due to unforeseen cutbacks, and he will get even closer to Xylens. Unknown to Raul, Xylens is searching his mind, and he will not shapeshift until the time is right; he needs to get stronger, but in Earth time, it will be three days. If only the marker could get stronger, it would speed up his process for freedom.

Unfortunately for Raul, Xylens already knows Raul will be on shift when he starts his quest to return home.

With his new clearance level, Raul has access to information he could not access before, information that infuriates him; when he gets home, he will not sleep well, and his mind is in turmoil between right and wrong.

Unfortunately, the government is holding technology back that could help the planet. However, Raul's ideology would change after these new revelations if he could only think of a way to free Xylens. Little does Raul know that he will inadvertently help free Xylens from his captors.

9

Four individuals are frozen in time in the UK, blanketed by a mist that has not moved for twenty-four hours. The situation is not as cut and thrust as Asku had told them; they have no sense of time. But, kneeling motionless in this void, could they all have made a monumental mistake?

Meanwhile, worried partners, now panicking, contact the police; rightly so; everything they have done is out of character; why did they not say anything to anyone? By the first light of day, police cars arrive, and the rumour chain starts to travel around the town within hours. The police dogs followed the most recent scent, which led them two miles away from the field. Four mutilated bodies have been found, and a discarded glove was found; in effect, one of the rambler's gloves dropped by accident. Local news outlets had to quell the anger with the response; no one had been found. Police officers are still searching in groups spaced apart for maximum coverage. Also, local officers were dispatched to the families' homes to ask questions the partners did not want to hear, probing their everyday lives and looking for the slightest hint of improprieties. Instead, the four were drawn into something they did not question, causing their families untold trauma. As usual, the crowds gather like vultures around a carcass, hoping to catch a glimpse of the macabre. But unfortunately, it is not the attention the four need now; if someone gets into the field, all will be lost. So the crowd starts to mumble between themselves and general comments from them about the strange mist in the field.

Then suddenly, the sky became darker till it was virtually black. People were cowering to the floor in fear, expecting an apocalyptic event; they looked at each other, shouting, 'it's okay, it is a solar eclipse,' then seeing that nowhere else was affected, started to panic, some beginning to cry.

Unprecedented rainfall flooded the area within minutes, followed by lightning strikes, and the crowd dispersed immediately, soaked through to the bone as it felt to them. All vehicles in the field were abandoned, it was impossible to drive them out of the quagmire, and farmer's tractors were called to assist in their removal the next day. Even the stoic police officers found it impossible to work, calling for backup so they could leave the scene; any evidence they felt they could have retrieved was now gone forever. The incident has become the talking point of Haltwhistle, as the downpour was only located around the cursed field, adding more nuance to the field's mystery. Once again, nothing on the advanced weather warning systems, questioning the validity of the systems, urgent diagnosis, and maintenance was called for by senior management, now severely embarrassed. One hour later, this strange phenomenon stopped, the area still overcast; the sun shone brightly elsewhere. Like all things that are different in this modern world of mobile phones and the internet, this phenomenon has gained the attention of non-existent government services, a red flag the four do not need, especially Xylens. They will monitor chatter to see if anything else happens; if it does, coincidence is not in their book of probabilities, and an investigation team will be dispatched immediately.

The only beneficiaries of this strange phenomenon were the local public houses thankful for this recent activity. The pub trade has spiked by 50%, grateful for the extra income due to a recent pandemic. In addition, the constant chatter over the drinking tables has made the locals drink more; the public house's tanks will need refilling to keep up with demand. It is the first time the landlords have smiled in several months as the locals banter with them.

The following day, the sun is shining, and most people fall out of their slumber in a good-natured way; strange how sunshine changes people's moods. That was till they saw that foreboding cloud over the field, more noticeable from a distance; an air of fear started to run through the town of Haltwhistle. Phone calls to the police had trebled since 6. AM and the police try to calm people down before paranoia takes over. But, by 9. AM, the cloud had disappeared, and the fickle human race could get on with its day-to-day tasks; the cloud was now forgotten, pushed to the back of their minds. The sun was intense, and the adjoining field where the vehicles got stuck was now remarkably dry; police officers looked in wonderment, 'what the hell is going on,' remarked officer Goode.

Officer Daye looked at him in abject silence, shrugging his shoulders; they walked up the lane; the eerie silence was broken as more people arrived to assist in the search for the four missing people. Everyone looked astonished at the mist within the field's boundaries, which has gained quite a reputation in the last day or so.

No one wishes to approach it now; a wide berth taken by the public, DSI June Billows, was given the job of investigating these strange happenings in the field.

She gathered her team at the field entrance, and the silence was broken by DSI Billows shouting out tasks to individuals.

Curiosity is starting to bring out-of-towners to the field, yet more unwanted attention; eight men step out of a minibus with good intentions; this field is becoming quite the attraction. As they walk down the lane, heading directly toward the field, DSI Billows bellows in their direction to get away from a possible crime scene, and cupping their hands to their ears; they pretend not to hear; then, she notices the cloud getting darker. Billows instincts come to the fore, and she shouts to everyone, 'everybody out quickly, now,' they turn to see the cloud and run to their vehicles.

The visitors take no notice, oblivious of any danger they might be in, and two individuals reach the corner of the field; laughing, they turn to their colleagues with glee.

'Photo, take a photo; from one of the men, this caught the lightning strike which killed them both. June Billows and the search team rush to the fallen men, but the lightning strikes continue, forcing them away, not believing what they are witnessing. They cannot reach the men, and their colleagues are distraught; June calls for further backup. She can hear sirens in the distance; the ambulance and fire services are on their way with specialist equipment; within fifteen minutes, the place is awash with more people. All safety precautions are taken to get the bodies out; people are in shock; this area will be cordoned off for the foreseeable future.

Red flag number two has reached the department of special projects, and phone calls are made to special

Investigators Roger West and Shaun Howlett.

Roger and Shaun met ten years ago, thrust together when they investigated a house with a questionable ghost. They found it was an elaborate plan to extort money and force the owner to sell the house for a quick sale and maximum profit. The nephew is due out of prison shortly. Then they bonded over several bottles of lager and have been close friends since. Investigating any strange phenomenon, nerves of steel and humour you can cut with a knife. Both are curious to find out the truth and have an uncanny ability to think outside the box. Both are from the de-coding department of a government agency that does not exist; it was noted they both had similar skill sets for analysis and investigation. Their first real case baffled the department for months; strange sounds emitted from a forest in Surrey; they analysed the data they had gathered. Unfortunately, the answer is far too simple, as past investigators went out with sound equipment to no avail. After checking the weather and wind speeds, the sound only happened at a particular wind speed and temperature, the wind blowing in from the Northeast at twenty-six mph. The sound emanated from one tree; the branches angled through time would vibrate at a certain speed creating the sound; case solved, the A team had been formed. Luckily they lived in Teesside, not far from Haltwhistle, around ninety minutes travel time on a good day. All information is downloaded to their encrypted computers, and coded pagers beep with the coordinates.

Shaun sent a text to Roger, 'pick you up in twenty minutes,' a simple 'okay' was the answer, wondering what the next little adventure would be.

10

Xylens is starting to feel stronger, unsure why; the feeling of leaving by the evening two days earlier than anticipated is overwhelming.

Raul's mind is playing mind games with him; the junction between right and wrong is a fine line, and the fear of going to prison is weighing heavy on his mind. The confusion that if you do the right thing, your entire life as you know it will be gone, your family torn apart for something that is the right thing to do. Even though he divorced five years ago due to the secrets he has to keep, he is still in contact with his family. Raul drives toward the black site with a heavy heart as if in a dream state; he has gone into auto mode, driving the same route for years, never faltering, always arriving with five minutes to spare. Passing Bob on security as though he was not there is out of character for Bob; he notes this in his log book; years of being in the military have made him aware of small changes in people's persona. Raul enters the hall, puts his case on the table, and walks toward Xylens, his pass now allowing him to get even closer than before. Moving his head from side to side, it is as though he can feel Xylens pain; being surprised by this only adds to Raul's confusion. Xylens has entered Raul's mind, and he can see he wants to help voluntarily, even he is startled by the change in twenty-four hours of Raul's mind. With Raul's newfound empathy for Xylens, the shapeshifting will be a lot easier as there will be no challenge as he enters Raul's body. The closer Raul can get to him, the easier the transition can take place Xylens plants the seed for him to come closer at 5.30 am.

Raul's shift is twelve hours long, from six in the evening till six in the morning, hence the 5.30 entry time; this will allow Xylens to acclimatise to Raul's body form. The problem for Raul is that Bob, on security, has made his concerns known further up the command chain, and superiors are having a meeting to ask questions that Raul may not want to answer. Once again, that fickle finger of fate intervenes, and a more pressing matter is brought to the table; they will discuss Raul after the weekend. A memo is sent to Raul via e-mail within the same working complex; it seems a phone call is too personal, such as how humans interact now. The e-mail reads,

'Mr Rodriquez, please attend a meeting at 8. PM, prompt at Mr Endrys office, subject to be discussed on arrival. PP. Miss Wright (secretary).

Raul hated the bureaucratic system of power but sent a curt response, 'will be there prompt' and left it at that, and it was as though he knew he would not be there.

Unknown to Xylens, he will receive an extra boost to his energy levels from an unexpected source before he transitions to Raul.

II

Shaun has just arrived at Roger's abode, beeping the car horn to gain his attention; Roger wishes that he could send a text instead of annoying his elderly neighbour. Both questioned whether they should have had that amount of beer the night before; a home barbecue with friends can do that to you. The new expensive barbecue was the talk of all Shaun's friends, and when the smoked pork of five hours or so melted in their mouths, a call to give up the day job and open a new business, people would queue up to sample his wares.

The door opens, and a bleary-eyed Roger gives a thumbs up; reaching the vehicle, he says, 'can I sleep on the way,' Shaun was hoping for the same thing but lost out again as Roger got his call in first. So halfway to Haltwhistle, Shaun decided to ramp up the eighties music on the car CD, saying, 'how good life was then, bro, wishing they were born in the early seventies.' Not one to wake up easy, Roger shakes his head and agrees as his senses come together; then, his foot starts to tap, and his hands begin to move all over the place. Shaun, thinking got you, wake up you bastard, breaking into a conversation to keep him awake.

'Did you read the e-mail last night?'

'Yep, this could be a strange one for once; I am actually intrigued.;

'Are you nervous?;

'What with a big guy like you with me, we can hold hands.' Both laugh, thinking I hope not.

Roger and Shaun have a success rate of around 95% on investigated cases. The other 5% are unanswered phenomena, with no resolution, cases not solved, but as the years pass and more information comes to light, they will be. Other teams, only

80%, so the A-team get sent to strange paranormal activities, with little intervention from their superiors, who usually want results so they can close their latest file. The journey is uneventful other than changing the music to some classic rock music to pump up the adrenalin. The sun is shining with spasmodic cloud formations, creating unusual patterns, strangely one looking like the United Kingdom; they both look at each other, the hairs rising on their arms.

Both are now moving their heads up and down like two old rockers; drivers of other cars acknowledge them. Then, with wry smiles, 'oh, they were the days,' as they remember their youth and misdemeanours of the past.

Shaun turns off the A69 onto the B6322, and they can see the strange mist in the distance. They look at each other and smile; this one is already fascinating as they reach the entrance to the lane.

There is a cordon of steel around the access to the lane; local authorities have placed steel barriers around the entrance, and officers were stopping anyone who wants to gain access. So the first job will be to get past the jobsworth, two officers with stern faces, obviously chosen because of their attitude. People stare at Shaun and Roger as they exit the top-of-the-range Mercedes SUV, which is more noticeable because of the rare bright red leather interior.

Both men were dressed in dark blue suits, white shirts, and matching dark blue ties; the only thing missing was the obligatory sunglasses.

Onlookers sarcastically mentioned 'that it is the British version of 'men in black,' their shoes polished so that your face could be seen in them, now comparing them to ex-servicemen.

Roger turns to Shaun, throwing a coin in the air, 'tails and I am lead, heads it is you; Shaun laughs; this has been going on for the past ten years. Roger catches the coin and places it on the back of his left hand, covering it with his right hand.

'Okay, show me; it had better not be that double-sided one you used for three years.'

'Oops, sorry, the wrong pocket; you win then, sir.'

Shaun laughed, 'arsehole,' Roger walked toward the officers as Shaun ran to catch up to him.

They both have heavy leather backpacks, which looked odd for two men wearing suits. A five-minute conversation ensues with plenty of card waving and frantic calls to various departments so that Shaun and Roger can gain entry to the lane.

While waiting for entry, Roger asked for a clear fifty-metre exclusion zone, so no one could see what they were doing. However, the local authorities did not wish to spend the money until Shaun mentioned the official secrets act. Forty minutes later, the police cordon was moved to fifty metres, to the annoyance of two stern police officers. Shaun and Roger entered the lane with no prying eyes to see what they were about to do; if anything happened, they Informed the officers to abandon the site if they were not back in twenty-four hours.

The officers are surprised by this statement, and a sense of panic forms in their heads, both thinking, 'what have we got involved with now.'

Shaun and Roger walk the first half mile, discussing the probabilities of this phenomenon; as they get closer, they notice the cloud is getting darker. Seeing this, Roger stops Shaun, 'hang on, let us walk back for a minute.'

'What the hell are you talking about, Rog.'

'Watch the colour of the cloud as we walk away; please just do it.'

'Okay, but I am not happy; we have a job to do.'

Roger pulls him back, and within ten metres, the cloud gets lighter, 'bloody hell, well, I never,' from Shaun.

'It is as though it is protecting the field, like a safety barrier; this is interesting, my friend.' After a short discussion, they decide to carry on up the lane to see what will happen next, already being told about the two unfortunate people who have died and another four missing. They walk down the centre of the old lane, which has had more people on it in two days than it has for two centuries. With every step they take, the cloud seems to get darker; their minds must be playing tricks on them, and then inexplicably, they stop at the centre point of the field. They place the backpacks on the floor and take out their white coveralls, putting them on, then they fully zip up and then pull a hood over their heads. As they move forward, both hold different instruments, one to measure frequency and the other to measure gas levels and content. They get closer to the metre-high hedge, one eye on the hedge and the other on the cloud, and stare in amazement as the hedge begins to part as if inviting them in.

The frequency meter is off the scales, and the gas analyser cannot tell if the mist is okay to walk through. Nevertheless, both men have encountered strange events before, and each event is a challenge.

They attempt to take one step back, and in doing so, the hedge return's to its solid state. Taken aback by this, the hedge seemed alive, but why did it open and close? As both look at each other to gather their thoughts and form a plan, a voice in their heads tells them it is okay to move forward. They look at each other in astonishment; that soft, gentle voice is soothing, mellow in tone, strangely hypnotic.

Walking toward the hedge, it opens again, and they notice the clouds have got lighter; stepping through the gap, they are in the field before they know it. It was like a personal invite onto the dance floor; who will they tango with today?

Unknown to them, they have a more substantial genetic marker than the four, which will help Xylens increase his strength. As they enter, the mist is a barrier from the outside, a shield in effect to keep anyone inside safe until Xylens task is over and for them to do their mission.

Inside as they stand motionless, the hedge closes, and the mist behind them looks like a thin wall between them and the outside world. Both look left and right to see the kneeling bodies of Joanne and Denise; instinctively, they separate Roger running to Denise and Shaun to Joanne. On reaching them, both men automatically check for pulses on their wrists, astounded to see the amulet appear and disappear into their wrists. Finally, both men fall to their knees and are in a suspended state like the others.

The transference of the amulet to the men meant they were in contact with the women, allowing them to see Xylens in their minds.

The six people can communicate between themselves, the newbies astounded; what the hell have they uncovered? But, like Raul, they can feel his pain and desire to return home.

Contact with an alien being came unexpectedly for the first time in their lives; both were amazed they could hear each other. Unknown to them all, they can work as one or individually in their task ahead.

12

Now in a state of suspension, strangely not frightened, unable to move, they have accepted what might happen to them but feel no malice from Xylens. Roger and Shaun will take a journey of discovery that will question everything they think about alien lifeforms, now getting visions of Xylens home planet. Then a feeling as though they are being transported through a portal. They were passing planets in their peripheral vision at an unbelievable rate of speed. All are in contact with each other by thought, now seeing something no human has seen before. All are in awe; from this day on, they will have a different outlook on UFO phenomenon reports if they survive this encounter. Within seconds, they could see Xylens planet. It looks much larger than our Earth and is flanked by two moons, a different sun in colour, but like our Earth, a world of oceans. Lands of greenery and trees, both men are mesmerised by the vast fabric of various constructions; it is as though they are standing on a cliff edge looking around, so vivid are the visions. The beauty of the vast wonderous landscapes on a far greater scale than on Earth. No roads, machines were flying through the skies, a metropolis of cities, and yet a sense of contentment, no signs of wars or destruction. Even though they could not feel or touch Xylens, they could see why he was desperate to return home.

On this planet, there is no violence, no robberies, and no drugs to blight society, but in this utopia, there has to be a semblance of control to achieve this unity; the question is, what?

Shaun and Roger instinctively labelled this planet E2 in their heads for clarity between themselves.

The history of E2 went back thousands of years before the Earth existed and started similar to Earth.

Growing out of the abyss of pollution, the inhabitants over

millenniums had outgrown their human state, and their brains had become more intelligent.

As a result, certain parts of the body, which were little or no use, gradually disappeared, thumbs gone, remaining fingers elongated over time to compensate.

As the brain enlarged, heads grew larger, giving the illusion of a longer face, and tablets replaced food, delivered once in Earth year in timescales. Finally, the mouth grew smaller with all the nutrients the body needed. With this enhanced brain size, this race can do things no human can do just by thought.

There is no bodily contact for reproduction as we on Earth enjoy; they choose the sex of the child, and a tablet is given to each recipient, they embrace, and a child is conceived. Through this short contact, the tablet interacts, and within a specific timeline, a bead of sweat forms on both parties. The beads of sweat or sperm are collected and placed inside an embryo cubicle for the process to begin. They do not wait nine months as we do on Earth; in a matter of days, the child is taken home to start a life of servitude. Unfortunately, all is not greener on the other side, as only a few get to live a life worth living.

With this control system in place, the commissioners, who are the rulers of this planet, dictate the population growth and the direction the aliens' lives go. Even with their higher intelligence, the pills are given at such an early age that they do not know any different.

Some, like Asku and Xylens are pre-programmed for their tasks; Earth's development was a whimsical choice by the commissioners, a plaything when they found planet Earth.

Seeing that it had a 98% match to their own, they decided on an experiment; after all, it is light-years from their own and will not impact their world.

In many ways, even with their higher intelligence, they felt they would help this newly found planet grow, nurture, and bring it on, like a mother with a child. But they had interfered with the natural course of evolution on this Earth. In many ways, changing the planet's natural growth was a criminal offence in the eyes of the human race if they only knew.

Only the commissioners know of this error in judgement, and the information is passed on to their direct heir, with no records to implicate them. Like on Earth, the commissioners enjoy life to the full, as do the rich and powerful of our society, while the subservient survive an uneventful life. Underneath the underbelly of any society, there is still a need for protection from any outside intervention. Unknown to the masses, they have violent retaliatory recourse for anyone who might try to intervene with how this planet operates. If they can remember, it has been so long since the need to use violence. Either internally or from another species, protectionism is vital to survival at any cost. Each alien lifeform lives for two hundred years, and their bodies automatically disintegrate into dust particles when they die. These particles spread across the land in the wind, and all the nutrients go into the landscape, continually feeding the planet.

It only happens in a natural death; when it is sudden, the body stays intact, as in Asku's untimely death, enabling Earth's scientists to dissect his body.

In what seemed hours were only minutes to Roger and Shaun, even with the information overload, they had grasped their task to help the world if they could, but they were still unsure how to achieve this. Xylens has seen inside the heads of the human race once again, and for once in his life, there are questions to be answered if he is brave enough when and if he gets home. What is about to happen will change both planets, and both will go through changes they did not expect.

So the irony of the commissioner's intervention in the Earth's ecosystem could backfire on their own world, and a revolution could be coming.

Xylens could become a virus on his own planet, and E2 will change forever.

It is now **A Time for Change** for both planets.

13

Xylens is unclear in his thoughts, which he can blank out at will from his new allies, baffled by the freedom of this human race to do what they want. An ability to question everything and not be punished. But he can see the destructive element of good versus evil and the dangers it can bring. His kind has never witnessed violence in any form; such is the control the commissioners have over them. Is this something that his home planet needs? Should he attempt to change the balance of power? If he gets home?

He has not known fear before but senses it in his new allies, and he must find out more before returning home.

Xylens does not realise the length of time he has been a captive; without the tablet intake, he can think for himself; he is eager to learn more. He must prolong his stay to find out, to understand the term freedom of choice. While in captivity, the nutrients he had been supplied with on his home planet were washed away; when he was drip-fed to keep him alive. In a twist of fate, Xylens has been freed from his commissioner's hold over him; what can he do? He must find out how this has happened

The nutrients he has been designated in the black site are different from the tablets he was given on E2. Only a 10% change but enough of a variant to cancel the many years of addiction forced upon them. Unfortunately, that 10% can only be found on his planet, an additive unknown to Earth. He will scan Raul's brain to find that fundamental change; he must help his fellow lifeforms; they must be free.

But, as in the human world, there are more questions than answers, Xylens must be careful not to overload Raul's brain, which is much smaller than his, or he will be trapped forever till he dies. It is now approaching 5. AM, Raul is contemplating what to do with his family for the weekend. He sees them every two weeks, a condition of his divorce settlement.

At this time of his twelve-hour shift, Raul is tired, so his senses are low; he needs to sleep even after all these years, and he still struggles with his night shift rota.

More noticeable by the spilt coffee on the table due to his tiredness, he needs to get home to sleep. For the past few months, he has contemplated leaving his job, requiring a challenge to stimulate his brain. He is slowly writing his handover notes, which have not changed much over the recent months. Other than the date at the top of the page, such is the monotony of the job lately. Little does Raul know that in the fine print on his contract, he is only allowed to leave if the management wants him gone. So Raul is trapped in his place of work, and he does not know it; this is one part of freedom of speech that Xylens does not know. Finishing his notes, it is nearing 5.30, and Raul has an urge for one last look at Xylens; having sensed his pain earlier, it was to say goodbye mentally for the weekend, and he will see him on Monday. As he walked closer to Xylens, even through his tired eyes, he could see a sudden sharpness in Xylens eyes; now more intense and interested, he moved closer. The rest of Raul's work colleagues were in the locker room, preparing to go home, gathering their lunch boxes, phones, and car keys, leaving Raul with Xylens alone.

While Raul stares into Xylens eyes, he overlooks the orb transfer into his body, and then Raul shudders; a cold sweat runs down his forehead and a strange feeling in his bones. Raul will try to explain this feeling to his ex-wife when he sees her later in the day, and then a sense of nausea comes over Raul, wanting to vomit; this passes as quickly as it came. Raul is about to turn and notices that the intensity in Xylens eyes has gone.

Did he imagine it?

Turning around, he walks to his desk; in doing so, he nearly falls over, 'what the hell is happening to me?

It must be too many spices in the leftover dinner, having re-heated in the microwave. Xylens had shapeshifted to Raul, but the human race, has a different gait, and he is struggling to walk.

Xylens outer body will remain for three days before it gradually disintegrates, like a snake leaving its skin behind. The scientists on-site will accept his time is up, unaware Raul will be missing for days, ignorant of his actions. Finally, after fifteen minutes, Raul's relief arrives, and he is allowed to go to the locker room to get ready to go home. Colleagues ask if he is okay, 'looking a bit pale, Raul, anything wrong.'

Raul shakes his head, 'I think I must be coming down with something; hopefully, it will clear up over the weekend.'

Unintentionally, Raul has given an alibi for the next few days, and no one will question it when he does not come to work on Monday. Going back through the usual security doors and finally reaching Bob at the x-ray point, a knowing nod from Bob, 'see you on Monday, Dr Rodriquez, looking a bit pale. Are you okay?'

Raul puts his hand up, 'feeling a bit unwell, Bob, that's all.'

'Sorry to hear that; see you on Monday, hopefully.'

Raul takes his case and slowly walks to the main door; Bob notices his strange walk but puts it down to Raul feeling ill; for once, Bob has failed in his due diligence. As Raul reaches the final security check, he puts his ID card on the sensor and walks into the daylight, a sudden involuntary gasp from within him.

Xylens is not used to the intake of the Earth's atmosphere, and Xylens is now free. Raul, unsure why? A tear falls down his cheek, 'must be overtired,' he thinks.

As Raul walks to his car, Xylens is now more comfortable in Raul's body, taking in the surroundings, and when Raul gets into his vehicle, Xylens is astounded by the archaic technology. First, Raul turns on the ignition, and the engine's sound is something Xylens has never heard. Next, Raul switches the radio on, and the sound of music comes out of the speakers. It soothes Xylens; why does his planet not have this noise? Expecting the vehicle to rise from the ground and fly, Xylens now realises how far this planet is behind his own, thousands of years before they will get to their evolution status.

So Xylens goes into standby mode to allow Raul to get home before making himself known.

Raul must get home to sleep; his ex-wife and kids are coming at 4. PM, he must get some sleep and tidy up before they arrive. But unfortunately, when he arrives home, sleep will be the last thing on his mind, events will take over, and a race against time will ensue. Raul parks his car on the pristine driveway.

Living by yourself gives you plenty of time to do your chosen jobs. Not the continual list his ex-wife would give him. It is ten minutes past seven when Raul puts the key in his door and once again wonders how he got there, and he starts to worry if he is losing his mind; he has no memory of the drive home. As he walks through the door, it is as though he is in slow motion as Xylens comes out of standby mode and takes in more information. Not one for having coffee so early in the morning, a sudden desire to do so overwhelms him.

Xylens has smelt this inside the black site; Raul takes a sip and instantly vomits, Xylens is not accustomed to any taste and recoils within Raul.

At this stage, Raul can hear a soothing voice in his head; rushing to the bathroom, he looks into the mirror, then throws water over his face to wake himself up. Again he looks into the mirror; all he can see are the eyes of Xylens. Then that voice again, he shouts at the mirror, 'what is happening to me,' as he cries in desperation. Finally, Xylens voice comes back to him, calming him and telling him to sit down. Raul slowly walked to his living room and, as if hypnotised, closed all the blinds and curtains around the house and ensured all the doors were locked before he sat down. Neighbours were accustomed to this, knowing he worked regular night shifts. With his head in his hands, Raul listens to the voice in his head; he thinks he is going mad; Raul wants to scream, but no sound comes out; the voice tells him to breathe slowly. Xylens waits until Raul starts breathing normally and then starts to tell him what is happening. The situation gradually becomes a question-answer scenario in his head; Raul is astonished at what has happened.

Being a scientist, this has gone far beyond his wildest dreams, and there will be no sleep today. Finally, after two hours, Xylens explains he can live in his body for seven Earth days any longer, and he will be trapped inside of him forever, and Raul will slowly die with him. Xylens has told him about the other people in the UK who are trying to save the planet by altering how energy can be created away from fossil fuels. Even though Raul is an intelligent man, he is struggling with the concept of what is happening. Trying to explain these people cannot change time; if they did, he would not be talking to him now; this is impossible. And it goes against all that he has learned and knows.

So, could he be losing his mind?

Can he accept the consequences of a mental breakdown? Xylens is now questioning what his commissioners have told him and decides to transcend from Raul's body. Xylens is taking a risk because his species can do this several times within a short period, but each time makes him weaker and even more dangerous now that he has not taken any nutrients from his own planet. Xylens tells Raul to stand up, perplexed. Raul obeys, closing his eyes; that cold sweat forms on his forehead; he shudders, and moments later, he opens his eyes; standing in front of him is Xylens, those intense eyes an alien lifeform from another planet. His first reaction was he should ring the facility or the police for help; these feelings soon went as he looked into Xylens eyes again. With his mouth open, Raul cannot believe his eyes; what is standing before him; thankfully, he is not going crazy. Weeping tears of joy, he collapses back into the chair.

Xylens cannot understand these human emotions, as it is something his planet does not possess, long gone due to the intake of tablets.

14

Six people are just coming to terms with the information overload and the monumental task bestowed upon them. They have learned very quickly that they can work collectively or as individuals. Xylens is already aware of the timescale they must alter; it starts with the seventeenth century. It is hard to believe that the human race's problem might have begun by solving how excess water was removed from mineshafts. The introduction of a steam engine to pull the water from the shaft was so successful other inventors jumped on the process to create other engines for different applications. Soon the need to bring coal to the surface became paramount to quicken the pace of evolution, and the industrial revolution was coming. Unfortunately, fossil fuels are abundant on this Earth, which, unknown to the people of the time, would pollute the atmosphere, and the human race was ignorant of its effects. Then in the nineteenth-century crude oil was found; this became known as black gold to some people, making many individual people wealthy in a short time. It was the greedy man's new drug, perpetuating questionable cabals, which have become the byword for greed and control. This evolution of motorised machines set the world toward self-destruction. They were searching for new forms of fuel that could be produced to drive these machines at a cheaper cost. Looking to ease the workload on the human body, making it easier to go from point A to point B, to make the use of time at the workplace more efficient, once again, the emphasise on money and profit.

And the world blindly carried on without caring about the environmental consequences. It was recently highlighted during a pandemic when millions of people stayed home, and pollution levels dropped because machine operations dropped to a bare minimum.

And yet another bonus to the wealthy investors, they found

something else happened when the oil was warmed up to different temperatures.

The by-products created could be used for many different applications, in some cases, as many as one hundred products. Investors shook their hands in glee, sitting in their ivory towers while the world gradually died. The list goes on from petrol, diesel, paraffin, paints, plastics, perfume, shampoo, etcetera.

The realisation that our six heroes might have to go back hundreds of years is daunting, even if they are only going in their subconscious minds. The mindset of their ancestors will not be able to cope with any suggestion in their heads, and they will think they are going mad. After his conversation with Raul, even Xylens questions his validity and his planet's role on this small planet called Earth.

But a solution could be closer at hand if they can all talk to each other, including Raul, it will be dangerous, but it must be done. Seven people and one alien must join together to form an alliance to help the Earth. Denise, John, and Peter have just seen through Raul's eyes an alien called Xylens standing before him; he is the same as Asku, who Joanne had seen at the farmhouse. On E2, all lifeforms are the same, cloned from one source, yet another control feature of the commissioners.

With each tablet, a different additive is used to create the job that the lifeform will do when it reaches maturity.

Everything is automatic in many ways; they have become robotic in their mannerisms, no questions asked, and then they become dust and waste floating into the planet's ecosystem. Xylens is now becoming more aware of their fruitless life; anger is building, but first, a solution must be found to help this small planet.

Today will become the first day that this world will start to change as Xylens suddenly comes forward with a possible solution, which has been on Earth since 1947. Xylens tells everybody through Raul that his broken craft is in a dark place near where he was kept. He could sense it; another part of their evolution was that they were sensory to any craft they flew. The energy source that his home planet had produced to fly their craft was limitless and clean, a slight variation to fusion that could be controlled easily and without danger to anyone.

Everyone is in awe of this statement; why have the authorities not told the world to free us from this catastrophic abyss the world is heading to? Self-evident that the money machine will be affected, and the bottom line will get smaller; such is the control, just like Xylens planet.

Seven more individuals are becoming angry now; they must do something, but how can they help?

Xylens informs them that he must get back to his craft; he knows it is broken and unable to fly, but every craft has information to help re-build it on board, a small chip with details on how to repair it if required. The chip can be placed into any computer and automatically aligns with its program.

There is no need for different systems; everything in the universe is binary, Xylens tells them.

Everybody instantly questions that the authorities must have found it by now. Xylens calms them down, telling them only his kind can access it. And, believe it or not, they themselves can, due to their strong genetic marker. Different parts of the craft hold specific information for repairs with other outcomes; every possible cause and effect can be repaired. This is because if the craft was captured, all the information about the craft could not be used against them. But, once again, the commissioners are protecting all they own, always afraid to lose control.

Then Xylens surprises them by informing them they have their own powers if they believe in themselves, and they will all need to use them to protect all. Xylens mind is awash with questions, everybody not believing what they have heard. Once again, that soothing voice calms them, he will answer their questions one at a time, but time is of the essence they must act quickly.

Roger is the first to ask, 'what do you mean, powers,'

'Every human can do it; your race calls it telekinetics.'

Denise rushes in, 'What is that?

'The brain can do great things if you free your mind; it will develop over the next thousand years as your race starts to understand your capabilities.'

John now astounded at this revelation, 'but how can we help you.'

'I need to get to my craft and will need your help to achieve this.'

Joanne was more pragmatic, 'will it harm us in any way.'

'No, it will probably enhance how you look at things afterwards, a newfound ability you did not know you had.'

There will always be a sceptic, and Peter is shown to be the weak link, 'I don't know everyone, for crying out loud, he is an alien from another planet, can we trust him.'

Raul interjects, 'look, everyone, I am with Xylens; he only wants to get home, oh and by the way, he wants to help us save our planet.'

Shaun, now taken in with the wonderment of the situation, 'I say we help; this is a one-time situation where two different species help each other, I suppose a universal first if we survive.'

Roger butts in, 'what do you need us to do, Xylens? Is that your name?'

'I can put you all in sleep mode until nightfall, as you will need to conserve as much energy as possible for the task ahead.'

Suddenly, their heart rates start to slow down, like a bear hibernating, except for Raul; Xylens needs as much information about his workplace as he can. Raul explains that he knows nothing about the rest of the site, as there are restricted areas that they have to avoid so that no other information can be passed to an enemy, such as an alien lifeform or enemy of the state.

Xylens explains that inside Raul's head is a minefield of new information, and he will have seen things which are automatically stored in his memories. He needs to open it up. Xylens touches

Raul's forehead, and he can see the site in his head from all angles; he notices a large hanger against a small mountain range. His senses tell him that is where he needs to be this evening.

It was only seconds, but Raul was unaware, coming out of a trance, not knowing what information he had given Xylens.

15

It is three-thirty in the afternoon; time has passed far too quickly for Raul; tiredness is long gone, running on adrenalin. Then a beep in the distance; turning to see his phone light up, he has received a text message from his ex-wife; she is running a few minutes late. Then, adding a note, 'we need to talk. I have left the kids with my mother.'

Instant panic from Raul; she could not be involved in what was just about to happen; he could not forgive himself if anything happened to her. He explains to Xylens that Sara is his ex-wife, the mother of his children, and she will be here shortly. Raul replies to Sara's text

'I have an issue and must go back to work; sorry, will next week be okay.' Ten seconds later, another text, 'I have just pulled up outside. I will be with you in one minute.'

Xylens can see that Raul is tense and about to panic and automatically transcends into Raul's body; just then, the doorbell rings. Raul feels that shudder, and nausea comes back for a second, Xylens voice in his head calming him down. Raul walks to the door, and on opening the door, his ex-wife is standing before him, more beautiful than he has ever seen her before; he has not seen her for a month due to work schedules. Their divorce was amicable and always friendly; they had just drifted apart due to work commitments. They had both lost weight intentionally, going to the local gyms in different parts of the town.

They kiss; it is the first time Xylens has felt instant emotion, as they do not have this on his planet; he is immersed in their thoughts.

Not sure if this is good, but he can feel how pleasant this interaction is; he wants to feel more; even an alien has feelings, so it seems. Sara steps back, 'looking a bit pale. Raul, are you okay,' it seems he will hear this more regularly while Xylens is in his body.

Raul explains that he needs to go to work; Sara tells him this will only take an hour, but it might be a little longer, depending on his response to her request. Sara starts by telling him that, in recent months, she has regretted their divorce; the time apart has given her time to reflect on their relationship. Is there any chance they could rekindle the flame? The children also miss him; she grasps his hand, 'please can we try again.' Raul's head is in turmoil, he still loves his ex-wife and children, but they could all be in danger if he helps Xylens. Inside his head, two conversations are taking place; Sara can see he is hesitant, so she grabs him by the hand and leads him to the bedroom.

She kisses him more passionately than ever before; Xylens stops talking; he will take part in something none of his kind has ever done for thousands of years, an event he will cherish for the rest of his life. But unfortunately, none of the six will witness this event; Xylens can cancel these thoughts from everyone else.

Before Raul stands, Sara they kiss again and start to take each other's clothes off; Sara had bought some new red lingerie, which Raul had asked her to do on several occasions when they were married, but she would not. So instead, often saying, 'I will choose what I want to wear, not you.'

It was one of the few contentious issues in their marriage. So to see this beautiful woman in front of him, looking so stunning, a tear ran down his cheek.

Sara placed her hand on his face and kissed him again; both fell onto the bed. Xylens will feel for the first time two humans copulating, and this experience is intoxicating to Xylens. He had never felt passion and intensity like this before the euphoria when they both climaxed. Once again, this lifeform is starting to question the very existence of their race with no emotions or feelings. Thirty minutes later, two happy humans were laughing and talking about the future again. Raul forgot about his visitor, and Xylens stayed silent, waiting for Sara to leave; the one-hour visit lasted ninety minutes, and both were happy about the outcome. As Sara got up to go, 'I will bring the children tomorrow; they will be so happy.' Both are smiling at each other, but Sara could sense some apprehension from Raul; she has known him long enough to know something is wrong.

'What is wrong, Raul? Have I done something?

'No, it is this problem at work, and as you know, I cannot talk about it.'

'Okay, ring me tomorrow.'

Raul thinks that if all goes wrong, Sara will have plausible deniability, unaware of Raul's actions.

Raul smiles and watches Sara drive away, waving as she turns the corner. However, the joy of what had just happened was soon broken when Raul heard Xylens voice again.

16

As if flicking a light switch on, Xylens brings everybody back into the conversation; they only have a short time to create a plan. But first, Xylens will need to explain how they can use their minds to achieve things that, at the moment, seem impossible. Even though they are thousands of miles away, they can cross the gap by concentrating as one entity. Roger is trying to inject some humour into the situation, 'oh, like a giant head,' this was a reference to an old TV series from years ago regarding aliens. Only Shaun got the connection as they both liked the same TV programs, laughing mentally, but it was greeted in silence. Xylens explains what he can do, telling them he is currently inside Raul's body. He carries on; his species can shapeshift and take the form of another human looking exactly like them; nobody can tell the difference; this helps if you need to move between your species. We have other abilities, which you will see later tonight, but to achieve what I need to do, I will require all your strength to help your human race survive. Within seconds of this enlightenment, they start to question if Raul will be okay. And Xylens explains that Raul is only a passenger, a vehicle to get him to the facility; he will take another body form to get to the craft. Roger comes into the conversation, 'when you get this mysterious chip, how will this help us.'

Xylens responds, 'seven people will have the means to move this information around your world; listening to my captors, I believe you call it the internet.'

A hesitant Shaun interrupts, 'the government watchdogs will try to stop it, though.'

'But Shaun, we work for the government; in a sense, we will be committing an offence, won't we.'

'No, we would offer an alternative energy source; in the current climate, it should be welcomed. If it stops the world from burning, surely we can stand some of the heat.'

It would only be the oil and gas consortiums that will panic, but life has told me they will turn it around to give them more profit; I guarantee they will take it on board if it goes public. Everybody agrees it is a risk worth taking; Joanne chips into the conversation. Have you heard of newspapers? It will be the biggest scoop of the century; unfortunately, we cannot put our names to it; the repercussions are enormous. Also, how could we explain how we received the information? After a few moments to deliberate the situation, they all agree it must be done for the good of the human race. Raul is secretly thankful he will not need to enter the facility and is only a carrier for Xylens, but how can he avoid being seen? Xylens can sense his hesitancy, 'do not worry, our other participants in the facility will not realise their involvement; they will have no memory of any events.'

Xylens tells him, 'no harm will come to them; it is short term; it will only affect them while I am in their vicinity, and when we come away from the facility, it will return.' Raul's inner tension subsides now, knowing no one will be hurt. Xylens, still within Raul, tells him it would be better to sleep for a while to gain much-needed strength for the task ahead of them. Explaining his limitations of leaving his body again to shapeshift to another body also weakens him far more than being in Raul's body. Raul, now exhausted, lies down on the unmade bed due to the visit from his ex-wife.

He instantly falls asleep, a different type of sleep for Xylens, whose senses are now on constant alert and ready for any situation. Likewise, the others in the field automatically go into sleep mode as Xylens rests.

Meanwhile, back in the UK, tensions are rising outside the field entrance at Haltwhistle, where barriers were erected. Although the two agents went inside the field hours ago, there has been no sign since they instructed the rest to stay outside. Instead, even the two sour-faced officers are showing signs of concern. Then the sound of excitement as they turn around to see four unusual vehicles trundling towards them, led by a Range Rover, blue and white lights flashing. Officers Goode and Daye start to walk forward; Goode says, 'this is not good, government vehicles, all black, no signage.'

Daye responds, 'guess we will be going home then, I can guarantee it.'

The lead vehicle stops, and the officers can see the passenger door open; a pair of highly polished shoes touch the ground, followed by ironed, creased black trousers and the biggest man they had ever seen. Standing tall at 2.1 metres, the tailored suit comes directly from Saville Row; he is clean-shaven with a square jaw and handsome features. His hair was dark brown, with a wisp of grey hair on the right side of his temple. He has piercing blue eyes and is in his mid-fifties with a manner that demands attention. His name is ambiguous to the man's size, 'my name is Don Small, who is in charge.'

Goode replies, 'no one, we are just guarding the area to stop the public getting into the field.'

'You can both leave now.'

'We cannot till our chief superintendent tells us to leave.'

Don liked that the officer respected the chain of command.

'Name and phone number of your chief, please,' the man's size added to his authority; both could tell he was not a man to be dismissed lightly.

So the officer rings his Superintendent, 'Officer Goode here, sir, reference the problematic field at Haltwhistle. I have someone who wishes to speak to you.'

Don Small walks to his car so as not to be overheard, and a conversation ensues amicable at first; then, both Goode and Daye can hear the raised voice of their chief superintendent. Then, finally, Don moves the phone from his ear; the two officers are surprised but admire their chief, who was fighting his corner for his men to stay onsite. After a minute or so, Don calmly gives the chief superintendent a number to ring and returns the phone to Goode, 'he will ring back in two minutes, and then you can leave.' Goode and Daye look at each other, both amazed at the calmness of this man; sure enough, the phone rings, and Goode answers, 'leave the site now and come back to the station immediately.'

'Yes, sir, on our way,' a quick nod to Daye, and they make their way to the police car, 'who did that guy tell the super to ring from Daye? Little did they know Don Small as full authority from the Prime Minister, no questions asked. As they leave, they can see ten men get out of each of the other four vehicles with strange devices and faces covered, heading towards the field entrance. They notice the mist and cloud above the field, looking dark and angry at this point. Don Small is a problem solver; in his mid-forties, the wisp of grey on his temple adds even more mystery to his character. However, many think it must have been a bad experience to cause the grey hairs on his temple because this man does not frighten easily.

He was another ex-forces man who came to the attention of clandestine services and was recommended for this position for his steely nerve under pressure.

He was always methodical in assessing situations under pressure; it seemed time stopped around him while he resolved any problems. He often felt it was from an outside force but could not pinpoint how or why. Once all his men had entered the field, he gathered them up to issue instructions; they all had great respect for Don, willing to lay their lives on the line if required. All were selected for their unique abilities and skill sets and were the best of the best in their chosen field. Don tells them all what is happening with the limited information they have, and they have a window of twelve hours before they can enter the field. With the mention of going into the field, a sudden lightning strike hits the ground a hundred metres away. A wry smile from Don, 'This will be a challenge, boys. Are we up for it.'

A roar from his men as he tells them to surround the field, ten on each side, and stay twenty meters away from the hedge row until further notice. Don called into action due to the protocols he had set in place eleven years ago after two colleagues died in one such unusual encounter.

It became known as the Devil's Hole incident after a local farmer noticed his beef stock was slowly depleting while in their milking pens.

Naturally, this reached the ears of Don's department, and two people were dispatched to investigate.

Although, due to manpower restraints, both were only on the job for one year, the job was deemed an enquiry-only situation. On entering the barn, all seemed okay. As usual, the cows were being milked, and both colleagues kept in touch with the head office via headset radios. Bob Small and Pam Little, head office, always laughing when they put Little and Small on a case, described everything they could see, and a body cam fitted to their shoulders so that head office could get the barn's layout and precise information over the radios. Within five minutes, the raised voice of Bob (Don's son) shouted into the headset. A sinkhole was opening up directly behind them on the barn's floor, Pam and Bob's screams haunt Don's dreams every night, and it was that night the grey hair formed. When he entered the barn two hours later, all that was left were the right hands of Pam and Bob. There was no hole in the ground, but in Bob's hand was the bodycam he was wearing when analysed, a creature that looked like the Devil himself; Don vowed till the day he died he would hunt this thing down. The ground was solid, x-rays revealed nothing, and the history of the land did not indicate pagan activities; Don may never see this again, but if he does, he is ready mentally now. In the past eleven years, there have been reports of similar incidents in Europe, and Don is waiting for the next incident in the UK.

Hence the new protocol, all operatives must check in every hour unless priority notice has been given before the activity starts. Roger and Shaun had contacted head office before they entered the field and, for some inexplicable reason, had asked for twenty-four hours of silence.

Don had only found out about this unusual request before he was sent on his quest to assist his men.

A decision made by his immediate boss may well have jeopardised Roger and Shaun's lives. Don will abide by their request, but he and his men will storm this field for answers in twelve more hours.

17

It is time for Xylens to wake everyone up; all are mesmerised by this alien's powers. But, deep down in Roger's mind, he is acutely aware that Xylens alien race could destroy planet Earth by the abilities he has witnessed. In the back of his mind hoping Xylens could not sense his anxiety. Then suddenly, Xylens enters his thoughts, telling him his planet is peaceful and has no desire for conflict. I can contact you individually so that your concerns are not overheard. Xylens knows he needs as much cooperation as possible from this backward planet to get home. These are problems he has not encountered before: the constant request for information and the need to know what is going on. Now constantly wondering about his planet's mundane existence, what his race does, what they achieve daily, and why they exist. These are all questions he needs to find answers to when he returns to E2.

At this point, Raul is starting to stir from a deep sleep, akin to a power nap, surprised by how refreshed he feels, having only slept for three hours. Raul starts to get ready and prepares a flask of strong coffee; he must stay awake this night of all nights. On the one-hour drive back to the black site, Xylens can sense Raul's tension once again, and he calmly explains his intentions. But Xylens now realises how weak Raul is and must make a calculated decision, or all will be lost, and his freedom is at risk. The journey in the dark is quite different from his journey in daylight, with the constant buzz of traffic speeding and car horns blaring in the distance due to road rage.

The silence is deafening, and the traffic is down to a bare minimum. Xylens can see the constellations as the sky is clear, with not a cloud in sight; even he is mesmerised by the beauty of the night sky.

Then the headlights of an oncoming car surprised him; he was not used to this type of transport, and everything was unfamiliar to him; the high beam of the lights dazzled his eyes, and he struggled to re-focus his eyes. Then, with Xylens in Raul's body, the car swerved to the opposite side of the road, missing an oncoming vehicle by millimetres. Although Raul does not quite understand why it happened, he looks in his rearview mirror and sees Xylens eyes; the penny drops to his present predicament. Five minutes later, Raul could hear the sound of a police car siren, and in his rearview mirror, he could see the blue and red lights as the car approached at speed. In Raul's mindset, the police must be going to a crime until the loudspeaker bellows for him to pull over, unaware that the innocent driver they nearly ran into has contacted the police of a possible drunk driver on the road. He voiced concerns about the driver who nearly ran him off the road. Finally, both cars pull up to a stop, Raul in his mind telling Xylens what he thinks has happened, and the other driver must have reported him to the police. Xylens has now come across a system of control he did not comprehend; they do not have anything like this on his home planet.

Xylens can sense the weakness in Raul, and his anxiety levels are creeping up; he will break down in front of the officer. Raul has never interacted with the police, and the thought of them finding out what is about to happen terrifies him.

The officer gets out of his car and walks towards Raul's car, placing his hand on his holster as per police procedure. This action makes Raul panic, wanting to confess everything, and the officer has not yet reached Raul's car. The officer requests Raul to roll down the window, his right hand still on his holster, holding the grip of his gun. At the sight of a weapon, Xylens goes into protection mode to defuse the situation. At this point, Raul shudders, and he can see the officer convulse; Xylens has transferred to the officer, and an internal discussion takes place inside the officer's mind. The officer was confused about what was happening to him and tried contacting his department via his radio handset. Raul can see the paleness on his face, and then he feels Xylens return to him, who tells him to carry on.

'But the officer, what have you done.'

'Let us say he cannot remember why he is here.'

'No, we cannot leave him.'

'If you want this planet to survive, we must carry on.'

Xylens is now seeing the problems of freedom and being able to choose, which he has never known; could this be why the commissioners hold them back?

The officer slowly walks back to his vehicle, opens the door, and sits down behind the wheel; he turns off the recording camera, turns the car around, and heads back up the road. But, unknown to Raul and Xylens, the vehicle camera recorded a white orb entering the officer; only for a second will it ever be seen, and with no arrest, will they bother to look. Although the black site is five miles away now, Xylens is in contact with the people in the UK, describing how they can mentally project their thoughts to him.

Finally, Raul drives up to the security gate; the guards know him well as they are long-term site employees; this in itself can create problems as, with familiarity, you forget your basic checks.

'You don,t usually come in on the weekend, Dr Rodriquez, from one of the guards.'

'I have a few important issues I need to sort out, Bruce.'

At this point, a phone call should have been made to confirm that Raul had clearance for an out-of-hours visit. But familiarity as got Raul and Xylens through the gate

It was a passive look at Raul's pass, and the automatic gates opened; they were in; he drove one hundred meters and turned left as though he was going to the main carpark. At this point, Raul is unsure what to do; in his mind, he thought he would be outside the fence and not inside. Then Xylens tells Raul he must go back to the security cabin, so he can shapeshift into the senior guard, who has access to most of the black site. Xylens explains he only needs to be within fifty meters to achieve this. Xylens is getting close to his limit of shapeshifting, now starting to feel slightly weak; this is why he needs the assistance of his UK allies. The encounter with the police officer was an unwanted distraction, and he hoped it did not weaken him too much. There are plenty of security guards around the black site, all ex-military, but Xylens needs a senior guard who controls the staff. He is positioned in a portacabin one hundred meters to the left of the main gate. Xylens is now forcibly having to move Raul forward to the portacabin, and this is not what he wanted to do, but fear tends to overcome common sense as Raul is starting to realise the implications of his actions to come.

Blocking his thoughts from the others, Xylens now has control of Raul, who is now in what looks like a hypnotised state.

Now oblivious of his actions, Raul knocks on the supervisor's door, and with the sound of a chair falling over, it seems he has woken up Brad Lee, the man in charge of tonight's crew. A flustered Brad opens the door, mainly because he has told all his colleagues to contact him by radio only. He brushed the breadcrumbs from his shirt, some catching in the obligatory line of pips on his shirt. This showed his past years of service to his country Xylens was unaware of this. Brad vaguely knew Raul when he occasionally stood in for Bob at the x-ray machine.

'Oh, hello, Dr Rodriquez; this is a surprise; I have no notification of you coming tonight. Are you okay? You look pale.'

Then Brad started to convulse, a bead of cold sweat on his head, and he staggered back into the cabin. No time to contact anyone by radio, Xylens has taken over him. Still in a trance, Raul turns and walks back to his car, impervious to all around him; he sits in his car in abject silence, waiting for Xylens to return. Time is of the essence; while Raul is alone in his car, the chances of detection are high. Such a high-profile site has more security than most military facilities. At this point, Brad, under Xylens control, leaves his cabin, informing everyone by radio comms he is on a walk around to check if they are doing their jobs. A few sniggers on his radio, many saying, 'We are going to hide; try and find us, boss.'

The more astute ones thought, 'why the hell as he told us that, surely it would be best to surprise them and see if they are doing their job properly.'

Second in command, Travis Brown, was on the radio straight away, 'are you okay, boss? Why are there no surprises this week.'

It is a conversation Xylens could do without; the more he talks, the more danger he is in, and he could easily slip up. 'Decided you all could do with a night off, but I might be lulling you into a false sense of security.'

'Okay, boss, take care.'

Brad gets into the security vehicle and automatically drives toward some huge doors, spreading one hundred metres across and at least fifteen metres high. The doors are visible from the main gate one and a half miles away; such is the size of the doors. He drives along the perimeter security fence line to indicate he is doing a perimeter check, passing two of his colleagues, who wave to him. Basically, self-checking that they are in their correct positions. Again, an involuntary wave back from Brad, Xylens is unaccustomed to this type of constant contact between each other. All these interactions are slowing him down, and as time gets short, he must achieve his goal of getting back home. The site is dimly lit up for a facility of such high profile; the main reason is to avoid pictures from airborne craft and the prying eyes of adventurous people or spies. The poor lighting has given Xylens an unexpected advantage as they get nearer to the large doors. As they approach them, standing guard is John Compton, an ex marine with his obligatory AR-15 in his hands.

Automatically he grips his gun tighter; this is unusual that site security comes this far down the site. Then, finally, Brad steps out of his vehicle. John knows Brad from his military days and eases his grip on his weapon, 'bit out of the way, Brad.'

'I needed a break, John, just a change of view; how are you,' as Brad approached him, he took his hands off his weapon, and it swung down to his right-hand side, shaking Brad's hand. John puts his hand in his pocket and takes out a packet of cigarettes; as he is about to offer Brad one, he takes a short pause. 'Are you okay, Brad? Even in this light, you look a bit pale. Do you feel okay?'

Then, John convulses the bead of sweat so commonplace now; Brad automatically turns and returns to his vehicle. The six in the UK are witnessing something no one else has seen and are about to see a part of a craft beyond their wildest dreams. Unfortunately, if the government ever found out, they would face a lengthy jail term. They can now sense Xylens is getting weaker, and all must concentrate on helping him; in unison, they think of Xylens, and he feels a sudden burst of strength.

John turns and stands in front of a door by the side of the larger ones, with a card reader and keypad for access. John slides a card down the reader and inputs a six-digit number; the door mechanism opens, and he walks into the building; the door closes automatically. Once inside, Xylens could see this place was vast, and the craft could not be seen; even to him, it was an eerily quiet place.

First, there was no sign of people working, and then he could see different rooms to his left and right with tinted windows; he could not see if anyone were in the rooms.

Most of the workforce is at home. The craft has been in this facility for so long that nobody gives it a second look unless a visiting dignitary is invited, under exceptional circumstances, after signing the official secrets act paperwork. Hence, the bare minimum workforce at the weekend will help Xylens get to the craft.

Once again, this common frail mindset of the human race, if you see something so often in one place, it never seems out of place, and they sometimes forget it even exists.

When Xylens transitioned into John, security control staff were changing for an evening meal beak, so no one noticed the white orb move from Brad to John; several questions will need to be answered by the morning.

18

After three hours, Don Small is now showing signs of agitation, which is not typical for this man, deciding to walk the entire perimeter of the field. Two more hours will have passed by the time he completes his walk around, talking to each of his forty men, helping to keep them motivated for the possible unknown encounter ahead.

By the time he reaches his starting point again, the agitation has not stopped; the thought of something sinister is happening. After walking the perimeter, he cannot understand how this mist seems encapsulated within its boundaries. It is the first time he has encountered such a phenomenon, and after checking with head office and weather agencies, there have been no recorded events of this type ever. He was quietly running scenarios through his head, trying to assess what might happen if they breached the hedgerow and crashed into the field. Even in the darkness, Don can sense a change in the mist; the clarity seems to have deepened. Shining his torch into the depths of the mist, it seemed to swallow the beam of light, with no reflected light coming back. As Don started to walk toward the hedge row, a loud crack as a lightning strike hit the floor five metres from him; this surprised his colleagues around him; Don raised his arm for them to stand down. Don can now guarantee that this is purely a protection device, so no one can stop what is happening inside the field. Therefore, he must take a calculated risk, which could endanger at least three of his men; he explains his thoughts to his men, his hypothesis that the lightning strikes are protecting the field.

He needs three volunteers to walk forward on his order to see if it happens on each side. No surprise to Don, every man volunteered; such is the respect he has from his men. He tells them to talk between themselves and come back to him in five minutes; it only takes two minutes. Likewise, the lead agent on each field side volunteered; Don thanked them and confirmed that they must all walk forward simultaneously. Finally, Don stepped back and, with an intake of breath, told them, 'on my count to three, walk forward, but do not touch the hedgerow,' a slight pause. Then, Don started his countdown, talking into his radio handset, 'one, two, three.'

The three men were stationed at the twenty-metre mark and started walking toward the hedgerow; when they reached the five-metre mark, three lightning strikes hit the floor simultaneously behind them. Don had positioned himself to look down one side of the field, and this strike confirmed his suspicions it was protecting the area, 'what the hell can be going on in there,' he thought to himself. Don thanks his lead agents for their help and explains what he thinks is happening; they are all surprised by his theory, and he tells all to go back to their trucks till further notice. Don now worried for Roger and Shaun, wishing he could get confirmation they were okay. The thought that they will be gone forever if he does not do something soon. His men march past, and each lead agent stops to confirm what they have all witnessed; Don thanks them, ensuring they will need to sleep for the next four hours if they can. Don hangs back and walks up the lane, unsure why there is no real need to, feeling he must go for some strange reason.

Walking up the lane, he stops inexplicably, as all the others have before him, at the centre point and shines the torch toward the hedgerow; it opens up just as it did for Roger and Shaun. Don staggers back in awe of what he has just seen; at his hesitation, the hedgerow closes.

Don was not a man who used swear words to express his feelings, but a few filled the air that night. Memories of his son's death were brought to the fore when the hedgerow moved. As he stared in disbelief, looking around in the darkness, he could not see anyone else who may have witnessed this event. Then suddenly, the clouds moved, and a full moon lit up the field; in the back of his mind, 'this cannot be happening; what the hell is going on.' Don sits on the ground, trying to gather his thoughts; he is used to strange things happening, and it does not make him feel afraid; he is curious indeed.

In most cases, there will be a simple explanation. Another ten minutes passed, and still sitting on the ground, he heard the familiar voice of Roger. Excited, he spins around to greet one of his proteges; nowhere to be seen, he puts his head in his hands, 'what the hell,' the comment broken by the sound of Shaun's voice. He is about to scream into the air, 'I'm going mad,' cut short by an interruption from Roger, 'all is okay, sir, we have everything under control.'

'How did you know I was here.'

'We think the field allowed us, so you do not breach it.'

'What the hell is going on.'

Roger tells him, 'the lightning is keeping us safe till its job is done.'

'What it is alive.'

'Not exactly, sir.'

Don starts to talk aloud, thankful his men are in their trucks, not hearing this, and hopefully are sleeping. Shaun interjects. 'sir, use your thoughts; we can communicate by thought.'

Silence from Don, not wanting to believe what he hears; this is impossible even after all these years of strange occurrences; he finds this hard to believe.

His mind stutters, 'are you both okay, are you harmed in any way.'

'Are you sitting down, sir?'

'I am now; what the hell is going on.' Don listens in disbelief to Roger and Shaun's voices, explaining that the four metal detectorists are with them and are safe and well. They have agreed not to tell Don about Xylens and his quest for freedom and to say they are all well and everything will come to light when they return. We cannot believe how we communicate with you; it must be something to do with the mist. Little did they know that this ability would stay with them forever and save their lives on many occasions in the future. But the human race is inconsistent and, on many occasions, will not believe the truth when they are told. In Don's mind, they could be getting coerced, but they have not used any safe words for any given situation embedded in their psyche. Don is in turmoil, and his usually stoic persona is being tested; he is a man who is used to problem-solving quite easily.

Yet his men tell him they are in no danger, and he must believe them and stand down; he turns and slowly walks to his vehicle in silence, still worrying for his men in the mist.

19

Xylens is now in the body of the security guard John Compton, having entered the large building via the side door. His eyes searched the building; accessing John's mind, he discovered his craft was over half a mile away. As they walk forward twenty metres, they come to a set of barriers; at these barriers, the floor drops fifteen metres, and he can see rail tracks, heavy machinery, and vehicles moving. A security guard below waves to John, and his radio comms crackles into life, 'Hi John, a sight for sore eyes, must be too cold outside, I guess.'

'Yep, just having a ten-minute warm-up.'

'See you in the canteen in one hour.'

'Yep, see you there.'

Xylens is still trying to get used to the human form's mannerisms; the barriers proceed on the right-hand side five metres from the wall, a continuous pathway, into the dark abyss ahead of him. The lighting is dim, and Xylens is puzzled by this, but it has been designed to get brighter when more people are in the complex to save on electricity, ironically.

The ten-minute walk to his craft will seem an eternity to Xylens, as his form creates an affinity to each craft they use, forming a bond so they can work as one. As he walks toward his craft, he can see in some of the rooms, taking mental notes, even after all these years, noticing parts of his craft are being dissected for re-engineering purposes. As with any planetary mission, it was a calculated risk that they might be caught. They never thought it would happen; after all, they are far superior beings.

Passing another two workshops, the sudden realisation that some of their technology could be used as superior weaponry for warfare. Xylens feels sick that they may have inadvertently created an even more violent planet. These emotions and the ability to think for himself are overwhelming to him now; in his old guise of being under the commissioner's control, this would be non-existent. However, he must get his disk before he ends this situation; he approaches another set of large doors. Still, he was surprised by the lack of people in what he would consider a critical installation. One of the main reasons for the lack of personnel is that the facility is so old that congress deemed a sizeable budget cut would take place; this already happened to Raul's department a couple of days ago. After all, the facility has such a reputation no human could penetrate the complex. Once again, familiarity has created a window of opportunity for Xylens to get inside. One more time, John swipes his keycard and types in different numbers on the keypad, also, having to use the eye retina scan, Xylens returns John's vision, and the scan is complete. Finally, the door opens, and for the first time in seventy-five years, Xylens can see his shattered craft.

A sense of joy and despair at the same time, emotions he had not felt before, and again a single tear falls down John's cheek. A man wearing a white coat, seated at some monitors, swings around on hearing the door open and close, 'who are you? This area is out of limits to you; get out.'

John carries on walking, not hearing anything; the man is shouting obscenities in his direction; he runs up the stairs to confront John. Then standing in front of John, he can see the eyes of Xylens.

He staggers back and trips, falling down the stairs and hitting his head. Xylens priority is to get the disk and set something in motion to end this madness of war.

A set of stairs have been erected to get into the craft through the damaged side, which is partly missing shearing off on impact. It was missing because if not connected to the craft it evaporates, so no evidence of the vessel can be found. In many incidents, if there are no survivors on impact, the whole ship vanishes because it cannot sense them being alive. But Xylens was nearby, and the ship could sense him; hence this gave his captors time to re-engineer their technology.

The six people back in the UK have witnessed the man falling down the stairs; unsure if he is okay, they have become involved in a possible murder or at least manslaughter by default if he does not survive. They try to break the bond with Xylens, but he has honed into them too strongly, and they cannot break free. Nevertheless, Xylens is so near to the next step of his freedom that he must carry on. The craft is not large by any means, measuring ten metres by fifteen metres; his race had designed this for the most efficient profile to travel long distances. Inside a cryo chamber for both beings, programmed to open in emergencies for long-distance journeys. An array of controls that human engineers have still not decoded, symbols of star constellations still unknown to the human race. It will be many years into the future before humanity will see these symbols of distant galaxies again. The two seats encompass the alien's form, so it becomes one; there are no switches or buttons, and the astronaut's brain controls everything.

It is the main reason the engineers cannot break the code to start it; only the fusion fuel cell was found at the rear due to the damage to the craft. The fusion fuel cell has been re-engineered to power up the facility, giving free electricity to the complex; this technology has not been given to the populist. Once again, the emphasis on control is similar to Xylens planet, so both worlds are the same but different; it is much slower progress on this planet; the seeds are there, and they will come; it seems inevitable to him.

John climbs the steps to the craft to access it, Xylens hearts beat faster, seeing the controls have not been dismantled; this will enable him to achieve his goal.

Xylens needs to access these controls and must transcend from John's body for a short while; in doing so, John stands rigid unaware of what is happening.

Xylens is getting weaker, more noticeable now he is struggling to immerse his hand into the craft's main fabric; for the first time,

Xylens can feel pain he has not known before. Nevertheless, he carries on; he must get this disk and leave; time is running out; it takes a full minute to get the disk; in normal circumstances, it would only have taken seconds. Then he moves to one of the seats and programs the craft to self-destruct in one hour. Finally, with the disk in hand, he returns to John's body Xylens emerges from the craft; he can see the man on the floor starting to get up; the rest in the UK have witnessed the man is okay and collectively give a sigh of relief. The man was still groggy and looking around, and he could see nothing wrong, his memory vague at the moment; then he heard the door close.

At this point, a colleague who had spent excessive time on the toilet, located at the other end of the room, walks into view.

'Hi Chris, are you okay? You do not look okay.'

Chris turns, 'I'm not sure, Dale, don't feel well at all.'

Dale guides him into a chair, then goes to the fridge and brings back a bottle of water; Chris slowly sips the water.

At this point, Dale notices blood dripping down Chris's neck, 'what the heck have you done,' to Chris.

'Nothing. I do not feel right; what is wrong with me.'

'Stay there. I will ring for a medic, and it looks like you have hit your head on something.'

'I can't have; I have been sitting at my desk all shift.'

Chris rings the onsite medic located one floor up, and she will be there in five minutes, emphasising to Dale to keep him hydrated. This interaction gives valuable time for Xylens to escape; by the time the medic arrives, he has reached the door to freedom. John Compton walks toward Brad's vehicle; the driver's side window opens, and the orb transitions to Brad again. John turns and retakes his position guarding the entrance, oblivious to his involvement inside the facility. Brad starts the vehicle and drives back the way he came from, heading toward Raul's car, guided by Xylens, waving to his colleagues again; they respond smiling, thinking the boss is quiet tonight. Driving to Raul's car, he parks behind him, gets out of his vehicle, and walks to Raul's car. Opening the front driver's door, and getting into the front seat, Xylens transitions again; he is getting weaker and weaker. Finally, they must get away to give him time to recuperate.

Brad leaves and walks back to his cabin, leaving his car; this is against site protocol, as it must be parked by his cabin for a quick response to an emergency. He waves to his two colleagues in the security house covering the site entrance, and both comment that it is the first time they have seen him out of his cabin for weeks. At this point, Raul drives to the entrance and stops at the gate; one guard comes out and requests to check around his car.

'Can you open the trunk, Dr Rodriques,' he duly obliges.

'All okay, Dr Rodriques, looking a bit pale. Are you okay?'

'Just tired, Jeff, too many long days and nights lately.'

'Okay then, you had better be on your way home to bed then.'

The gate opens, and Raul sets off to go home; twenty minutes have passed since Xylens set his craft into self-destruct mode; Raul will be long gone by then. In the meantime, the medic has transferred Chris to her medical room, where he is rambling about something or someone being in the facility. Jane, the medic, thinks the knock on his head may have caused him to be confused and asks him to calm down. Unfortunately, his agitation continues, so Jane contacts the command centre to explain his ramblings, who scan security cameras and notice John Compton, who should not have been there.

Forty minutes have passed since Xylens has set the self-destruct button, and four internal marine security guards are sent to arrest and bring John Compton to the command centre.

Unfortunately, while they were arresting John outside, Chris started to vomit and had a seizure; in the medical room, an agonising ten minutes later, Chris died due to a blood clot in his brain.

When they arrested a confused John at his post, five men witnessed the loudest lightning strike ever to hit the mountain containing the facility, rushing inside the building for safety.

20

Six people in the field of contention at Haltwhistle are thankful that their task is completed, knowing the man in the USA was safe? They gave each other an imaginary congratulatory tap on the back, all smiling and thinking it would be over soon. However, they have not realised they are still required to help Xylens to get to another craft; now, all are in danger; if Xylens fails to get to the other craft, they will be trapped within the field till they die. Xylens and Raul are driving home; with every mile that passes, Xylens is getting stronger, and he will recuperate quicker once Raul goes to sleep. Unfortunately, Raul is unaware of what Xylens has done, and if he manages to sleep, he will have a rude awakening. It is seventy minutes since Raul left the black site; as he reaches home, he parks on his driveway. Now thankful it is all over, and Raul can finally go to sleep, stepping out of his car, he looks skyward at the sound of several helicopters flying toward the black site, searchlights scanning the entire area. He starts to panic, and his heart starts to race, which awakens Xylens; Raul wrongly assumes they are looking for him at this stage. Xylens tries to calm him, but he is not listening. Raul opens his front door and starts running from room to room, throwing things into a travel bag, gathering toiletries and some clothes, and hunting through drawers to get as much loose cash as possible. Xylens is not used to a federal state, and the way the police system works, Raul is trying to explain that the authorities will be knocking on his door if they put two and two together.

Xylens voice starts to calm Raul, 'take a deep breath, slow down, tell me what you mean.'

Raul is sitting on the edge of his bed, still unmade due to a romantic liaison with his ex-wife, 'When I entered the facility, my access card automatically tells them the time and date I have been on site.'

'So if anything happens, they will go through the CCTV and video surveillance cameras.'

Xylens re-asserts that it will be okay to reassure him, 'You will not remember anything; an unknown entity had taken you over.'

'But how can I explain that to them if I cannot remember.'

'Exactly.'

'But I don,t understand; what should I do now.'

'First, how long would it take for your police force to get here.'

'Fifteen minutes to one hour, depending on transport, whether a helicopter or car, I don,t know.' Raul starts to shake, and the tears flow, 'oh no, what have I done.'

'Other than transport an alien lifeform into your facility, nothing at all,' even Xylens, in the short time he has interacted with the human race, has grasped irony and sarcasm. It did not go down too well with Raul, his agitation reaching a new high, 'we must leave now.' Rushing to his car, the odd shirt falling to the floor from his travel bag, he throws it on the back seat, jumps into the driver's seat, and starts the engine, tears still flowing. A neighbour on the early shift coming home sees Raul in distress, 'are you okay, Raul? Looking a bit pale.'

'I am okay, Mr Diaz, just stressed.'

At that moment, a gust of wind slams the front door shut. 'For goodness sake, I am locked out of my house now; the keys are on the table.'

Raul reverses off the drive, a car horn blasting out loud from his rear as he nearly crashes into another neighbour's car, who is on his way to work. Raul is waving his arms frantically in the air; apologetically, he speeds away. Xylens asks, 'what are you doing? Where are you going.'

'I must get away from here quickly before the police arrive.'

Slowly Xylens, explains that his job is not complete yet; Raul slams his foot on the brake, the car sliding along the tarmac to a standstill, early morning traffic swerving to avoid a collision. Finally, Raul screams out loud, 'what do you want from me? My life is ruined now, and I will have lost my job; my wife will probably leave me now; I wish you had not come into my life.'

Xylens calmly tells him, 'it will soon be over; everything will be okay, as one alien to another, it will be okay; I need to get to a place about five hundred miles east of here.' Strangely this simple statement calms Raul, and he starts to think logically, 'what would the authorities do to find him.' So he begins to troll through crime films in his head and starts to write things down in a notebook, a sense of humour coming back, 'this is why I kept the notebook in my car,' it was one of his kids who had left behind. He writes it down in order,

1. Must ditch the phone
2. Cash only, no card transactions
3. Change cars, how? (Sara's car)
4. How does he explain this situation to her?

He continues driving and is twenty minutes away from Sara's apartment; he cannot ring to tell her he is coming.

He had already thrown his phone out of the car a few miles back. Now that Raul is starting to think straight, Xylens has gone into sleep mode to recuperate. Raul drives into the multi-story carpark three hundred metres from the apartment block, parks the car in a secluded corner, and walks to Sara's apartment, carrying his travel bag. Luckily her apartment is located on the first floor next to the lift; he rings the doorbell several times, but it takes three minutes before she reaches the door. Looking through the door eyeglass to see who it would be at this hour of the morning, surprised to see an agitated Raul, she opens the door. 'What the hell, Raul, what's wrong?

Sara invites him in, and she notices the travel bag, 'Raul, what is going on? Why the travel bag.' Raul guides her to her lounge area and sits her down; Sara responds, 'I am worried, Raul; what is wrong with you? Why are you here.'

'I can't explain, Sara, but I need your car urgently.'

'But why, what's wrong? What's going on.'

'I can't explain. It will put you in danger.'

'Oh, my God, what have you done.'

'It's hard to explain; please give me the keys to your car.'

'No, not till you tell me what is going on.'

'I can't, and you would not believe me anyway.'

Sara raised her voice, 'try me, Raul, try me for God's sake.'

Raul stops talking as Xylens enters his head, telling him, 'I think after your night of passion, she will be able to accept your problem.'

'It will be difficult to explain, Sara.'

'Go on, try.'

'Firstly, do not scream or go mad at what I am about to say.'

'I am getting mad waiting; Raul, stop messing around, will you? Get on with it.'

'Right here goes, yesterday evening I was taken over by an alien,' Sara jumps up, 'Raul, stop lying to me,' He grabs her shoulders, 'look into my eyes.'

Sara stares in disbelief as she sees Rauls's eyes change and faints back onto the chair where she is sitting. A few minutes pass, and Raul gives her a glass of water; she looks at him, astonished at what she has just witnessed.

'But how Raul, oh my goodness, we are all going to die.' Raul calms her down, 'you have been watching too many crazy films, Sara; it's not like that, Xylens just wants to go home.'

'Good grief, it's got a name.'

'Sara, calm down; please let me take the car.'

'Not till you tell me how it happened.'

I would love to, but time is not on my side; I need to get away from here, and now, it will take far too long to explain.

'Well, you can tell me on the way then.'

'What, you cannot come with us; what about the kids.'

'They are with my mother till Monday, and I was going to decorate.'

Xylens tells him it will be the quickest way to move forward instead of arguing; 'it will give you someone to talk to on the way.'

Raul tells Sara to pack a bag, leave her phone and only bring cash.

21

John Compton has been hauled into the control room to answer his actions, 'what have I done? I have been at my post all evening.'

'You have been seen inside this facility between 01.00 and 02.00 hours, John. Can you explain why?

'Respectfully, sir, I have been at my post all evening; I did not leave till I was falsely arrested.'

Captain Rae takes John into another room with wall-to-wall screens, 'Look at the screen to your top left.'

John could not believe his eyes, as he could see himself walking around the facility and into the room where the craft was located. In the craft room, they witness the altercation with Chris, and then Chris falls down the stairs; luckily, John had made no contact with him, and then he was seen entering the craft.

'But sir, that is not me; I did not enter the building.'

'Why did you go into the craft, John.'

'You have got to believe me, sir; I would not do anything to jeopardise this facility.'

Captain Rae has known John for many years, serving in Iraq with three tours together, and he wants to believe him, but the evidence is beginning to look overwhelming that it is him. Then the phone rings; it is Jane, the medic, informing him Chris has died; the Captain tells John of Chris's demise, who is visibly shaken by the news.

The Captain continues with his questions, 'why did you go in the craft.'

'I did not; that was not me, sir.'

'Look at the screen, man; it's you damn it.'

'But sir, it cannot be me; I was outside all evening check security cameras.'

With John's constant denials and their past history together, Rae is starting to doubt the validity of the screen, and he must get to the bottom of this quickly.

Captain Rae requests footage from the cameras outside the building; as they look at the screen, they see Brad drive up. First, both are talking, and then something happens that they cannot believe; they look at each other in awe.

As they re-run the tape to confirm what they saw, one of the operators shouts to the Captain, 'sir, we have a problem,' not words the Captain wanted to hear.

On another screen, they catch a beam of intense blue light emanating from the craft, and they watch in disbelief as the beam hits the large interior metal door. The door disintegrates; there is no sign of the metal, no noise, and people start running to escape, expecting a loud explosion. Instead, the Captain hits the alarm button, and different horns and sirens all sound in unison for people to evacuate the building. Over the tannoy system, he shouts, 'this is not a drill, this is not a drill, everybody leave the building immediately, go to your designated muster points now. Then the blue light becomes more intense as it hits the larger doors, half a mile away, which also disintegrates. Both watched as the craft slowly disappeared, evaporating before their eyes as though it did not exist. Also, unknown to them, all the items they were re-engineering disappeared. Then total darkness, paradoxically, the craft was powering electricity for the site, and the sirens and horns went silent.

The only things that operated were anything with batteries till they went flat.

Then Rae and John raced for the exit in case something else was about to happen; the backup generators were overloaded by what had happened, and all the internal wiring was completely burnt out.

Emergency calls to Colonels, woken from slumbers and happy dreams, crashed down to Earth in a millisecond. More calls for authorisation to send emergency equipment to a black site that does not exist. The higher echelon is now looking for heads to roll, never blaming themselves for the budget cuts; they implored the government to do so. After all, nothing ever happens there.

Raul witnessed the sudden availability of supplies as the helicopters flew overhead, prompting him to go on the run, unaware that it would be several hours before the jigsaw pieces started to drop.

The human race has just seen the incredible power of an alien race and the dangers of what they might find if they continue their obsession with space exploration.

Also, as the craft evaporated, the scientist in Raul's laboratory witnessed the outer husk of Xylens body disappear. Again, there were frantic calls to superiours, but what could they do as daylight approached? Military troops were gathering as though WW3 was about to start. Xylens has undoubtedly left his footprint within this black site that does not exist.

22

Even though the six in Haltwhistle cannot move, a sense of pride re-verberates among them a job well done; one hour has passed, and the six are becoming unsure why they have not been released yet. Shaun took the lead to try and contact Xylens; with the help of the rest and a concentrated effort by all this time, communication was established far more quickly than anticipated. A two-way conversation over thousands of miles, they still could not believe it, just by thought alone, still seems incredible to them. Sarcastically Roger's humour drops in again; 'at least it will save on the phone bills; think how much money we could save.' The others laughed, thinking he was right; long distant mind calls to Australia are the way to go. They all noticed how quickly they could talk and respond, little realising their abilities were getting fine-tuned by the time this adventure was over. They will be different people with different outlooks on life.

Xylens is now trying to explain that he needs them for a few hours more, that his craft was damaged beyond repair, and that they are making their way to another craft, only hours away. Finally, Peter, who has been a silent participant up to now, other than when they needed to concentrate on helping Xylens, breaks his silence. 'Good grief, how many are they? This could be a bloody invasion, and we are helping them to invade; we have been taking for fools.'

It, unfortunately, triggered four of the six, who are now getting angry and felt they were being used and are now prisoners, trapped in a void they could not escape from, still motionless.

Xylens now realises that this freedom of choice can be a burden that can create problems, as everyone is on a different page; if you all disagree about other things, this exasperates his situation; he must control the narrative, or all is lost. The comparison between this world and his own is monumental, but which is correct? He will need to search for answers to a complex situation in which he has no experience.

Xylens can shut different people out of the conversation, so he communicates with Roger and Shaun, already knowing these are the strongest two mentally. He explains to Roger and Shaun, 'I want to return to my planet, as you would if you were on mine; we are not invaders as Peter assumed; please help me. Can you persuade them I need all of you to concentre? Two alone will not do; I am too weak without your help.'

'I can force all of you to help me, but all respect will be gone, and we will become enemies; I do not want that, and neither do you.'

Roger and Shaun agree that it would be of mutual gain to help each other and resolve the animosity Peter had caused. Xylens is thankful for their support and opens channels to the other four, an ability that Roger and Shaun find astounding. They open up to everyone and start to tell them that not everything they see and believe is true and partially explain what their jobs are. Then they explained to them that on many occasions, they have needed to use their gut instinct to carry on; we both think this is one of the times. Also, telling them that you have witnessed Xylens abilities, he could have, done something to us at any time; Peter interjects, 'but we have not finished his work; he could do anything to us.'

A curt reply from Roger, 'You could die tomorrow; either way, we are helping with or without you, Peter.'

Peter stutters, trying to reply; Joanne decides enough is enough and, as always, pragmatically says, 'we are all in here; we will not get out till Xylens allows us to anyway.'

Shaun shouts up, 'are we going to carry on then? I would say a show of hands to confirm, but a simple yes will suffice.'

A total of five said yes, except Peter, who stayed silent; this simple act of defiance will impact Peter's now limited future, as he will leave with no abilities. Unfortunately for Peter, only people who help will be rewarded. As the rest retune immediately to Xylens, they have agreed to help, Xylens tells them they will go back into sleep mode till he requires them, but can sense Peter does not want to participate. Ten minutes later, Peter is still conscious, realising the rest are asleep, he tries to contact them, but he is met with silence. His mind is now in turmoil, and for the first time, he has a sense of panic; where is he? What is he doing here? Why am I on my knees in a field on my own? I should be home, but where is home? Peter is starting to lose all semblance of what has happened to him, his memory gradually fading to nothing. He struggles to stand; his hands seem stuck to the ground; they are so heavy; what the hell is going on? Then looking at his right hand, he can feel intense pain in his wrist, wanting to scream, but no noise; his heart is racing so fast; what is happening?

Staring at his wrist, the look of astonishment as the amulet comes to the surface of his wrist.

Then it falls to the ground and disappears into the soil; his hands are now free, he frantically scrapes at the earth, and there is no sign of the amulet.

Realising he can stand up, he turns around; in Peter's mind, he can see that the field is overgrown with weeds and shrubbery everywhere. But, in fact, it was in pristine condition; why would he be here, his metal detector gone in an instant, as though it never existed? At this point, he steps back, falling through the hedgerow, two of Don's men rush to assist him, and lightning strikes either side of them; they stop as Peter staggers towards them. Then, a call over the radio for Don to come to the southeast corner urgently; Don walks quickly, his days of running are long gone, but with a brisk walk, he is there in ten minutes. Turning the corner, Don can see his men giving Peter some water and medical attention; he is not harmed physically, but when questions are asked, it will determine if Peter is okay or mad. Finally, they stand him up, so Don can talk to him; one of his men tells Don about him falling through the hedgerow.

Don asked him, 'what is your name.' there was abject silence as if he could not hear; Don looked into his eyes which looked dim and vague, as though he had suffered trauma. Again Don asked the same question, no response; Don called one of his men over, who could do sign language, but still no response; Don took an unusual decision to slap him, still no response.

Don shouts to two colleagues, 'get him to our special unit urgently; we must get answers out of him quickly, and use my car, go now.'

They scurry off with Peter, who is in what looks like a zombie state; both men are wondering what is going on in that field.

It takes twenty-five minutes; such is Peter's state, which seems to be getting worse by the minute. Then a call from Don on the radio, 'Jim as he got any ID on him,' wishing he had checked before they had left. So Jim started going through various pockets to retrieve his ID.

'Yes, sir, it is Peter Howes.'

'Thank you,' Don dials a number to give his head office an update, now nervous that a similar fate awaits the other five within this energy field. A return call to Don verified that Peter was from Portsmouth, and it was his car on the lane. Don was organising his men to do an assault on the field. Then the voices of Shaun and Roger came into his head again; these mind calls are unnerving, but he is slowly getting used to them. The timing was impeccable, as though he was being watched; he looked around as the sunrise hit his eyes, casting shadows along the ground. Then, he asked Roger, 'what the hell is going on in there.'

'All quiet here, sir.'

'What's the story with Peter Howes, then.'

'What do you mean, sir.'

'He has just come crashing through the hedgerow in a hell of a state.'

'Shaun and Roger are both surprised by Don's statement, 'can we come back to you? We need to check something out.'

'Don't be too long; things are getting tetchy if you do not want a full-blown assault on your hands.'

Roger and Shaun try to contact Xylens; their ability to do so is getting faster each time, and Roger contacts him immediately, coming directly to the point.

However, before two words were spoken, Xylens interrupted him, acutely aware of the question that Roger was about to ask.

Speaking first, he tells them that 'Peter has left voluntarily, of his own volition, with no coercion from him, and he would not listen; I told him there are risks if he leaves now.'

'What risks,' from Shaun, now concerned about himself and the rest, Xylens calmly replies, 'that Peter will have memory loss for a short time. Then he will be okay.' He has not lied to them; he missed out on some valuable information that, if pushed further, he would have told them more. His race can only tell the truth if questioned; to lie is a breach of their space code. Again an alien race controlling their own kind, similar to our dictators on Earth; these similarities were getting a bit too regular now. Shaun makes contact and creates an open line with Don, explaining that 'Peter will be okay in a few hours; they have assurances from a third party, which will become abundantly clear when we come out.'

'I hope so because this man is not in a good place now.'

'Thank you, sir; keep the Calvery away till we request it, but I don,t think we will need them.'

Roger is concerned about Don's statement, and, as usual, Xylens calms his anxiousness, 'do not worry, I did not want to tell you till I was about to go home. But all of you will have abilities you did not have before; when Peter left, those abilities automatically went; his body is now re-adjusting, that is all.'

Shaun and Roger are nervous about this new situation, puzzled by what it will mean to them all; it could be good or bad; they have not got long to find out now, as Xylens goes silent.

23

After many conversations with Roger and Shaun, Xylens drops to sleep mode inside Raul, who is now feeling like an old, well-worn jacket. The five-hour drive to the other craft will be short compared to his imprisonment; he should feel anger but can see if someone landed on his planet, the scenario would be the same. While he sleeps, Raul and Sara are coming to terms with Raul's decision to help an alien race; Sara does not know whether to laugh or cry, riding this wave of excitement. Finally, Raul moves the back of the seat down, telling Sara he has only had three hours of sleep since he left work, asking her if she can let him sleep for two hours and he will be okay.

The look of disappointment was enough for Raul to forego his sleep, realising she was after answers, raising the seat back to its original position. The smile was enough to tell him he had made the right decision for once. 'Go on, ask your questions, Sara.'

Sara responded with a whisper, 'what is it like having an alien inside you.' pointing to his stomach.'

'To be honest, when it first happened, I felt sick and had nausea; now I forget he is there.'

The thought that her ex-husband is a carrier of another being is complex for Sara to grasp, and she wonders if he has made the right decision. She realises that Xylens can communicate with others but has not made contact with her; she wonders why. The simple answer is she does not possess the genetic marker the rest have, which makes it much easier for Xylens to talk to them.

It could become a problem for him if she realises Xylens cannot enter her mind.

Raul starts to describe the beauty of Xylens planet, which is far greater in size than Earth; they are socially thousands of years ahead of us, but their technology is unbelievable. If Raul knew what it was like, he would instantly change his opinion. Also explaining he has been a captive since 1947, Sara recoiled in horror at this statement; a prisoner for seventy-five years, she wanted to be sick there, and then, pulling over the car, she got out and vomited at the roadside. Raul gets out to comfort her, wiping away tears; she could not believe our government could do that to another being. Unfortunately. Sara was unaware her husband was one of his jailors for the last twenty years; he dared not tell her now, or their relationship would be gone forever. He comforts her and guides her back to the car, 'do you want me to drive for a while, Sara.'

'Yes, please, we must get him home, Raul; we must help him, damn the cost.'

Inadvertently, Xylens has witnessed the human frailty for living things and now understands that a small minority only have the mental ability to start wars. Sara, still upset, tells Raul to drive; he knows she will be silent for some time now. It is the way she is till she resolves it in her head. So the many questions Sara was so excited to ask have now long gone, pushed to the back of her mind; they seem so minuscule now. So he is driving towards Utah, not knowing where to go, but is sure his built-in Sat nav will wake up and tell him in a few hours. Drive time is around four hours, so he settles down to drive, puts the car into cruise control, and takes his feet off the peddles, hoping it will be over soon.

Raul is impervious to the carnage that Xylens has left behind, and he turns the radio on; this was switched off when Sara wanted to talk.

He re-tuned to a news channel, and over the airwaves, there is an unfolding incident in Nevada, and a state of emergency has been declared, and there will be hourly updates as they come in. Raul starts to sweat and constantly looks into his mirrors; he will fall to pieces if confronted. Then the sound of sirens, he sweats more profusely; the police cars are coming towards him; what should he do? He pulls over. The police cars speed past him, heading in the direction he had come from; in his head, he thinks, 'of course, all services will be heading toward the black site area.' Now with an air of bravado, he carries on with his journey, knowing all resources will be focused locally in the short term. It will give him more time to help Xylens abscond this planet; he puts the car back into cruise control and heads toward Utah again.

24

Back at the black site, there are more generals than soldiers, all assembled at the front of the building, with lots of finger-pointing and arms waving. Oblivious to any harm or injuries that may have happened to the personnel. Twenty of the staff suffered minor injuries while rushing to leave the building, two with broken ankles tripping over items knocked over on the floor.

Before the enclave of Generals arrived in descending rank, all with enough pips on their tunics to cover a toilet picture gallery. John Compton and Brad Lee were frog-marched to a secluded part of the site for further interrogation, protesting their innocence to what had happened. These two men will be scapegoats for the hierarchy, so their hands are not soiled, and the term innocent until proven guilty will not apply until sufficient proof shows they are not implicated.

Captain Rae will also suffer a demotion for now; this incident happened on his watch, a situation way above their control and understanding; after all, millions of dollars of US money had gone up in smoke. The noise of helicopters is deafening; six suddenly part away, they are forming a circle of protection; coming into land is the President. Even the president said sarcastically.

'Good grief, I did not know we had this many Generals; I think we need to re-visit the military budget.' It was overheard by his closest aide, who smirkingly agreed, anything to keep his job. Coming down the steps of the helicopter, he is greeted by his Lead General, who brings him up to speed on what they think has happened until further investigations are made.

Looking for more gold braid, one Lieutenant Colonel mentioned the apprehension of the two culprits, an assumption of guilt without proof.

But neither have the technical expertise for such a task; they have accused Compton and Lee of installing a device that decimated the craft and doors way beyond their capabilities. Although, the device destroyed two bomb-proof inner and outer doors, with no evidence they existed. The craft disappeared before their eyes; they still do not know yet of all the periphery items that have also gone without a sign that they existed.

It will take a miracle to exonerate the three accused individuals; even the evidence Rae and Compton are trying to explain is falling on deaf ears. Brad Lee, like Compton, can not explain why he contacted him; he was in his cabin all the time, with no recollection of the past few hours. While they are subjected to a constant barrage of questions, also the standard one, do you work for the Russians? These two innocent people will have their lives scrutinised, no stone unturned; their past brought up memories of the service they gave to their country, now slowly being eroded to find a scapegoat. As the questions come thick and fast, externally, the military is erecting large metallic screens to protect what is left inside away from prying eyes.

Suddenly there are small private aircraft in the air, trying to see what has happened, with high-end cameras with incredible zoom ratios to see into the building. Two drones come into view, and a General orders them to be shot down immediately; one man, one rifle, and two drones fall to the floor in two shots; give that man a pip.

The drones are collected and crushed, and all evidence is gone. The situation is worsening by the minute, and a twenty-mile no-fly zone is implemented; at this point, the president decides his presence has been a good PR exercise and decides it is time to leave. He is telling his Generals to keep his aide posted with updates and mentally thinking about budget cuts to his military, which after what he has seen, is far to top heavy. Emergency contracts are made for specialist contractors to work on a top-secret site to repair all that was damaged; when called for, the system can take shortcuts.

Three hours have passed since the incident, and the interrogation is stopped; Lieutenant Dicks, who is watching the proceedings, can feel something is not right; having observed Rae's and Compton's interview, he feels they are telling the truth. He respectfully asks to speak to Rae, and his interviewer leaves, giving him five minutes. He asked a couple of basic questions before he asked Rae, 'do you have any proof that you were not culpable for what has happened?'

Rae explains about the recording, 'I cannot explain what we saw; you should make your own conclusion.' Lt Dicks asked where the recording was located; Rae replied, 'in the server room, Row C, cabinet six and four hard drives down,' he carries on, 'if it has not been fried by whatever happened?' Dicks lets the interviewer back in and leaves the room himself; then, breaking into a jog, he runs across the compound to another building two hundred metres away. Reaching the main door, he is immediately confronted by a guard positioned to let no one in due to the recent event. Unfortunately, not even his rank can get him through the door, yet another obstacle in the military wheel.

He must find someone to let him in, 'who do I need to contact to authorise entry then.'

'That would be Captain Rae.'

'He is incarcerated now, and I need to be in to help get him free.'

'Sorry, sir, for all I know, you could be going in to destroy evidence.'

Dicks cannot blame the guard; he is doing his job; down to the letter; he will need to bring someone higher ranked than the Captain to gain access. He returned ten minutes later with Major Colson, and as it happened, he commanded the guard in Iraq now standing on duty. 'Let him in, Jones; by the way, well done for doing your job properly, well done, I wish others had done the same today.' Major Colston leaves, and Dicks is stood waiting till Jones's broad smile is gone; a man with pride in his job, he finally lets Dicks into the building.

Dicks runs up the stairs two at a time, and conscious time is of the essence for Rae and Compton. He reaches the door to the server room, flashing his keycard, 'damn, what was the access code Rae gave me? Calm down, think, man, come on. Dicks has only three attempts, or he will be locked out; 179026, a red light beeps at the first attempt; he is sure they are the numbers. Second attempt: 197062, a red light; he only has one more shot. It has got to be correct: 179620, green light and the latch on the door clicks; on opening the door, there are rows of servers. The room is vast; this is not an ordinary server room; something else is going on here, he thinks, he knows the site is large, but this server room is ten times bigger than it should be. He has to forget about this at the moment and find the hard drive, 'good grief, which end do I start,' he thinks.

Commonsense tells him left to right, but this is the military; things are not easy; the door is central to the room; walking forward, he comes to rows, L-M-N he needs to go right to left. Then finding row C, cabinet six, and searching for the hard drive four down, Dicks removes the drive. But he now realises the pungent smell of burnt-out electronics around him; he had not noticed due to his adrenalin rush. He sigh's in disbelief, all his effort for nothing, but he must at least give it a try. Rushing back to the building where Rae and Compton are being held, Dicks request's a computer, and the connection leads to connect the hard drive to the computer. Switching the computer on, waiting for an eternity, he realised the battery was flat, and they still had no electricity. He wanted to throw the laptop at the wall in frustration, clenching his fist, wondering why life was conspiring against him. Three men's lives and careers are on the line, all for the sake of electricity seems ironic, as Xylens is trying to give them clean energy.

25

Raul and Sara are halfway to their unknown destination; Raul has calmed down considerably when Sara asks him to pull over; she will drive for a while so he can get some sleep. Sara takes over the driving; she looks across at Raul; she can now see how exhausted he looks and realises the significant risk Raul is willing to take to help this unknown alien. One and half hours further down the road, Sara can see a roadside café. In the distance and pulls over for much-needed coffee; as the car stops, Raul stirs, thankful for the stop, when he sees the roadside café. Knowing it will be dark in a couple of hours, they need some sustenance to keep going; they enter the café, which is quite crowded. Some customers are curious, turn around with a knowing nod, and then return to their conversations. Also, as with the human nature of herd mentality, they bow down and carry on eating; as they sit down, a server walks over to take their order. Placing their order, the server walks back behind the counter and turns the volume up on the TV. Everybody stops talking as the news channels update the public about the incident in Nevada but does not tell them what the incident is. Once again, protectionism is the government's byword so that people do not worry about it. They cannot be concerned if they do not know what is happening; the mention of a twenty-mile land and air inclusion zone pricks Raul's ears, wondering what Xylens may have done.

Then the bacon and eggs arrive for them both, a sudden thought from Raul, what will Xylens do when he attempts to eat the food, having vomited the coffee up a couple of days ago?

Luckily Xylens is still in sleep mode, gaining much-needed strength by the hour for his journey home.

The people in the café start to discuss the incident in Nevada, and as usual, conspiracy theories start to be addressed regarding the national emergency. Heated arguments between true patriots and non-believers, some saying they believe the government to be corrupt.

After finishing their meal, they decide it best not to get involved and must carry on to their unknown destination. As Raul returns to the car, Sara decides she will buy some items to take with them, and she purchases different sandwiches, drinks, candy, crisps and various papers. Raul takes over the driving. He noticed a motel on the opposite side of the road already in his mind knowing they would need it on their return journey home. It is another ninety minutes before Xylens stirs. Finally, he tells Raul to turn left into the desert and head towards a raised mound half a mile away. This mound only formed fifty years after Xylens unfortunate incident; it hides its true identity below the surface. Another surveillance craft slightly larger than his own could carry four beings. This craft was programmed to search for the remnants of Xylens craft, and the two beings inside are still in a suspended state inside their cryo chambers. As with any technology, no matter how advanced, it can go wrong, which is what happened when passing the sun; a solar storm affected some of its instrumentation. Both beings were not woken automatically, so they could take over and guide the craft to their objective. But their technology is so advanced that the craft was carried onto Earth, orbiting the planet for a signature so it could land.

There was no signature, so the AI of the craft decided to bring it down near the last signal that Xylens craft had given out. As it landed undetected, the craft set in motion a force shield around it so no one could see it. Then, as daylight rose, the surroundings were reflected, showing nothing was there.

Over the years, the wind had blown dust and debris up and around it forming the mound. But, even though it was only half a mile from the highway, nobody noticed.

The full moon silhouettes the mound, and darkness falls quickly around here; Sara comments on its strange beauty, unaware that the mound will disappear shortly. As Raul and Sara drive up to the mound, staying back fifty metres, they leave their headlights on to witness something no other human will see.

But half a mile away, officer Jenks is just about to tuck into his favourite cheeseburger and fries, complete with a large iced drink. The drink was placed in the cupholder by his side, the fries perfectly balanced on top of the dashboard, and the hearty cheeseburger was resting on his portly stomach. He had volunteered for traffic duty; he liked the power of pulling over people for self-satisfaction. Most colleagues were happy he was on the road; not being liked was something he loved. His demeanour was quite aggressive, telling those who would listen that it was a good trait, and nobody would argue the point with him. As he finished his cheeseburger and fries, with a modicum of grease oozing down his chin, a paper towel was supplied to wipe it away, which subsequently ended up in the passenger footwell of the police car. Then the police radio crackles; a disturbance at the roadside café further up the road; he responds he is on his way.

He started his vehicle and, with his foot hard down on the accelerator pedal for maximum effect, wheels spinning, and dust and small rocks flew into the air.

On his way, he notices a car's headlights half a mile into the desert and informs despatch to send someone else to the café; he thinks poachers are up to no good.

While Jenks heads toward the lights, Raul and Sara are coming to terms with the fact that their alien friend is about to leave. Raul and Sara get out of the car; the air is still warm with the sun just setting in the distance, the silence broken by the sound of crickets common in the area. Xylens thanks Raul for his help and tells him to warn Sara about what will happen when he leaves his body; Raul turns to Sara, standing nervously by his side.

'Sara, do not scream and shout, but Xylens is about to leave my body.'

'I'm not scared, but will you be okay? Will you get hurt?'

'I will be okay, there will be some slight nausea, and on the good side, I won,t be pale anymore,' trying to lighten the situation. A cursory half smile from Sara, hoping he would be okay. Then she notices Raul's stance stiffen, and an orb starts to come out of Raul's chest; Sara stares in wonderment at what she is witnessing. Then the orb began to change into Xylens body form, and strangely it was Raul who asked Xylens if he was okay; then a conversation took place inside Raul's head, which Sara could not hear. Sara could see the gentle eyes of this alien and wished they could have helped sooner. Xylens turned to wave goodbye, but Sara rushed forward and hugged him with her bag of goodies to give Xylens; as though he was a child going on a school trip.

Sara explains you can show your kind what food we eat, and the papers will give you an insight into our different politics, which in fairness, is brutal.

Xylens put his arms around her; emotions flooded his brain, which he had never felt before, thinking they could not leave this planet to die. He blinks, and a small tear falls onto Sara's neck and quickly absorbs into her skin. Xylens steps back and touches her forehead, and she can hear him for the first time, and happy tears fall down her cheek.

He asks her to take care of Raul and that everything will be okay; he turns to walk towards the mound then some headlights come into view. He tells Raul to take Sara into the car as the headlights come closer, and as the car door closes, Xylens waves his left hand, and a dark shield forms around the vehicle; they cannot see anything. They attempt to get out of the vehicle, but they cannot, and then the voice of Xylens pops up in Raul's head, telling him, 'not to worry, all will be well soon.' Raul grasps Sara's hand and explains what has just happened. While in the darkness, they can hear the sound of the car getting closer.

Jenks is driving toward the headlights, which had just gone out, when Xylens places the shield around the car and is confronted with something he finds impossible to comprehend; before him, an alien seems to be waiting for him. Jenks is in a dilemma, confrontation or run, and arrogance is his forte; he slams on the brakes, headlights shining on Xylens, car and body cam working.

Then, as with most American police forces, he unholsters his gun, pointing it at Xylens and, rather than ask questions, instinctively fires a shot at Xylens, at which point a shield absorbs the bullet.

Xylens alien race will only retaliate if attacked; Jenks seeing the shell being absorbed, fires three more times. Raul and Sara are helpless in the car; on hearing the sound of gunfire, they instantly think the worse has happened, unable to give any assistance to Xylens.

The last thing Jenks saw was Xylens wave his left hand, and an impulse of light went through him and towards his vehicle, and he and the vehicle were vaporised, and no evidence was left at the scene.

Xylens, in just a short time, has witnessed the good and bad of this small planet Earth.

The shield disappears from around Raul and Sara, unaware of the violence that has just occurred; maybe if Raul knew the immense power Xylens processes, he might not have been so helpful. But, even before they stepped out of the car, their memories would be erased when Xylens left Earth.

Raul and Sara wondered why Xylens was outside, thinking he was still inside Raul, both shrugging their shoulders about to ask the question that never came as Xylens turned to the mound. But, instead, he spread his hands apart, and the rocks started to move away from the mound, both in awe of what they could see, which to them was impossible. Then, walking forward, Xylens disappears into the protective shield that has surrounded the craft for twenty-five years. Inside the craft, which had automatically switched on, all the auxiliary services had been on standby so that the cryo chambers were operable. Xylens could see his fellow beings and thought it best to wake them when he was away from Earth. Xylens checked the cryo chambers to see that all the relevant readings were okay and his new-found colleagues were safe.

Even advanced aliens had moved on with technology when he

left his planet, and he struggled to re-configure the controls to his mindset. After several minutes of unusual frustration, his own lifeforms could stop him from returning home, and he is so near to leaving this little planet. Then the craft accepts his genetic code and the chair wraps around him; the joy from despair to freedom was indescribable, emotions non of his lifeforms have felt due to the pills.

Outside, Raul and Sara wondered why it was taking so long; it seemed an eternity to them. Then they could feel the Earth starting to shudder; it had taken Xylens ten minutes to familiarise himself with the craft.

They stepped back to stand behind the car, frightful of flying debris; as the craft rose, hovering two metres off the ground, there was no sound, no heat. Raul was surprised by this, wishing he could see inside. Then what looked like a porthole opened, and they could see Xylens; Sara grabbed Raul's hand in excitement as Xylens bowed his head forward and waved his hand goodbye; in an instant, he was gone.

They stood there in silence, happy yet sad they could not tell anybody; in fact, no one would believe them anyway. Finally, they got into the car, made their way to the highway, turned right, and headed towards the café they had been in only a few hours ago. Fifteen minutes down the road, both look at each other and simultaneously say, 'why are we here? How did we get here.' With no memory of the last twenty-four hours.

Raul pulls over, head in hands, searching for clues in his mind; little does he know these memories will come back in his dreams.

Sara bombards him with questions that neither can answer, and they decide to carry on; not knowing where they are, Sara asks Raul, 'how many miles on the car.' Looking at her perplexed, 'what for Sara,'

'I got the car serviced yesterday; how many miles Raul.'

He gives her the mileage; Sara responds, 'for crying out loud, we have travelled over seven hundred miles, Raul.'

'But how could we do that without knowing what's happened to us?'

Sarcastically Sara's curt reply was, 'It must have been an alien abduction; it's the only answer.'

'Now you are crazy,' forgetting he had assisted in keeping an alien a prisoner for the last twenty years.

They continue for another hour when Sara tells Raul, 'I don't feel well at all.'

Raul can see the lights of the motel ahead, 'we will stay here for tonight; and maybe you will be much better after a good night's sleep.'

Raul pulls up to the motel, parking outside reception; he walks in and mockingly requests the penthouse suite, not knowing why he did so; this night is strange indeed.

Instead, the man in reception gives him the keycard to room 105, five doors to his left; Raul returns to the car, asking Sara if she is okay to walk to the room. They walk to the room, and the biggest thunderclap roars across the sky. Lightening hits the area where the mound used to be; torrential rain starts to fall; Raul says to Sara, 'this is just like one of those old horror movies, spooky, eh.'

Raul uses the keycard and looks inside the room, 'I guess you get what you pay for.'

Sara follows him in, also not impressed with the room; she sits on the bed.

'How are you feeling now.'

'I don,t know; I have never felt this way before.'

'What do you mean? Do you need to go to a hospital?'

'No, it's just that my hormones are on fire; I have never felt so aroused.'

'What do you mean, sexually.'

'Yes, oh my God, I need sex now, Raul.'

Grabbing Raul, she starts to do things she has not done before; for Raul, it is like a pleasure dome of sexual experiments.

For the next two hours, both are locked in positions of pleasure neither has experienced before.

Sara somehow held back Raul's ejaculation till they climaxed together. Finally, they both woke up in each other's arms, not remembering anything other than Sara feeling ill. They decide to shower, then they notice some bruising on both of them, 'have we been in an accident, Raul.'

'No, Sara, I think we would know about it.'

'It's just that we are both covered in bruises; why?'

'What the hell, Sara, where have we been.'

Unfortunately, they will never realise what happened that night, but memories will be jogged unexpectedly in a few months. Finally, they get dressed, check out, and continue their journey home; Raul must get to work tomorrow.

They walk over to the café across the road to get breakfast and coffee for the journey home. Once again, they sit at a table; the server ambles over to their table, the same one from the evening before.

'You must have enjoyed the eggs and bacon to call back so soon.'

'Have we been here before,' from Sara

'Yes, last night.'

Raul and Sara did not want to startle the server, and Raul said, 'I told you we should not have had that whiskey; you know how it affects our memory.' Winking to Sara, so they are on the same page. Both were now worried about the loss of twenty-four hours from their lives. Then on the TV, the police are requesting information about officer Jenks, who has gone missing, last reported sighting, looking to question some poachers off the highway last night.

Raul grabs Sara's hand, 'I think the sooner we get home, the better.'

Sara agrees, 'but let me have breakfast first,' her priority is to eat, which is unusual; she does not normally eat in the morning; 'after all, look at my figure.' Raul now worried about too many coincidences in the last twenty-four hours, and they must get home as soon as possible.

Raul gets up to pay; having paid, he places the change into his pocket; in doing so, he finds a strange disk in his pocket. Baffled, he puts it to the back of his mind and will look at it when he gets home. Sara grabs the car keys and will drive some of the way to keep her mind busy. They both step out of the café; the sun is shining; the skies are a clear blue with no clouds to be seen; life feels a little bit different today as they head home.

26

Don Small is reflecting on recent events; he is used to the unknown now; nothing seems to surprise him anymore, but there is something different about this situation. He has just received feedback regarding Peter Howes; the signs are not good, with medical and psychological specialists predicting he will be in a mental institution for most of his life. His brain is in turmoil, with ramblings they cannot understand yet. Don is now worried more than ever for the safety of Roger and Shaun and whoever is still in there; He has never been so indecisive before should he storm the field. Don makes the decision he has to make, and time is not on their side. He opens comms to his men to get ready for a full attack on the field as his men gather to line up. They are prepared for the order to storm the field, with the odd one looking to the skies, hoping not to see any lightning today. Don looks to his left and right to make sure his men are ready; he is about to give the order when he sees the mist slowly starting to disappear. As the mist is receding, he hears Roger's voice in his head, 'we are coming out. boss,' never has he been so pleased to hear those dulcet tones. Coming out of their suspended state, they see the amulet fall to the floor and disappear as they look at the floor. Standing up, they can all feel a small disk in their hands and immediately place them in their pockets; they all have a valuable secret to keep now; no one must know. As they rise, they automatically make their way to where they came into the field; there is minimal conversation as they try to get things into perspective in their heads.

Don holds his men back, having just been advised by Roger that all are coming out; Don sighs 'thank goodness,' in his head, telling his men to stand down.

All of them stare in astonishment as the hedgerow parts to allow its captors to be free; even Don's men, accustomed to strange anomalies, stand with their mouths open. Then a roar as Roger comes out first, followed by Joanne, Denise, John, and Shaun bringing up the rear in case things start to go wrong. The mist disappeared in an instant as soon as they all came out; once again, everyone was amazed. They turned to look at the field where they had been captors for twenty-four hours. The field suddenly started to be overgrown with weeds, and the hedgerow started to grow inwards, having not grown for two hundred years.

Some of Don's men advise Joanne, Denise and John they will be taken to a specialist medical facility to check them out after their ordeal. The three laughed in unison, 'what ordeal, nothing happened,' Don's men noted they all spoke as one; this was too unusual to miss, and a message was relayed to Don. Receiving this message, Don calls over Shaun and Roger and asks, 'how are the both of you after the ordeal.'

They both answer in unison as well, as though they are one; Don is even more concerned than usual. As per Don's protocols, they will be taken to separate facilities to be de-briefed to quantify all data and ensure no misdemeanours have occurred. The police and all relatives are informed that their partners are safe; unfortunately, the call to Peter's mother will be a sad affair, and strong counselling will need to take place.

Joanne, Denise and John are whisked away to different military bases for interviews; everyone will give the same answers without mentioning Xylens.

Don contacts head office to express his concerns regarding Roger and Shaun; there are no signs of trauma outwardly. But he worries about their mental state, 'what the hell happened in that field.'

He thinks they might start to talk more freely once separated, and it will be the next day before they can question them. Overnight he created ten questions as an experiment. He did not want to do it as he trusted Shaun and Roger implicitly, but something happened in that field, and they must find out before it was too late. All are not prisoners as such but have been separated in different medical centres within a fifty-mile radius. Don has requested a conference call with them; they will only hear his voice so that all questions can be answered simultaneously. Each conversation is to be recorded and time-stamped for comparison, Don did not want to do this, but his best men could be compromised in some way. At ten-thirty, the call is made to the five recipients, and they are all informed that they can only hear his voice and that their answers will be recorded. The interview was over within thirty minutes; all the recordings for visual recognition were sent to Don's e-mail address from the other facilities. He meticulously went through them one by one. All answered each question the same, as though they were one entity. By the end of the day, this was impossible, surely. He wants to bang his head on the wall. Instead, Don tells the medical staff to monitor them for the next three days and inform him of any changes.

Within twenty-four hours, the talking in unison would disappear; this was due to the residual time lag of contact and questions with Xylens. However, whilst they were in their separate facilities, they found they could still talk to each other by their thoughts, speaking individually to each person and opening up a conversation as a group talk when needed. Roger and Shaun could deal with this situation, but reservations between the two that, with the rest, it could be too much for them. Shaun asks everyone, 'did they receive a disc or was it just him,' he is thankful all the rest had them. He advised all to keep quiet until he and Roger could fathom how to use them. Roger chimes, 'Be aware there will be cameras in the room, so do not mess around with the disc.' All are now grateful that they can communicate this way and are now curious how long it will last; little do they know it will be for the rest of their lives, and it will be challenging to see if it is a gift or a curse.

27

Raul and Sara are driving home without a care in the world, oblivious that they have helped an intelligent lifeform find a way home. Over the radio, there is still constant chatter about an incident in the desert, but no details are available. Finally, looking at each other, Raul says to Sara, 'I wonder what is going on; it sounds like it is at my place of work. What could have happened for all this attention to happen.' Unaware, he has become a person of interest to the authorities.

Xylens destruction of his craft and some electrical supplies happened over thirty-six hours ago, with a flood of electrical contractors and local site engineers trying to re-energise parts of the black site. Gradually emergency electrical supplies have been connected up temporarily to various areas to enable essential services to operate, but seventy per cent of the site is still down. Again the human race's self-reliance on electricity in their daily life; what would happen if this was not available?

Two hours ago, Lt Dicks finally got the hard drive connected to the computer; he, along with the comms tech, could not believe what they could see on the screen. Compton and Lee are still adamant they have no idea what has happened and are confined to separate locked rooms, still protesting their innocence. Lt Dicks has used his mobile phone to take a snapshot of the computer screen and is heading to speak to Captain Rae to verify his findings, and he asks the comms tech to say nothing. Shrugging his shoulders, 'who would believe me, sir.' Rae, like the others, is confined to a guarded room with two armed guards; they allow Dicks into the room.

Dicks apologises for the delay, but 'without electricity, it seems the world stops nowadays.'

Rae accepts his apology resolutely and asks him, 'did you find anything, sir,' always following the chain of command.

'Yes, it confirms what you have said, but I do not know how to take it up the ladder; even here, there are still many sceptics, I'm afraid.'

'What do you mean, sir.'

'In all honesty, it is too hard to believe.'

'You have proof in your hands. Sir.'

'What do you think it is, Captain Rae.'

'What do you mean, sir.'

'Can you explain what it is on the screen?'

'No, sir, it is a white orb; that is all I can say.'

'My point, Captain Rae, how can we explain this phenomenon? A trick of the light does not get you free and only brings more questions.'

'But my career and reputation are on the line, and my life is in your hands.' Words Dicks did not want to hear; his curiosity brought him into a situation where three men's lives had become his responsibility.

'Can you think of any more cameras that would have picked anything up?'

'No, sir.'

'Think, man, your life and others are on the line; surely there must be more.' A few minutes pass as Rae mentally goes around the site in his head, 'Sir, there are separate cameras in the security cabin at the front gate.'

'How will that help? Everything electrical got fried.'

'But, sir, that was supplied from a different sub-station, a recent upgrade to separate from the main power supplies, for disaster recovery for an incident like this one.'

'How does that help, Captain.'

'That is where Brad Lee was located.'

'I'm listening, Captain.'

'The cameras monitor all traffic in and out of the facility; we can timeline Brad Lee from when he left his cabin.'

'I suppose it is worth a try, and we have nothing to lose in this current situation.' Dicks turns to go to the door,

'I suppose you had better wish me luck, Captain,' as he walks out the door. It is eleven-thirty in the morning as Dicks strolls across the site, looking over his shoulder, constantly aware he could be called to find out where he is. He knocks on the door of the security cabin; a new security crew have been allocated due to recent events. A brash new supervisor with an arrogant attitude, trying to make his mark but only annoying everyone, stands towering over Dicks. Seeing his rank, he automatically stands to attention, now defining his ex-military affiliation with Dicks; he looks at him and salutes.

'Your name is.'

'David Banks, sir.'

'Can I come in? I need to look at any recordings from midnight of the twelfth until the incident closed the site.'

'Yes, sir, please come in,' Banks sits at the monitors, and Dicks sits to his right. Banks resets the recording to midnight of the twelfth as they scroll through; headlights appear on the road to the site, and they get brighter as they get closer. Then, finally, the cameras pick up the car registration automatically registered to Dr Raul Rodriquez.

Dicks questions why he would come at this hour and why, as nobody else said anything, more questions than answers yet again. To date, no one has checked what time Raul entered the site.

Furthermore, crucial mistakes were bound to happen with most things beyond repair. Too many top brass were visible, and many feared for their jobs; this was the start of an ongoing disaster if not for Lt Dicks and Captain Rae's intervention. Finally, it was noted how familiarity allowed Raul through the gate with little checks and no phone call to check if he was scheduled to attend. They saw that the guard did write down his entry time; this one act might save their jobs. The car drives through the entrance and then disappears out of sight; a couple of minutes pass, and the camera picks up Raul walking to the cabin. Reaching the cabin, he knocks on the door; it opens and the cabin's lights behind Brad light up the doorway. They both look astonished and see a white orb transfer from Raul into Brad. Banks staggers back, knocking his chair over and looking at Rae for some explanation, who looks at him and says, 'classified, Banks, classified.'

Rae asks Banks to freeze the frame and again takes a snapshot of the incident; Rae is now building a picture of what may have started this situation. Finally, he asks Banks to carry on scrolling through the recording to see if Raul has left the facility. They noticed that Raul had turned around, but something was not right; how he walked and the few minutes he was on the camera, a blank stare as though hypnotised.

'What the hell is going on, sir.'

'I wish I knew, but we will get to the bottom of this.'

'What do I put in my handover report, sir.'

'The truth everything you have seen; I will countersign the report as a witness for you.'

'Thank you, sir.'

'Right then, Banks, let us carry on looking through the recording, please.'

An agonising thirty-five minutes pass before the headlights of Brad's vehicle come into view, but instead of parking in his allocated parking bay, he turns right away from the cabin. Then a full six minutes later, Brad comes into view, and they both notice he has the same walk and stare as Raul, walking toward his cabin. As he enters the cabin, Raul is stopped at the main gate, security doing their correct procedures for once, checking the car inside and out, including the trunk. Raul looks calm as he trundles down the road, unaware of what is about to happen, with Xylens having left an unexpected parting gift.

Dicks leaves the cabin perplexed at his findings, as it looks as though all the people involved did so involuntarily; he must move this information up the ladder of command. But, unfortunately, within this system, everybody is guilty till innocence is proven, and Dicks will become under suspicion as well. His efforts could be in vain as paranoia rises its head and valuable hours are lost tracking the real antagonist.

28

Forty-eight hours after Don's question and answer scenario with Shaun, Roger, Joanne, Denise and John, he requests another meeting to check if they all are okay. Once again, a conference call is set up, but this time it is different; their answers are similar but out of sync as they come back to normality. So much so that Don authorised all to be released to go home, but unknown to Joanne, Denise and John, they will be under constant surveillance for the foreseeable future. If they have a sixth sense, it will undoubtedly come to the fore to avoid any form of detection. Denise, Joanne and John head home to their loved ones; if they thought the questions from Don were evasive, families could cut to the bone more quickly, especially when they cannot, at this stage, remember properly. The discs are a constant reminder of something that happened in the field, feeling they must hide these from prying eyes but not knowing why; maybe a sign in the future will help them. There are strange signs on the disc, and they seem to feel they have seen them before. Over the following few months, relationships and marriages will be tested, with one potentially ending in divorce. When they were released, Roger and Shaun were called to Don's office to answer questions the others did not get asked. Don's office is located near Westminister; this in itself is not what they wanted; to be summoned generally means demotion or being relieved of duties. On the way, they discuss the various questions they could be asked and form a plan of ignorance, as their memories are vague about the whole situation but get more evident by the hour.

They decide they must tell Don about Xylens, how he got into their heads, and why they helped him without telling him about the disc at this stage.

The sat nav gave a travel time of four and a half hours, and they agreed to swap driving at the halfway point; they decided to listen to the radio instead of their favourite rock music. The journey was uneventful till they reached the M25 ring road around London; within ten minutes, they fell in line behind yet another tailback of heavy traffic. Unaware at this stage, a constant barrage of eco-activists has blocked the road junctions yet again. An irate ambulance driver beeping his horn, with the sound of his siren, lights flashing, traffic nose to tail with no space to manoeuvre. Screaming at people to get out of the way, he is stuck till some people manhandle their cars sideways to enable him to go down the hard shoulder. They were trying to reach someone who had had a heart attack in this traffic on his way to his wife, who has terminal cancer. Unfortunately, later in the day, the news tells of his sad demise due to the actions of the eco-zealots. These activists are trying to achieve a non-existent eutopia that is impossible to change if the rest of the world will not follow their indoctrination. They pull off at a junction they are not used to, and the sat nav automatically changes, but it will be another two more hours before reaching their destination due to delays; they both curse under their breath. A muted phone call to Don, updating him, and by the tone of his voice, they could tell he was not best pleased. Having arrived at P.H.Enomenon offices, a front for a government unit that does not exist. Shaun and Roger arrive at the car park; as they get out of the car, they instinctively look up to the third floor to see the scowling face of Don Small.

They sigh deeply and head toward the rear entrance door; Roger sarcastically says, 'if our keycards don't work, this will be a short meeting.' Shaun turns white; he loves his job; he passes his keycard through the reader, but nothing happens; he turns to Roger, 'I think we are out of work.' Roger started to laugh; when they stopped to rest and have a coffee break, and while Shaun used the toilets, he had rung reception to play a prank on Shaun. He tells Shaun to wave to the reception girls, Jayne and Anne, looking up, and he sees them giggling; he turns to Roger; a simple 'arsehole' is all he hears as the door opens. They enter, Jayne and Anne stand up and hug them both; Roger slips a twenty-pound note into Jayne's hand,

'You and Anne have a drink on me,' she smiles and kisses his cheek; Shaun asks, when are you going to ask her out; Roger blushes, which is rare. Then, walking away flustered, Shaun whispers, 'revenge is sweet, my friend.' Roger nods in agreement; they reach the lift, the door opens and out strolls Don, looking at them both, 'come with me now, conference room.' They follow like lost sheep, and the girls start giggling again; Janye turns to Anne,

'Like lambs to the slaughter, I hope they survive; otherwise, no more free drinks.'

Don takes them to the conference room, telling reception, 'no calls under any exception till we come out,' the girls nod in unison; this is rare for Don to take this line. Roger and Shaun sit down opposite Don,

'Right, I could go through the bullshit of separating the two of you to get some truthful answers, but out of mutual respect for all of us, I want you to come clean, and for God's sake, now, or else your careers are toast.'

Roger spoke first, 'but, sir, we are not too sure ourselves; most of it is a blur, as you know.'

'I know both of you, and your mental strength is far stronger than the three civilians, so I need more answers.'

Roger and Shaun are now finding out the benefits of talking without speaking, as their thoughts are all they need; they agree to talk about Xylens but not the disc.

Don was annoyed with this silence and was about to lambast them when Shaun spoke first.

'What we are about to tell you is unbelievable even to us, sir.'

'My God, Shaun, we work with the unbelievable; nothing is out of bounds; you know that every day we are sent to check the unbelievable.'

Roger interjects, 'Sir, we were under the control of an alien lifeform.'

Don's answer surprised them, 'thank goodness I thought both of you had gone mad.'

Both gasped at this revelation, forgetting how level-headed Don is, 'now let us work together and see if we can resolve this; oh, by the way, you have not asked about Peter Howes.' Again, both are devastated by their lack of compassion, forgetting he did not come out of the field in the right frame of mind. Don explains that Peter will probably be in a mental institution for the rest of his life. Some parts of his brain have been destroyed, irretrievable for no medical reason, and doctors are baffled how it could happen. Both were shocked at this information and now worried that some of what Xylens had told them was untrue; it was a risk they had to take to save the planet.

'So sorry to hear that, sir, but we seem okay,' from Shaun.

'We will need to do weekly cat scan checks on you both to make sure there are no after effects; an appointment has been made for tomorrow at 10 am for Roger, 11 am for you, Shaun; both of you will be there, or you are fired, do I make myself clear.'

'All too clearly, sir.'

Don was not going to fire them, but his position needed strengthening to get the required results.

'Right then, let us carry on; which one will tell me what happened.'

Again Roger and Shaun have an internal conversation, and Roger agrees he will tell Don what happened. However, Don breaks their discussion, 'before you tell me what happened, how the hell did you get into the field in the first place without being struck by lightning.'

'The hedgerow opened up as though we were invited in, sir.'

Don shook his head in disbelief, 'carry on, Roger.'

'Once we entered, we noticed Joanne and Denise in opposite corners; they were kneeling as though they were praying, sir, so we separated and ran to them.

'Okay, plausible so far,' he indicates for Shaun to take over.

'When we reached them, we also kneeled to check their pulses; as we did so, a metal amulet appeared from their wrists and dissolved into ours.' The surprise on Don's face was a joy to behold, even for both of them.

He returns to his story, 'after this, we were in a suspended state, unable to move, and this calming voice came into our heads, and we found we could all communicate together, as you later found out, sir.'

Don nodded in agreement and waited for Shaun to carry on.

'I don,t think you will believe the next bit, but here goes, inside our heads, we could see another earth; it looked twice the size of ours, and with two moons different in colour, it was fantastic, so beautiful, sir.'

'Right, stop now,' Roger and Shaun reeled back, unaccustomed to Don's tone.'

'Both of you go to opposite ends of the table, with the pads in front of you.' Don was trying to break their momentum to see if he could get a reaction.

'Why, sir.'

'Do it now, and I want you to draw this lifeform you claim talked to you.'

They proceeded to draw a perfect portrait of Xylens, both minds working as one, they had no artistic skills before, but these drawings were perfection, both starting and finishing simultaneously. Don walked around the table, looking in awe at the speed at which they drew the portraits, both finished at the same time; he gathered them up. He told them to return to their seats; he sat down to look at the drawings, amazed at the accuracy; he thought one was a photocopy of the other. Showing Roger and Shaun the drawings, even they could not believe what they had done, having no great drawing skills before.

'Proceed,' from Don

'Xylens wanted to go home and needed us all because we had the same genetic marker to communicate with him and form a strong mental bond to enable him to leave, sir.'

'Why did you not refuse.'

'We could not; we were trapped in limbo, helpless, sir.'

'Could you not break free.'

Sir, it was impossible to move other than talking through thought.'

'Prisoners then.'

'In a way, yes, but it did not feel that way; looking back, sir, if we had, could we have finished up like Peter.'

'What do you mean, Roger.'

'We could all talk to each other and see what was happening through his eyes; he only wanted to go home.'

'What! Why are you telling me this now.'

'It is just coming back to us, sir.'

'Where was this lifeform, and how long had he been here then? Enlighten me; as you know, I am sceptical of this type of thing.' Shaun takes up the rest of their story,

'You have heard of Roswell, sir.'

'Don't go there, Shaun, that is impossible. It happened years ago, bloody hell, before I was born.'

'We know it is hard to believe, but we have no reason to lie; our jobs are on the line.'

Don is starting to get frustrated; with his fist clenched, he bangs it on the table, 'good grief, how do I tell our superiors that both of you have left me in a no-win situation.'

'But sir, it would be the same answers in a court of law; we have nothing to gain by lying.' Don concedes to their argument, and he sighs, 'carry on, Roger,' by rotating them, he is watching closely to see if their demeanour alters, but they are stable. The only option is a lie detector test or truth serums, and then he is stepping into the realms of spyware, 'good grief, he thinks, what the hell am I doing? Get back to reality.'

Looking on his computer, he brings up Roswell on the internet search; upon reading it, he becomes even more sceptical, 'that can,t be right; it happened in 1947.'

'Yes, sir, Xylens told us they automatically die when they reach two hundred Earth years.'

'You realise, we are talking about an American, black site base, the international repercussions, the fallout could damage our fragile relationship.'

'Sir, this lifeform had been a prisoner for seventy-five years; he was in the wrong place at the wrong time.'

'Right then, both of you have a coffee break, come back in an hour, get reception to book a hotel near here; I have a few calls to make.'

'Yes, sir, from both of them,' they leave the conference room and head towards two giggling receptionists, always happy to see them.

Shaun passes on the information to Anne, and a few minutes later, Anne tells Shaun they only have double rooms left. Do you want to share with a wry smile on her face?

Even Shaun blushed up, or was he hopeful of an evening of bliss, 'separate rooms please, Anne.'

'Meals in the hotel. Do you want a table booked,' he looked over to Roger, who nodded yes; after the long travel down, he did not fancy the dazzle of the London nightlife tonight. Jayne turns to Roger and calmly asks him, 'if they would like two beautiful women at their table, lets us say eight o clock then.'

'It is the twentieth century; how could we refuse such a fantastic offer,' while adjusting his demeanour, talking to Shaun by thought, 'London is nice, this time of year.'

They both smile, but the moment is broken by the booming voice of Don, 'See you here at nine in the morning.'

'Yes, sir, from the both of them,' wondering why he changed his mind. Both kiss the hands of Jayne and Anne as a fond goodbye, 'see you at eight.'

As they leave, Jayne and Anne are flustered and share erotic dreams of the night ahead for the next hour.

29

Lt Dicks is trying to find the right people to talk to, being pushed to one side as tunnel vision and paranoia are reaching new heights. In this capitalist world, the financial impact of Xylens intervention is running into the billions of dollars of damage; an extraordinary emergency meeting in capitol hill is taking place, and decisions are to be made on how to re-fund this black site or even close it. Who else will suffer when budget cuts are made, one department at least will go, from twenty people to four. Especially as they do not have an alien lifeform to watch over, which has not yet been noticed due to recent events less than a mile away. The blame game is rife, suggesting their enemies have a secret weapon of immense power and destruction; could it be Russia or Iraq? Yet the evidence is close at hand if they would only listen to Dicks; he has a USB in his pocket with all the information required to move forward. Also, Don must keep quiet in the United Kingdom, or the fallout will be catastrophic to his team and three civilians.

As Dicks slowly walks over to the main office complex from Brad's cabin, his mind turns over what he has seen, but getting people to believe will be another matter. On entering the main office via his keycard, lower-rank soldiers saluted, he was low-level compared to the higher command chain, but there were new faces with dower features devoid of any humour from their look. It seems the men in black are here, with polished shoes, smart-pressed suits and no personality.

He sits down, having requested to speak to his superior and being informed it will be a long wait due to the current circumstances. Nevertheless, he tries to explain he may have information pertinent to what has happened. The men in black are showing signs of anxiety and seem to be waiting for someone; he wonders who, not wishing to be in their shoes. Then, preparing to wait, he sits in the reception area; one hour passes when he notices three men are being frog-marched toward the office.

The issue of a military complex such as this is loyalty to your country; any misdemeanour to the contrary is treated as treason. Unfortunately, the three men are being forced to walk across to the main office, in full view of everyone, and are being treated as such. But, again, this need to apportion blame without proof; their colleagues witnessed this debacle and already want to kill them without trial. As the three men continued to proclaim their innocence falling on deaf ears, it reminded Dicks of the kangaroo courts of the wild west or the Salem witch hunts; he must do something. As Rae, Lee and Compton are forcibly pushed through the door for everyone to see, the men in suits become more aggressive; they move forward to arrest the three men. Dicks moved forward and shouted, 'these men are innocent.' One man in a suit hits him firmly in the stomach; they do not care; they have three lambs to the slaughter, and then a fight ensues between the military staff and the men in suits. Until General Bright threw a chair through a window, everyone turned, and he bellowed at the top of his voice.

'Stop, and that is an order; what the hell is going on? It is bad enough that outside is falling apart around our ears; it will not happen here; I want an explanation and now.'

The men in suits are still trying to get to the three men, Dicks gets up from the floor and salutes his commanding officer, 'sir, this idiot struck me; I was trying to tell them these three men are innocent, but as usual, sir, they are guilty without a trial or evidence.'

'What do you mean, Lt Dicks.'

'I have evidence for your eyes only, sir.'

'Come with me now, Lt Dicks and Sargent Lone. Can you put our suited colleagues in room 13 now? Lt Dicks, Captain Rae, come with me and get these men something to drink now.' A corporal leaves and returns with a choice of coffee or water; Lee and Compton accept them gratefully. Dicks and Rae followed the General to his office, and the General slammed the door behind them.

'After the last few days, Lt Dicks, what is it you have that will help solve this nightmare.'

Dicks handed over the USB, 'if you could look at its contents, things will start to unravel, sir.'

'What is on this item that will solve my problem.'

'I would rather you witnessed it yourself, sir; if I told you, I don't think you would believe me.'

'I hope this is not a waste of my time, or your head will roll further than Captain Rae and his colleagues.'

'Sir, three men's careers are on the line; I can assure you they are innocent of any wrongdoing.'

General Bright inserts the USB and opens the file, 'Right, Lt Dicks, what are we looking for? Please explain.'

'Sir, we are watching Brad Lee, head of perimeter security, driving up to Compton; when he gets out of his vehicle, watch the close interaction between them both.'

'I do not see anything, Dicks, are you messing with my intelligence? It will be the last thing you do.'

'Sir, watch closely; slow the speed down.'

In doing so, the General could see the orb transfer from Lee to Compton; he looked in amazement, transfixed on the screen playing it over and over, turning to Dicks,

'What the hell is that, Dicks. How did it get on my facility.'

'Sir, I think an alien life force took over Compton and Lee, and they did not know what they were doing.'

'Do not talk, crap; it is impossible.'

'Sir, we had a craft in our hanger for years, but it is not there now; untold damage to the facility is the only possible answer, sir.'

'Do you have any clues, what happened, Lt?'

'No, sir, but we have another suspect.'

'What the hell? Get on with it, man; which bastard caused this catastrophe.'

'If you carry on to the end of the recording, sir.'

Bright scrolls through the recording till Rae tells him to stop, 'look at the vehicle coming to the gate, sir; unfortunately, the security staff did not do their due diligence as far as I can see.'

'What do you mean, Lt?'

'From what I can see, they did not check the vehicle, and I cannot find any record of them phoning his department to check if he should be here.'

'When you leave here, Lt, get me their names; I want their arses in my office in the next four hours.'

'Yes, sir, but we must carry on with the recording; it will only take a few minutes.' Captain Rae will be forever grateful to Lt Dicks; by the end of this day, one man's faith in him and his colleagues will be justified. The General looks at the screen, 'again, Rae, what am I looking for.'

'The man you are looking at is Raul Rodriquez, a physicist in our research laboratories; he was not due in on the day of our incident.'

'My God, find the bastard now.'

'Sir, can you carry on with the recording? Watch how he walks and look at his face; it seems he is hypnotised; his eyes do not blink.'

'Good grief, you are right; what the hell is going on.'

'I know we should not assume, but I think all three are carriers of one single orb transferring between them and did not know about it; that is why they cannot remember anything.'

'That is some wild theory, Lt, and in many ways, I hope it is true, or we could be going to war with an unknown aggressor; the rumour mills are working hard to start one.'

'I hope so too, sir; these men are innocent. I am willing to bet my life on that.'

'Let us hope it does not come to that, and I do not want to lose an officer to friendly fire; if you know what I mean, capital hill is brutal for scapegoats.'

'Yes, sir.'

'I will make some phone calls to get this Rodriquez guy in my office by the end of the day.'

'What about Compton and Lee, sir.'

'They and Captain Rae are relieved of duties until we can verify this situation.

They will be confined to this facility; unfortunately, Captain Rae, you will all be in separate rooms without discussions inside or outside sources. Do I make myself clear?

Rae salutes the General and leaves the office, then waits outside for Dicks, to thank him for listening to him.

Dicks saluted the General, turned to leave, and was stopped before he reached the door, 'thank you, Lt, for your exemplary work; I think when you leave the military, a job in police work could be your next profession.'

Dicks smiled, 'thank you, sir; I will look for a good reference from you.' The General picks the phone up as Dicks leaves; by the time he and Rae reach reception, the men in suits are being ushered aggressively out of the door. Then Rae, Compton and Lee are escorted away, Dicks allays their worries, telling them everything will be okay.

A national alert to all law enforcement has been issued to find Raul Rodriquez and detain him alive at all costs has been set in motion.

30

On board an alien craft, in which Xylens has put into autopilot, he has programmed the cryo chambers to drop temperatures, enabling his new colleagues to come out of their suspended state. Although the progress is slow, he has plenty of time; even in hyperdrive mode, it will take several Earth weeks to reach his home planet. Enabling him to forge new friendships with his two co-pilots, friendship is a new word he has now found, and he wants to share this experience with them. Sadly it will take two hours for Nyle and Byne to be fully functional, so Xylens decides to look in the bag Sara had given him. Pleasantly surprised by its contents, and with the various papers, he can show his new colleagues what a diverse planet Earth is. It will help with Xylens plans to change their world if he can recruit these two new allies. Also, there were packets of what looked like multicoloured tablets; they were sweets for him to try and see if he could taste them; it was a kind notion from Sara, he thought; suddenly, Xylens realised he was picking up human emotions, yet again. Xylens knew what they were, having trawled through human minds; he had pictures in his head when they thought about food, drink, and other strange things, wishing, in hindsight, he had asked when he had the chance. But these sweets will help in the indoctrination of the new world order, and he will dispose of the nutrient tablets and put the sweets there instead, explaining they were leftover from his craft. Xylens is getting excited; the rush of creating a new faction that could change their subservient life has become uppermost in his mind.

In many ways, the commissioners will wish he had died on the small planet Earth instead of welcoming him home as a hero.

Searching through the papers, he could see the contrast between different opinions, and he was fascinated, even though he could see how there could be friction between opposing views. But, through Sara's intervention of kindness, she has given Xylens the means in which to create division on his world.

To him, absorbed in the papers highlighted how far away their technology is from theirs, but everyday living is fast-paced and does not seem to achieve anything. The time passes quickly, and Xylens is startled by the alarm on one cryo chamber; turning round, he sees Nyle stir first. He feels excited inside again; these emotions long gone are coming back, and he will be able to communicate with his own kind for the first time in seventy-five years. As he walks over to him, Nyle looks shocked and sees Byne in the other chamber; he has a sense of panic; what could have happened, 'who are you? Where did you come from.' Trying to grasp the enormity of the situation, we left as two, and now there are three.

Xylens tells him to 'stay calm until his colleague awakes, and all will be revealed.'

Nyle stares transfixed on Xylens face, 'I have seen you before, I am sure of it.'

'Wait till your colleague wakes, do not rush things.' At this point, Byne starts to stir; like Nyle, the response is the same. 'who are you.'

'I will wait till you are both stable and wide awake.'

A short while later, the questions started to flow, and as soon as Xylens mentioned his name, both Nyle and Byne stared at each other in disbelief.

Then, flustered, they explain that their mission was to try and find him and Asku. Xylens explained that the crash had killed Asku, and he had been in a suspended state, a prisoner for the last seventy-five years. Until a turn of events came together to enable his release, I made visible and verbal contact with other life forms, which helped me escape. Then Nyle asked how did you get onboard? We did not land on the planet.

Xylens is surprised by this statement, 'can you get into the craft's flight log.' Byne walks over to one of the pilot's seats, and within a few moments, a hologram comes up and lists the last ten significant events that have happened to the craft. Anything in blue was minor, nothing of concern; the red indicated a critical event and the time code the event occurred. Nyle and Byne were surprised by the time codes, the first significant event four months before the craft automatically landed on Earth. The first alarm indicated a failure in the time sequence to the cryo chambers, which had automatically set the chambers into manual. The fail-safe systems cannot override this, meaning it could only be opened manually; hence when Xylens came on board, he could operate the controls to free them. If he had not come aboard, they could have been there a lifetime, and when released, if they had passed their life cycle of two hundred years, they would have disintegrated immediately. Once this alarm was instigated, all the other alarms following became red due to no control of the craft, and the craft went into automatic to land at its pre-ordained flight plan.

Nyle and Byne look at each other, trying to grasp what has occurred, as they have just realised that they have been on Earth for twenty-five years.

Xylens two new colleagues have not yet realised that they are having an open conversation, which is different to their lifestyle back home. When Xylens pointed out what they were doing, both could not understand what he meant. Xylens tells them about the tablets and how they control their life every hour of every day; we are programmed like this craft to do a job without question. They argued for ten minutes till Xylens shouted, 'stop,' then he pointed out, 'do you not see what I mean.'

With a vague look on their faces, Nyle speaks first, 'I don't; what do you mean.'

'Do we question anything on our planet,'

'No,' from Byne

'Exactly, you are putting your idea forward, to put your point of view forward.'

'We still do not know what you mean.'

'Listen, you are thinking for yourself; you are arguing. Would you do that on our home planet?'

Both looked at each other in astonishment and liked this interaction; they asked Xylens what they were doing, and he responded, 'free will, the ability to choose what we want to do.'

'How can this affect us? What do we do with this free will.'

'Grasp it with both hands and free ourselves from the commissioners, who control everything we do.' The talking will continue during their journey home, but it will take strong hearts and bravery to achieve their newfound goal.

But if Earth's history is anything to go by, all wars and social conflicts start with a tiny minority with an opinion different from the norm.

31

It is six pm, and Roger and Shaun are booking into the hotel; the rooms are opposite each other, handy for that early morning call; one is bound to sleep past the alarm.

Both enter their rooms, 'give you knock at seven-forty-five; we will have a quick pint before the ladies arrive,' from Roger; Shaun nods in agreement. Both set their alarms, and a quick nap is required for the evening ahead after their long day, which could get longer. They both wake simultaneously, unaware of how in sync their bodies are after recent events. Both are getting ready, but when one thinks about the other, it is like an open invitation to talk by thought; if the other accepts the invite. They are excited about the evening ahead; being involved in their line of work is challenging to establish relationships due to its secrecy. Luckily Jayne and Anne know all about them; maybe they will learn something about their superiors, second-guessing themselves, they already know they will not. It is seven-forty-five, and a knock on the door; both open the door simultaneously to see the ladies standing before them with a night bag and a change of clothing for the morning. After discussions when Shaun and Roger left the office, they both realised that Jayne had the hots for Roger and Anne for Shaun. They look at each other and smile; this is the twentieth century, and ladies are more forward than in their parent's era, hoping they have not made a mistake over a night of passion. A kiss on the cheek for the ladies, a sign of respect from Shaun and Roger, old hearts in young bodies, but desire will soon take over for all.

They head for a meal, courtesy of P.H.Enomenon's business card, conscious that they cannot overindulge, as government accountants are very stringent, and the public purse is to be watched.

A wonderful evening by all, drink being kept to a minimum; they need all their energy for the night to come. All realise this could be a dangerous liaison, colleagues at work if it turns sour, repercussions tend to get out of control, so they agree to take it one step at a time, as they live over two hundred miles apart. So they head to their rooms, and the night ahead is bliss for all; Jayne and Anne giggle like little girls at the breakfast table, so pleased they took the bull by the horn and committed to the evening. All agree they hope they can repeat the evening again; hopefully, sooner than later, phone numbers are exchanged over the breakfast table, and they separate and go to the office separately.

Anne and Jayne arrive at the office with a glow on their cheeks as they walk to their desks; Don appears the women look coyly at him, both upbeat he can sense something has happened by their demeanour. None of his business, of course, consenting adults; in the back of his mind, he hoped they had a pleasant evening. Unaware his proteges are involved, he asked Anne, 'have you seen Roger and Shaun yet? Have they arrived?' She stutters, and Jayne jumps into the conversation, 'they will be ten minutes, sir,' Don turns and goes to the conference room, smiling as he goes through the door. 'They think I'm daft,' he smirks as the door closes; two minutes later, the reception phone rings, 'tell them to come to the conference room as soon as they get here, Jayne.'

'Yes, sir.'

Shaun and Roger arrive; the women are slightly flustered as they tell them, 'Don is waiting in the conference room; he likes two sugars in his coffee, it might calm him down,' from Jayne. Not what they wanted to hear, so Roger makes the coffee, 'I will get on his good side,' Shaun puts his finger in his mouth to indicate he is going to be sick, the women laugh, and then the conference room door opens.

The dulcet tone of Don's voice, 'get your backsides in here, please,' not wanting to show them up in front of Anne and Jayne. With coffee in hand, they sit opposite Don; sensing something is amiss, Roger passes Don his coffee with two sugars, hoping it will sweeten the situation.

'Well, we have a problem.'

'What do you mean, sir.'

'Unfortunately, your timescales line up with a significant incident in the USA; the world's intelligence services are buzzing about it. As you know, nothing is a secret in this internet world for long.'

'Sir, how can that be? What has happened.'

'They won't say, but we will find out.'

'I can assure you; we were not involved in any incident.' from Shaun.

'I believe that you think you were not involved.'

An adamant Roger qualifies Shaun's statement; 'we are not involved, sir, they talk in their heads, 'what the hell happened? We must contact Raul.'

'At the moment, you are both suspended till further notice; go home till I find out what the hell has happened.'

They both try to protest, and Don raises his hand, 'go now; otherwise, it will get worse, I assure you both.'

Jayne and Anne were surprised as the meeting only lasted a few minutes and even more surprised when Roger told them they had been suspended until further notice. This has never happened to their knowledge, so they are worried about Roger and Shaun's welfare, and their newfound relationship may have ended before it started. The men are lost for words and visibly shaken by Don's reaction; what have they been involved in that has made him take this decision? It will be a long journey home, and they will question all their choices made in the last week. They say their goodbyes to Jayne and Anne, who now realise their night of bliss could have been a one-night stand which all did not want. Jayne presses the release button to allow Shaun and Roger out of the building just as they are about to leave. Don bellows down the corridor, 'Don't go home, book a hotel for a couple of days; I forgot about your hospital appointments,' a muted squeal from Jayne and Anne. The men punched the air, and Roger smiled at

Jayne. 'can you book us a hotel, please, the same as last night, and would you like to come for a meal and bring your beautiful friend,' the women blushed. The women had smiles from ear to ear all day, and most of the staff noticed the change in their behaviour, no questions asked. Roger and Shaun walk to the hotel, thankful they do not need to go home; most men of their age would drown their sorrows in drink, but the evening has too much to offer, but why spoil a good thing? They both agree they must contact Raul, but with an eight-hour time difference, they must select a time when Jayne and Anne are not with them.

They both agree they must join together to reach Raul, and between five and five-thirty, UK time will be nine to nine-thirty US time.

32

It is late when Raul and Sara arrive at her apartment complex; Sara parks her car, and Raul is about to leave straight away, but the last twenty-four hours as brought their relationship to a new level. So she invites him to stay the night, as the kids are still with her mother till tomorrow; after the previous night, how could he refuse? This new promiscuous Sara is the woman of his dreams now, and the night is much better than anticipated; he leaves the apartment, and his mind is in a state of pleasurable delirium. Never in all their years of marriage was it ever like this; her sexual desire had reached a level he could not believe. Sara has told Raul to use her car for the next few days; he drives home, unaware there is a nationwide alert for him to be arrested alive. Unfortunately, US law enforcement tends to shoot first and not get answers later. The drive home is uneventful as he parks on his driveway, realising he left the house keys inside when he panicked to get away. Again, he was about to phone Sara, and again he realised he had thrown his phone away on his way to Sara's. The tension started to build; he was about to get in the car and drive back to Sara when he noticed the spare key on Sara's car keys; he had gone from despair to joy in milliseconds. He lets himself in, walks straight into the kitchen, puts the coffee machine on, and turns on the TV to see what all the fuss is about; then, he sees his face on all the TV channels as a person of interest, not to be approached at all costs. At this point, his home phone starts to ring, and his heart races should he answer.

It constantly rings. Will it not stop? Then a sigh of relief as it stops; thirty seconds later, it rings again, cautiously Raul picks the phone up, 'hello.'

'Raul, you are all over the TV; what have you done,' from Sara.

'Sara, I have just left you; I have done nothing.'

'Oh, my God, I hope it is all a mistake.'

Raul tells Sara not to panic, but inside he is screaming, 'what have I done,' still not remembering the last couple of days. As he puts the phone down, he runs through his head the last couple of days, but with the gap in his memory, not remembering the drive of seven hundred miles, what the hell could have happened? Then he hears voices in his head, 'oh my God, I'm going mad; then, as if a switch was turned on, he starts to remember. The voices of Shaun and Roger are so familiar, 'Raul, it is Roger; I am with Shaun. Do you remember us?'

'Vaguely, how can I hear your voices? Neither of you sounds like American.'

'Nationality is not the issue. Can you remember what has happened in the last few days' from Shaun?

'I'm struggling to understand how we talk like this, and my mind is all over the place.' Suddenly Roger feels the disc in his pocket and instinctively tells Shaun and Raul if they have theirs, and both reply yes. He tells them to touch it, and as they do so, visions of Xylens and the last few days flood their minds. They can not believe what they see, stunned at the spectacle opening up before them. Happy they helped Xylens leave, but annoyed and angry at the deception of his destruction of the black site.

But in hindsight, in the short time they were in contact with him, seventy-five years a prisoner can do something to your state of mind. They did not know his intention; he said he was only going for the disc.

Then they remembered; he said they could not lie, stupidly the realisation, no one asked what he would do after he retrieved the disc. So something must have happened for him to change his mind and cause such destruction. That simple question must have been a distress call; the next thing they hear is the calming voice of Xylens. All surprised by this intervention, Xylens explains that the three of them had the strongest genetic marker, and he could communicate over a greater distance and would soon be gone from their solar system. It was noticeable has his voice was dipping in and out the further his craft went; Xylens took the craft out of hyperdrive, explaining to Nyle and Byne why, and they nodded in agreement. Amazed at this new interaction with another human-type lifeform, all three have promised to minimise any information to the commissioners. Finally, Xylens informs Raul, Shaun and Roger that they will have other abilities in a short time that will help them in life. All were surprised at this news, wanting to know more, but time was running out and Xylens, needed to give his reason for what he had done. He explains that 'like any other planet and species, there is a need to protect yourself against other violent species if required. Unfortunately, what I saw in that building, where my craft was being re-engineered, angered me; they were trying to re-engineer our weapons for greater destruction on your planet. We are thousands of years ahead of your ecosystem, and your kind is primitive compared to us.

The amount of power in our weapons could wipe out your planet, and they were trying to re-create it; too many lives could be wiped out in an instant.'

The three men fell silent for a moment, as though time had stopped, the magnitude of this event hitting home quickly, and the thought of what could have happened was unimaginable. A sense of gratitude from the three men, thanking Xylens for his intervention. At this point, his voice faded as the craft was again put into hyperdrive.

Should they tell the authorities Roger, Shaun, and Raul now have a burden to carry for life, but Roger and Shaun are obligated to disclose this to Don, or all is lost for them? Of course, the Americans will not confirm or deny this accusation, but they will be curious about where the information came from and how it was acquired; this will be a decision for Don to make. Finally, they agree to tell the truth before this burden drags them down; at this point, Raul informs them the police will be at his house shortly, and he will bury the disc in his garden. As Raul buries the disc, he gives Shaun and Roger a mental picture if they need to get to it, hoping it will be buried forever in the back of his mind.

Returning to the house, he is washing his hands at the kitchen sink when the loud expectant knock on the front door comes.

'Raul Rodriquez, come out of the house; you are surrounded; come out now,'

He takes a deep breath and walks to the door, and before he can open it, the door is kicked down by the police; consistently over-exuberant, they find Raul on the floor with his hands in the air. A gunshot is heard from the neighbours; what is happening at Raul's house?

33

Instead of mentioning five names constantly during the ongoing investigation, and to simplify things, they have been given the file name of the Haltwhistle five. It is six pm in the UK when five individuals feel a searing pain in their stomachs, and as they grasp their stomach, they feel a trickle of blood and at the same time have a vision of Raul being shot. There is no injury to them, a simulation of what has happened to Raul, and it will require a change of clothes only, all grateful for that. They now know how their unusual bond will be for life and instantly open up links to each other to understand what is going on. At this stage, they do not know if Raul is alive or dead, as he is unresponsive to their requests. Roger and Shaun block out the other three to confirm they will not burden them with their knowledge regarding Xylens. After all, less than seven days ago, they were happy-going people with families with everyday worries; this would be far too much for them. Shaun calms them down, saying that this is probably something that will wear off over time, crossing his fingers. But if they have any worries to contact himself and Roger, through their newly acquired abilities while it lasts, do not write anything down, or phone anyone, etcetera; in a way, this is now our secret, between us all. So they break off communication, and Roger and Shaun try to understand what might have happened to Raul. They already know he is weak in character, but the situation of what he has just learnt might give him some steel in his back. Previous to this event, both of them attended the hospital for their scans, and hospital staff told them that Don requested the results for his eyes only.

While they are getting ready for another night of bliss, they both receive a text from Don, and he would like to see them at Hyde park in the morning at nine-thirty, at the usual spot. It is something the men have developed over time if they want to discuss things for their ears only. Shaun and Roger know it is a matter of concern, as these meetings are rare. However, they have learnt to separate everyday life from work and enjoy another evening of pleasure, each learning more about the other. Finally, the morning arrives, and like clockwork, everyone gets ready to go their separate ways; the women were surprised when they told them they would not be in the office later.

'Remember, we are technically suspended,' from Shaun, Jayne and Anne kiss them, still in the height of euphoria; this short relationship is fantastic for them. Next, Roger receives a text from Don, 'Bring coffee with three sugars.' Always a sign it is important, he informs Shaun, who is getting ready in his room; he was thinking, 'how can two people make such a mess in a small hotel room? The park is a short distance away, and both are trying to second guess what it could be about that requires a meeting in the park. Thankful it is a hot sunny day, they sit down on the park bench, which seems to have been reserved for them; the few times they have been here, no one has sat on the bench. A couple of minutes pass as they gently nod to people walking by, and in the distance, Don stands out in the crowd, literally towering above many individuals. He sits in the middle of them and pretends to wipe the snow off his head before a roll of puns and sarcasm comes his way; out of the office, formalities do not exist.

'What do we owe for the pleasure of this meeting, boss.'

'I don't know whether it is good news or bad, to be quite honest.'

Both men turn to Don and, in sync, 'what do you mean, sir.'

'The cat scan has revealed an abnormality in both your brains.'

Roger and Shaun again speak in unison, slightly unnerving Don, 'What does that mean, sir? Have we got a brain tumour?'

'On the contrary, the hospital thinks your brains have grown, a significant change to be notable.'

'Do we have anything to fear?'

'The hospital thinks not, but being in the job we are in; my instant conclusion is that this is why you can do your communication thing.'

'Good grief, sir. Do they think it will go away,' both are hoping not; they quite like this newfound ability.

'Not sure, but it means you will need to stay and be monitored in the hospital for a couple of days.'

'Is that necessary, sir? Can we not stay at the hotel,' Roger realising their nights of bliss had just stopped for the both of them.

'No, it is the medical team that wants you there for constant monitoring, no if or buts, get your clothes; I have told them you will be there in one hour; hurry now.'

A dejected Shaun and Roger resign themselves to the blip in their love life and get up to go to the hotel. As they do so, Don informs them he has requested that Denise, Joanne and John be checked out locally at the James Cook hospital in Middlesborough; as we speak,

'I will update you later today.'

A reluctant, 'okay, sir, we will speak later.'

As the men walk away, Don does not want to convey his worries, as this has become a strange phenomenon he intends to solve quickly. Roger and Shaun ring their new love interests, explaining they will be indisposed for a couple of days, they cannot tell them why, but if they get close to Don, they might find out. Jayne and Anne know they will not find out as Don is the most secretive man they know; they will need to wait and hope everything is okay. The men book into the hospital, and in doing so, a buzz around the ward that the two men, whose brains are growing, reach the nurses, so much for secrecy they think in their minds. For the next two days, the men are treated to the best private care the government can pay for, the same respect given to Denise, Joanne and John in the North East of England.

Roger contacts Don to explain that the staff must sign the secrecy act or it will be over the news; Don dispatches various people who lockdown the ward, and all paperwork is signed. If any breach, it will invoke a prison sentence. The same information is given to his people in the North East, the Haltwhistle three, unaware of their situation. It was two pm, and the call Don was waiting for finally came; he was not too surprised. It was as he thought, now confirmed that all the Haltwhistle five have this brain abnormality. He requests the same care for the three as his men receive here in the South. The five are in open dialogue and are getting used to this newfound ability, and now a friendship is starting to form as they realise the possible advantages it may hold. The conversation gradually moves toward the discs and what other properties they might have.

Unfortunately, they have left them in a hiding place at their homes so that no one can find them, so contact with Raul will need to wait.

Over the next two days, further scans found that their brains have expanded another two millimetres, not large by any means, but the enlargement is around the whole brain. At this early stage of their brain development, they do not realise their IQ levels are increasing and soon, their ability to solve complicated issues far quicker than ever.

All five will have to learn how to control their newfound wisdom, or their relationships will surely be at risk; John, especially his wife, has already noticed the change in his behaviour. Being a maths teacher, he already found he loved solving mathematical problems, but suddenly, John could solve complicated scientific equations, something he could never grasp. John was starting to get big-headed about this ability, and it was slowly eroding the family dynamics. Denise and Joanne have not tapped into their newfound capabilities, and there has been no need yet, but time is short, and something will happen for them to use this ability bestowed upon them. Unknown to them, there is a slight discolourisation in their eyes, and their vision is getting crisper, especially their peripheral vision; things are coming into view far quicker from the side, no need to turn to see now.

34

Whilst these oddities are happening on planet Earth, onboard a craft in space heading home, arguments are taking place. Xylens, Nyle and Byne have read through the newspapers that Sara had left, and unbelievably all have developed opposing political views of individual rights. They have healthy arguments and enjoy opposing views, but soon realise these views can radically change your perspective of right and wrong. Within a short while, these opposing views will alter the way in which they mingle with family and friends, and like a virus, on a computer, it will spread like wildfire throughout the planet. The populist will grab this freedom of choice and create havoc for its commissioners. But they need to get back home first, and to do so, they need to use the cryo chambers in rotation; as the automatic system is now broken, the system needs to be operated manually. One must be available outside to operate the controls, and now after these arguments, the human trait of paranoia raises its head; who do they trust to open the chambers? They have an inert ability not to harm anyone unless attacked, but this new form of anger drives long-dormant suppressed feelings to the fore. Could one of them be a killer? Xylens has not seen any of his family for seventy-five years, so it is agreed that he and Byne will go in the chambers for the next quarter of the way, having already passed the halfway point. Xylens, as reservations, having already spent so many years in a suspended state but is coaxed into the chamber by Nyle and Byne.

Nyle sets the controls and manual timer for the cryo chambers, and the gases form around Xylens and Byne.

Nyle sits back and looks at the newspapers; who knew these newspapers would change his world? Nyle is reading the newspapers repeatedly, and strangely he is more interested in the violence portrayed. Never before has he witnessed this type of violence; the ability to harm another lifeform intrigues him.

He looks at Xylens bag and places a hand inside to see what other wonderment it offers. The familiar rustling sound of a simple bag of crisps comes to his attention, and he bursts the bag of salted crisps. He realises they are a food item, breaks one, and places it into his small mouth; and he winces at the taste at first, then the flavour goes around his senses. Five minutes pass, and he passes out; Nyle will sleep for most of the journey, for the salt is slowly freeing him of the nutrients given to him via the tablets. The salt neutralises the nutrients taken for a lifetime, but there is a downside to this freedom from the pills not yet known. The cost of this freedom will be a change in their life cycle, and they will lose fifty years of their life. Many will wonder if this is worth the price to pay for freedom; there will be unrest for several years, and the question not yet answered is whether it will be for the better. Nyle awakes, staggered by how long he has slept, blaming his time in the cryo chamber; it must have altered his body clock. Looking at the timer on the chambers, it will be another ten minutes, and it will be his turn to go into the chamber; not that he needs it now, but he will do so; he does not want to make Xylens and Byne suspicious. Coming out of the chambers, both Xylens and Byne will need some minutes to re-acclimatise. As Nyle was about to enter the chamber, he told his colleagues to try the food from the open crisp packet.

A familiar sound was in the background; their planet was trying to contact them; they were within range of communication. So three delighted lifeforms are nearly home, and a sense of relief and excitement for different reasons, between them all.

35

As the police burst into Raul's home, a trigger-happy police officer instinctively fired a shot at Raul; luckily, he was moving, or it would have been a kill shot. Worse, he was unarmed; he as never owned any gun and had a hatred of them when his father was murdered many years ago. So many questions will be directed at the police department, and as it was a blanket request, he was to be taken alive, with no priors for violence, one officer at least will be asked to leave the force before a lawsuit is brought against them. The bullet was a through and through, but the pain was so intense Raul was unconscious. An ambulance was called for, but with the democratic system of capitalism, what insurance had he taken out, soon overruled by the military's might?

Within ten minutes of this request, a military helicopter was landing in an open area between two houses, military personnel rushing over with a medic and stretcher. Neighbours are horrified at what is unfolding as the military barge past the officers; the lead operative demands who is in charge, names and badge numbers are taken, and as they leave, he says, 'If this man dies, there will be criminal charges.' A bead of sweat forms on the forehead of the officer responsible.

One sarcastic neighbour tells his neighbour, 'looks like Raul's house will be for sale shortly,' strange how this human race can make light of many situations. The neighbours are now curious about what role Raul play's within the military. The guessing game has started, and within a couple of days, Raul will be promoted to General by the neighbours.

Raul is jostled into the helicopter, and the men take care not to injure him anymore, unaware of how vital this cargo is. The updraught of the helicopter seemed to find every bit of debris, as it was thrown all over the place; a hefty bill for new windows will be sent to them shortly.

News of his injury reaches command at the black site, phone calls are made to a higher authority, and the chain of command goes all the way to the pentagon.

More medical staff at the black site are waiting for Raul's arrival; they rush him to the medical centre; when he wakes up, he will be tied to a bed in cuffs. With a wound like this, most individuals would be awake in a matter of hours, at the most, but it will take a couple of days for Raul, hence the reason his friends in the UK could not contact him. Forty-eight hours passed, and in those hours, Raul's body was doing something not expected in a human being. When he wakes, standing before him, a nurse is about to check his wounds; he stirs and, looking up, asks where he is; a simple reply from the nurse is, 'the facility medical centre Raul.'

'Why am I here.'

'The police shot you.'

'What, where? I cannot feel anything.'

'I am about to change the dressing for you, and as she removed the bandages, the nurse went silent; she left the room and returned with the senior Doctor on site. Doctor Leach looks at the wound, 'can you call for General Bright, please, nurse Hilton.'

Nurse Hilton goes to the main desk and phones the General's secretary, 'can you get the General to come here as a matter of urgency, please, Jackie.' In a matter of minutes, General Bright walks into the room.

'What is the problem, Doctor Leach, that you could not tell my secretary.'

Leach shows Raul's non-existent wound, with no scar tissue, as though he had not been shot; luckily, photos were taken on his arrival, and no surgery due to it being a through and through.

A raised voice from Bright, 'what the hell is going on, Leach? I want answers now, for crying out loud.'

'I can't give you answers I do not have, sir; it is medically impossible for what has happened, sir.'

'Raul looks at them perplexed, 'what is wrong with me? Why am I here? Why am I handcuffed? What is going on.'

'Can you remember anything about the last few days, Rodriquez, 'from General Bright?

'No, General, I left work on Friday morning, and now I am here; what day is it.'

A stern look on the General's face, 'Doctor, can the patient be removed from here now.'

'His vitals are okay; I don't see why not, General.'

Bright makes a call, and within minutes two military policemen arrive; ten minutes later, Raul is handcuffed to a desk in an interrogation room, ready to be questioned. General Bright makes another call, and thirty minutes later, Lieutenant Dicks enters the room. Bright was impressed by how quickly Dicks got to the bottom of things with Compton, Lee and Rae and felt his insight would move things forward more rapidly. Dicks decides to take a softly, softly approach to try and develop a rapport between them. Firstly he wants to know if he knows anything that has happened in the facility, the blank look on his face was all he needed to know.

'I know you are a physicist; what is your role here.'

'I cannot tell you; I have signed non-disclosure and top secret notices.'

'I will get General Bright to give you temporary release from this, and we must find out what has happened here; national security is at risk.'

It made Raul stiffen what has happened, and he would do anything to protect our nation, 'get the General, please.'

Bright comes in; he was watching from behind the two-way glass; he explained this was a verbal release in front of Lt Dicks due to the current emergency; 'we must get to the bottom of this quickly.'

Raul is still in the dark, oblivious to what has happened, his mind shutting out certain things to not give away what he knows; his brain automatically hides the relevant facts, all part of his brain growth

'Can we carry on now, Raul? What is your job here.'

'I work in the building AL-1EN, which astounds me that nobody was putting two and two together, as it obviously spells alien.'

'Are you telling me that aliens exist, Raul?'

'My job was to watch and monitor an alien in that building, trying to find out how they function.'

Knowing what he has already seen, Dicks is still shocked by the realisation that his theory could be correct.

'Right Raul, take me back to Friday, walk me through that day; what can you remember.'

'It would be best to go back a couple more days; my job was to monitor the lifeform, which I might add has been here for several years.'

It took Dicks by surprise, 'what do you mean five or six years.'

'No seventy-five years, he was one of the original lifeforms from Roswell.'

'What? We have a lifeform here; I assume he is dead by now; is the body preserved.'

'Yes and no.'

'What do you mean by that, Raul.'

'There has always been a slight heart pulse, but the other lifeform was pronounced dead.'

'You are telling me there were two.'

'Yes.'

'Crying out loud, is this alien still here.'

'Yes.'

Dicks turned to the two-way glass and requested for them to see this lifeform, now annoyed because he knows General Bright as known all along. Dicks knows it is pointless arguing with the General; all his good work will undoubtedly be passed onto someone else. The General comes in and allows Dicks to release Raul from the desk, and a vehicle is ordered to take them to building AL-1EN. After what happened to Compton, Rae and Lee, Lt Dicks asks that the handcuffs be taken away, or he will again be judged guilty, which is human nature at work. The journey to the building is sombre; the three men get out of the vehicle and head toward the entrance, using the General's key card for access, the highest level he can access anywhere on the site. Once again, Bob is on duty and salutes the General and Lt Dicks; as they pass through security, he remarks to Raul, 'feeling better, Dr Rodriquez, you looked terrible on Friday, thought you were going to fall over; I see you have got your colour back.'

The General and Dicks look at Raul, 'what is security talking about, Raul.'

'It was near the end of my shift, and I felt ill but could not leave till my relief came.'

Going through all the various checkpoints, they finally reach Raul's workplace, Dicks is in awe at this facility; he has never been allowed in before. As they enter Raul's workplace, there are no salutes; these are civilian workers, but they acknowledge Raul, 'Have you changed shift? You are early, Raul.'

Raul waves; his colleagues can sense something is wrong; Dr Wong approaches; he is in charge of the dayshift, an excellent academic in the same vein as Raul.

'Can I help, gentlemen? As you know, this facility is out of bounds unless clearance has been authorised.'

Raul speaks first, explaining who the people are, and he is taking them on a personnel tour as they requested. Dicks speaks first, 'have you had any problems with your electricity supplies.'

'No, not that I know of; if you wait, I can check the handover log for the weekend.' Dr Wong comes back,

'Strangely, on Saturday night at around two am, how did you know.'

'Following up on an incident over the weekend; that is all; where are your main power supplies from.' Raul jumped in 'this facility is separate from the rest of the site, with it being such a large site it was separated years ago.' Bright and Dicks could not see any sign of this mysterious lifeform and asked where it was. Raul went over to the main control panel and flicked a switch.

The glass was a new type that created a frosted effect when de-energised; when electricity was applied, it became clear glass.

Bright and Dicks stood with their mouths open for a few seconds, trying to take in the sight of an alien lifeform in front of them. Wong commented, 'he always felt that way every time he flicked the switch.'

Then as if waiting for Raul, before their eyes, the husk of Xylens body slowly faded away, the sound of alarms going off around them, doors automatically closing so that the alien could not get away. Only Raul knew the truth, and he will not say anything till his dying day. The incident only gives credence to Dicks theory now. Bright started to shout for answers, but all he could see were panicked faces unused to any situation like this. Then he turns on Raul, 'what the hell do you know about any of this, Rodriquez.'

Dicks sensed the General was about to lose his temper; everything about this site was based on what had just disappeared before his eyes. How does he tell his higher authorities what he has just witnessed? Even to him, the chain of command can seem limitless. At this stage, it appears as though things are in slow motion, as people run around not knowing what to do. Dicks shouts for everyone to stop. Bright nods his head in appreciation; he will need to take control now. Bright, as now assumed his captor has died and gone to his maker, calmly asks for the alarm to be silenced. He told them nothing could be done and asked them to write a witness report so it could be analysed for information gathering.

Bright turns to Dicks, 'I want him back in interrogation; we will find out what happened at this facility by tonight, or he will not see the light of day for many years to come.'

'Yes, sir.'

'Before you leave this room, nobody, and I mean nobody, must know what has happened here today. Do I make myself clear, gentlemen?'

'Yes, sir,' from both men; they turn and head to the door; as they step into the corridor, they are confronted by the barrel of a gun; it is Bob on security doing his job. Dicks explains to him the alarm was triggered by mistake, 'the General is dealing with it now; please return to your duties.' A woeful nod from Bob, missing the excitement of being in a war-torn environment, slowly escorts them back to the front exit. It is midday, and while he is being taken back to his interview room, Raul can hear the voices of Roger and Shaun; they have just received visions of Xylens demise. Raul explains that they saw his old body, like a snake's skin left behind and that all is okay with Xylens; he is on his way home. A sense of relief from both men, now thankful for saving our world.

36

Back in the UK, Roger and Shaun have just finished a conversation, surprised by the vision they have both seen; as their brain grows, their abilities are becoming fine-tuned. Both are in separate rooms but are still communicating. They have decided that common sense must prevail and give Don information about their limited involvement in the incident in the USA. Both have had another scan in the last two hours, and the results have been sent to Don. He is pleased that no further growth of their brains has occurred and will request that they be allowed out in the morning. But, unknown to all, there will be another growth spurt in a week or so. A final upgrade, so to speak, Xylens did not want to overload their brains, but the future offspring of Roger, Shaun and Raul will have I.Q levels never seen before. As their children grow, they will influence generations to come and become the founder members of a subservient society.

Roger and Shaun receive a late text from Don, telling them they will be able to leave the hospital in the morning and that he will see them in the office when they get there. Five minutes later, they receive another text from Don, 'by the way, I have told your girlfriends, and they seem happy,' followed by a smiling emoji. They both think at the same time, how does he do that? He never misses anything. The following day they order a taxi to go to the office, and as they step out of the revolving entrance door, they laugh. They both agreed it's like a game of one foot in and one foot out, trying to avoid the door stalling as it touches anyone trying to escape the hospital.

As they step outside, both look to the skies in sync, yet more foreboding dark clouds. So is this going to be a bad day? Now always suspicious of any unusual cloud formation. The taxi arrives, and they make their way to P.H.Emenonmen; in Westminister, the taxi driver says he had never heard of them.

Are they new?

Rather than break into a long-drawn conversation, they replied six months in sync again, and the driver went silent, thinking it must be the medication they were on.

Roger and Shaun talk to each other mentally, comparing London's hustle and bustle to home life in the North East of England. Southerners call them Smoggies, a term from the industrial past long gone, the skyline ever-changing now. With many of these industries gone, steelworks and chemical plants are now taken over by tech groups and call centres. Nevertheless, they always smile when people from the south say how friendly the north is, always being greeted with a pleasant smile and a wave of the hand. Maybe the pressures of affording the ridiculous prices for houses driven by greedy entrepreneurs affect their mindset. Finally, the taxi pulls up outside the building, and they step out of the taxi; Shaun volunteers to pay the exorbitant bill of twenty pounds for a ten-minute drive around. Roger walks through the entrance door and is greeted by an excitable Jayne, and she kisses him; at this point, Roger realises their relationship might be moving to the next level. Shaun follows through the door, muttering under his breath at the price he has just paid; so annoyed, he asks for a receipt to claim it back. He looks up to see Anne, and her bright blue eyes, as she rushes from around the reception desk and kisses him, as Jayne had done to Roger.

As the giddiness dies down, they hear the sound of someone pretending to clear their throat, and they turn to see Don smiling.

'Glad to see the happy families, but can we get some work done now.'

Jayne and Anne rush to their desk, looking flustered, and as Roger and Shaun walk behind Don toward the conference room, they re-apply their glossy lipstick; they must look their best when they come back out.

Don tells them to sit down, 'right then, after your little rest, can we get back to reality.'

'Yes, sir, what has happened in the last forty-eight hours.'

'Intelligence is sparse, but I am confident your encounter within the field in Haltwhistle has something to do with it, but we will get to that in a minute or so.'

'What do you mean, sir, from Shaun?

'A strange question, but have either of you developed any unusual skill sets.'

'Not sure what you mean, sir, other than the ability to communicate by thought, no.'

'I have had John Downes wife Jane on the phone; he has had a personality change.'

'In what way,' a surprised tone from Roger.

'From being an ordinary maths teacher, he has developed into a maths genius solving scientific equations that he could never do before. Moreover, his wife was concerned about all the people involved with him.'

'Have we contacted Joanne and Denise, sir? Are they okay?'

'Silence, I'm afraid; I have asked some of our local staff to do a welfare check, just cover all the bases.'

'Speaking for Shaun, we hope they are okay,'

'I have sent staff, but can you use your abilities to contact them,' Roger and Shaun look at each other and agree they will try but cannot guarantee success if the other parties do not respond, 'and it would be easier if you were not in the room, sir,' from Shaun.

Don agreed, 'looks like I am on the coffee run this time,' and left the room. They try to contact Joanne and Denise, but being only successful with Joanne, they ask the question that Don wants to be answered. Unbelievably she responds, 'that only two hours ago, she saved her husband from injury.'

'What do you mean, Joanne,' from them both.

'Kevin was on the ladder painting the outside of the house, and he misjudged the ladder rung and slipped; he was falling; I shouted out and at the same time raised my arms as though I was catching him; it was like slow motion; I seemed to have the power to lower him by thought. I do not know whether to be glad or sad. I'm starting to shake now; it's finally sinking in that I saved my husband's life.'

'Bloody hell,' from Roger, 'is he okay, Joanne.'

'Like me, we are both in shock; I don,t know what to do; I'm scared.'

'Don't be scared; can you and Kevin come to our office in Westminister, please? I will text the address.'

'When do you want us to come, Roger.'

'We have some colleagues coming to check if you are okay. Will you let them bring you here today, please,?'

'After, what has just happened, I think we need to come, don't you.'

'I will leave word at the front desk, and they will arrange a hotel, etcetera; I will text details for you.'

'Thank you to you both.'

Don's timing is impeccable; as the door opens, he enters with a tray of three coffees and biscuits, 'any luck, guys.'

Roger proceeds to tell him what Joanne has just told them; it is the first time they have seen Don stumped for words. Then, after a short pause, the wheels turning in Don's head, he finally responds, 'Have you managed to contact Denise.'

'No, sir, we have invited Joanne and Kevin to the office for any investigative work, and we assume hospital.'

'Yes, that's correct; right then, back to you two, what can you tell me? Any recollections yet.'

Roger takes the lead, explaining how they were linked as one to enable Xylens to regain his strength, the easiest way to describe it is we were like a battery charger, gradually increasing his ability to leave after seventy-five years. Shaun takes over; 'sir, at this stage, we were under his control in the field, unable to move; it was impossible to refuse.' Shaun paused for a reaction, and it was not forthcoming from Don

'Carry on,' was all they got from him

'Then, we were put into sleep mode; it was like a light switch; we had no control at all.'

'I cannot understand why you could not fight it; both of you are experienced in the abnormal, looking for something different, your senses above all, what went wrong.'

'In all honesty, sir, we were ok until the amulet dissolved into our wrist.'

'Amulet, what f—king amulet; why did you not tell me about this before.'

'We thought we had, sir, both of them again in sync; this is something Don can still not get to grips with, starting to annoy him now; once again, he tells them to proceed.

'During this time, we did not know what was happening, but when we were woken, Xylens was somehow inside Raul's body, then we see him in different guises moving from body to body.'

'This did not unnerve both of you; this was happening.'

'Sir, we had no physical control; he was using our minds; it was as though we were one; it is hard to explain.'

'Gentlemen, it is hard to believe; it sounds more like a Syfy novel than real life; just carry on, will you.'

'It was then that we found they are sensory to their craft.'

'Here we go; what the hell does that mean, both of you, only one of you to answer; Shaun, your turn, before I lose my mind, tell me now.'

'Their lifeform is the pivotal part of the craft; without them, it does not fly.' They can sense the machine, and the device reciprocates; while both are available, they can sense and feel each other.'

'Good grief, their technology is unbelievable; no wonder you could not break free,' Don finally realises the dilemma his men are in, but how does he explain this to his bosses? Finally, an exasperated Don asks Roger to enlighten him about other events.

'The craft was unusable, and we only found out while we were in the hospital that while he was hoping to leave, he could see that the military was re-engineering their technology for war. They only use weapons as a defensive measure, but his weapons can destroy this planet, so he set his craft to destruction; it was to save our world.

We do not know what happened after that, sir, other than he found another craft somewhere; even we are baffled how many are here, if any.'

'At last, we have got to the bottom of it, but you have left me with a political nightmare.'

Roger decides to risk Don's wrath, 'not if you do not say anything, sir.'

For once, Don thinks he is right, and an old song comes to his head because it was the song he would sing at karaoke. It was the only one he knew the words to, 'Silence is Golden,' from his distant past.

37

Raul is staring at four grey walls, waiting for the return of Dicks; no need to turn his peripheral vision is now so acute he can see a speck of dust slowly drifting to the floor, so minute people with 20/20 cannot see it. General Bright has now arrived and talking to Dicks behind the glass window; they are discussing what they can prise out of Raul's head. Unfortunately, General Bright wants to go straight for the jugular; to get him to talk, he decides he must threaten him with the possibility of imprisonment for his wife as an accessory. Dicks walks into the room, giving Raul a cup of coffee and a sandwich, trying to create a softer tone, hoping this will work rather than the brutal use of Raul's wife.

'Raul, you know, we must get to the bottom of what happened here a few days ago, and it would be much easier on everyone if you could tell us about your involvement.'

'But I've told you I do not know anything; you have got to believe me.'

'Look, we have evidence; you are complicit in what happened.'

'It can't be true; you are lying; I do not know what has happened here; no one will tell me.'

Bright knocks on the glass window, Dicks turns and leaves the room, a camera monitoring Raul's every movement. Dicks meets the General outside the room and Bright comments, 'either he is the best liar on the planet, or he truly does not know what has happened. Get him to re-trace his steps from Friday, and maybe we can fill in the blanks between.'

'Yes, sir.'

Dicks returns to talk to Raul, taking a sip of his lukewarm coffee, nearly spitting it out; it never tastes the same as when it's hot, he thinks. 'right Raul, can you take me back to Friday, run through the day, when we last we talked you said you were ill if I remember.'

'Yes, that's right, I was tired. It was coming to the end of my shift; it would be around five-thirty in the morning.' Raul paused to think, and Dicks jumped in 'carry on, Raul.'

'Just trying to remember, ah, that was it; I had a sudden desire to say goodnight to the lifeform.'

'Is that something you regularly did?'

'No, it was the first time; I had never had the clearance to get that near before.'

Bright and Dicks listen more intently, 'how did you get the clearance to allow you to get close this time.'

'Strangely, cost cuts, a day or so before, some staff were laid off, and I was the next in line for a senior position, and the clearance allowed me to get closer than I have ever been before; it was fascinating.'

Dicks looked at Raul, and it was as though he was in a trance-like state, 'what do you mean by that, Raul.'

'I felt a sense of serenity, and the lifeforms eyes were so intense; after this, I started to feel ill; I felt nauseous and could not walk straight.'

'Then what happened.'

'I went home; the next thing I know, I woke up here in the hospital.'

'Okay, Raul, I will be back in a few minutes, Dicks leaves the room to talk to the General, 'sir, can we get security footage of Friday inside Raul's work area? We might get lucky, and we can see if anything happened.'

Sour-faced, Bright tells Dicks, 'I'm not too hopeful about that; security should have picked up something; we have not been informed of anything unusual.'

'Sir, no one picked anything up on the other surveillance

cameras.'

'Fair enough, I will make the call; we will look at it in my office, for our eyes only, Dicks.'

They walk over to Bright's office, discussing things that have happened, but will it be a happy outcome by the end of the day? As they enter the building, people start firing questions at the General, surprised they could not find him; after all, the place is falling around them. Finally, Bright turns around and shouts, 'be quiet, all of you, get out and make an appointment with Jackie; I have more important things to do right now, Dicks come with me.' Both of them head toward Bright's office, passing Jackie at her desk; Bright tells her to expect some calls; he does not want to be disturbed; just then, the phone rings, and he looks at Dicks, 'Let us hope we find an answer to this mess.' Dicks follows the General into his office and hears a deep sigh as Bright sits in front of the computer.

'Good God, I hope we can get answers; he opens up the screen; the security file has been sent. Bright clicks the icon, and they search through footage till they reach the time stamp at five twenty-eight; both watch and wait. Then, finally, they see Raul spill his coffee, get up, and walk toward Xylens, and when he reaches him, they see him tilt his head and then look directly at him. Then they look at each other in astonishment as they see the orb move from Xylens to Raul.

Bright stutters, 'how the hell can that be? That lifeform has been here seven-five years; why now, Dicks.'

'I guess the stars must have aligned for him, sir.'

Bright was about to shout at Dicks over his sarcasm, then realised the situation's irony, and he calmed down.

'Well, this will be difficult to explain; thank goodness for the taped evidence.'

'Does this mean we can free everyone, sir?'

'Unfortunately, not till we get the authority from higher up; I will arrange an extraordinary meeting, for tomorrow, you will be required to attend as my spokesman, and this will be behind closed doors.'

'But, sir, do you need me.'

'If you want these men free, I suggest it may become your priority, and I will send a memo that I have seconded you until further notice.'

'Yes, sir.'

'Oh, can you splice all the events together for presentation?'

Yes, sir, see you tomorrow; I will tell Raul he will be here till tomorrow at least.'

Bright nods in appreciation, and Dicks heads over to talk to Raul, Compton, Lee and Rae to tell them things are coming together, and it looks favourable they will be okay.'

38

Xylens, Nyle and Byne are within range of communication of their home planet, and Byne responds to them by explaining who they are; at this point, he does not tell them about Xylens. They gave the call sign number of the craft, and the communication went dead, Nyle trying in vain to get a response. The reason for the silence was they had no record of the craft number and were desperately searching in vain. That was until an old supervisor, in the latter years of her life, remembered the lost craft file, never opened since their craft was deemed lost in space. Another few weeks and she would have been gone, sent to end her subservient life at home with close family, and this file would have been lost forever. The supervisors at the air control centre, surprised at the amount of crafts lost over time, checked the number Nyle gave and opened communication again. Every craft was given a unique reference, and this reference was their guarantee for a safe passage home. A buzz around traffic control, the file contains information on the purpose of their search and seek task, to find Xylens and Asku, who are now regarded as cult heroes, going beyond their call of duty.

Many assumed them to be dead, especially when Nyle and Byne did not come back, now also on a similar status. The comms tech asks for their specific reference to confirm entry into the space zone; this vast expanse will still take them ten Earth days to reach home. After the reference is given, a loud cheer can be heard in the background, and then Nyle explains they have an extra package with them.

The cheers stopped instantly, and Nyle told them about Xylens; there was abject silence.

Twenty seconds later, they could hear quiet chatter, gradually getting louder, as they realised who it was, then a roar of approval, 'can we speak to him,' nervously from the comms tech.

Finally, Xylens speaks, and all he can hear is tumultuous applause in the background. It gradually got louder as more people who had heard the commotion came into the room. Then the question he did not want to be asked was, how is Asku? The applause stopped immediately when he told them about his untimely death, and they will pass the information on to his family. While Xylens felt human emotion, Nyle and Byne were non-plus at this point in their transition to form any emotion at this stage, but unknown to them all, Nyle is undergoing a life-changing effect on his life. The severity of the newspaper stories about murders in all walks of life struck a long-lost dormant urge to kill; the virus of humankind is about to reach a world millions of miles away. It is caused by the simple ingredient of salt on a potato crisp and other chemical by-products. It will dramatically alter their nutrient strain and affect Byne and Xylens differently if they eat the crisps. Feeling something is not right within himself, he mentions it is time for him to go into the cryo chamber, Xylens and Byne agree. Nyle steps inside, and Byne sets the controls. Xylenes watched as the controls were very different from his old craft; a sense of nostalgia came to him, like missing an old friend. They watch as the gases form around Nyle, then settle down to open a dialogue. Byne settles down; seeing the crisp packet, he tries a crisp, his reaction the same as Nyle's.

Byne offers Xylens the packet, who refuses, having seen his reaction to the taste. Although this refusal might save his sanity, Nyle and Byne will think differently about their world when they reach home. Ten minutes later, Byne falls asleep; this will become a quiet trip home, Xylens will engross his time looking through different papers, and his points of view will become far-reaching.

39

Sara is distraught, and her husband's face is all over the news; as a person of interest, friends and relatives are constantly on the phone, and there is no news of Raul's whereabouts. Finally, in her frustration, she throws the phone against the wall, and her hearing seems more sensitive lately; her body feels different now, and she cannot explain why? There can only be one reason, she will call into a pharmacist on the way to Raul's house.

Having already phoned for a taxi, she asked her mother if she could carry on looking after the children, explaining why. She needs to go to Raul's house for answers; arriving, she finds the door unlocked. A neighbour seeing her, walks over to tell her what has happened before she enters. Listening intently, she cannot believe what she hears; Raul is a physicist and has nothing to do with the military. Walking into the house, she can see the small blood pool on the floor, now angry that they could not be bothered to clean it up.

With a sickening feeling in her stomach, she rushes to the kitchen sink and vomits into it, wiping her face and then turning the tap on to rinse the contents away. Her mind was awash with fears that Raul may be dead; why had no one made contact with her? Who can she call?

Sara slumps onto a chair, her face in her hands; she starts to cry; how can she help Raul? Then she hears a voice, and she turns to look for Raul, the voice so loud he must be here, not realising it was in her head. She rushes from room to room, searching, running up the stairs two steps at a time, but nothing to be found; she sits on the edge of the unmade bed, never made up from the night when they made love and reconciled.

While sitting on the bed, she could hear the voice again; thinking she was going mad, she screamed; Raul could hear this and told her to talk through her subconscious.

Raul could hear her respond, 'What the hell.'

'It is okay, Sara; I am okay.'

'But, how, what is going on? How can this be.'

'It is a long story, but please do not tell anyone we can communicate like this; it is a story for another time.'

'But, the blood on the floor, what happened.'

'I got shot by the police, but I am okay.'

'I'm worried, Raul; what if the police come to see me? What should I say.'

'The truth, Sara, that is all you can do, tell them what you remember, even the missing time when we travelled seven hundred miles, and we do not know how, but only if they ask.'

'Where are you, Raul? Can I come and see you.'

'No, it is impossible.'

'Why?'

'I am in a military cell.'

'But, why? Raul.'

'A long story, I cannot tell you now, but believe me, I will be okay; it is a misunderstanding.'

'Are you sure, Raul,' I did not quite understand how they could communicate like this. Hoping Raul will come home soon before she goes mad.

'Yes, everything will be okay; I will talk to you later.'

Then Sara raises her tone, 'Raul, I think I might be pregnant.' Silence from Raul; it seemed ages before he responded, but it was in her mind only, 'Sara, that is brilliant; I'm so happy for us; it shows what reconciliation sex can do. Are you okay with it?'

'Yes, I suppose; I thought we would stop at two, but we went a bit wild if I remember, so I should not be surprised.'

'Wild, Sara, it was the best sex I have ever had; you were marvellous.' A chuckle from Sara, remembering how raw it was, 'I was, wasn't I, I don't know what came over me, but I'm glad it did.'

'When will you go to the doctor's, Sara.'

'When you come home, Raul, it would be nice for us both to go.'

'You are right, of course.'

'What should I do now, Raul.'

'Pick up the children and wait, Sara; it will not be too long now.'

'How will I contact you if I need to,'

'I do not know, and I suppose you think about me, as I did you, and it seemed to open a line, like a phone; I cannot explain why.'

'Okay, I love you.'

'Bye Sara, I love you too.'

Raul settles down in his cell, thankful he managed to do something out of the ordinary, a skill he is now grateful he has.

40

Don has told Shaun and Roger to hang around the office for a few hours while he moves what they have discussed up the chain of command. Roger takes a risk and suggests that 'Shaun may be right not to take it any further; the least they know, the better, sir.'

Don looked surprised that Roger jumped in, not normally confrontational, 'my decision, not yours, Roger.'

As Roger steps back, he says, 'plausible liability, sir; if they do not know, they can honestly say they know nothing.'

'I repeat my decision, now go to the hotel; I will call you with any updates.'

'Yes, sir,' both were annoyed. Don would not listen, but he is the boss, and they must abide by his decision. So they turn and leave and are greeted by two smiling faces, Jayne and Anne, sensing something is amiss but have learnt in this particular office to never push for answers. Their new love interests have booked hotel rooms for them, and then Roger mentions that Joanne and her husband Kevin will need accommodation. So Anne books them into a different hotel; after all, they do not want to spoil the night ahead. So instead, Jayne and Anne will go shopping for something special for the evening and enjoy every minute of their love trysts, while it lasts, at least until the bubble bursts. The women are not naive and realise it could go on forever or be over in an instant, but they are women of a modern world and will carry on with their lives. So again, the men make arrangements with them for the evening ahead.

Jayne and Anne kiss them, 'See you later, and wear the nice aftershave; it turns us on,' laughing giddily.

Stepping outside the office, the foreboding clouds have gone, and the sun shines across the high-rise buildings, reflecting the skyline like mirrors and casting shadows on the floor. They decide to walk to the hotel, then wish they had not made that decision, as disrespectful commuters hustle across the roads with dower faces, not speaking to anyone. 'Everyone seems angry here,' Roger says to Shaun, 'it's the metropolis, Rog; nobody wants to know anybody; they might interfere with their lives. I wish we were back in the North East and friendly faces,' Roger nods his appreciation of Shaun's insightful statement. Roger points out that at least two people are not like that; smiling, they turn the corner; the hotel is just ahead. On entering the hotel, the receptionist smiled, 'your rooms are ready,' the men looked at each other, smiling. Natalie informed them Jayne had requested an upgrade for repeat business, which they gladly obliged and hoped would be to their liking. Key cards are given, and they walk to the lift; Shaun mentions, 'it must be a good upgrade. It's on the tenth floor.'

Stopping on their floor level, the lift door opens silently; unfortunately, their rooms are at the end of the corridor; the benefit of a panoramic view across London was worth the walk. They entered their separate rooms next to each other, thinking this was miles better than the riff raft rooms, 'good grief, is it the same hotel? What money can do,' they thought. On the king-size bed are rose petals, chocolate on the pillow, satin robes and expensive wine on the table.

Both men are in sync in separate rooms, not knowing each is doing the same thing; as they sit in the sumptuous leather chair, they hear the voice of Denise.

'Hello, Shaun. Roger, do you need to talk to me.'

Not surprised, they ask, 'how did you know Denise.'

'Can not explain, guys; it was like a message in the ether that I need to contact you.'

They thank her for contacting them and explain why and the new abilities that Joanne and John have got.

A deep sigh from Denise, 'no, nothing like that; sadly, I could do with some excitement after our little adventure.'

Shaun then explains 'that something might manifest out of the blue, like Joanne when Kevin was in danger.'

Denise agrees, and as she is about to say goodbye, Roger breaks into the conversation, 'do you still have the disc in your possession, Denise,'

'Yes, it is safe; any particular reason, you ask, Roger.'

'Curiosity mainly, Denise. Are you near it?'

'What are you leading up to, Rog,' from Shaun; strangely, when he mentioned the disc, he was blocked from him; this was a safety mechanism built into the disc; they have become sensory to them like Xylens. Shaun is now worried about the impact these discs may have on them. Could it be a step too far?

'I have hidden it, out of sight and out of mind, Roger.'

'How long will it take to get it.'

'Five minutes.'

'Can you get it and contact me straight away, please.'

'Okay, is there a problem?'

'No, everything is fine; come back to me as soon as possible.'

As Denise leaves the conversation, there is a loud banging on the door; Roger opens the door to see an irate Shaun with a towel around his waist.

'What are you doing, Rog, shutting me out of the conversation like that,'

'I did not.?

'Yes, you did. As soon as you mentioned the disc, it went silent; for God's sake, tell me what happened.'

'I just asked Denise to get the disc.'

'But, why now.'

'Instinct, something is telling me to look at the discs.'

'What? is it Xylens as he contacted you.'

'No, listen to me. Have you got your disc?'

'Yes, it's in my bag in the room.'

'Bring it here, and I will show you something; it's buzzing around in my head.'

'Why the hell can I not see it then.' Roger shrugs his shoulders in abject silence; Shaun storms off to his room. Roger hears a scream as one female guest is shocked to see a man with a towel around his waist walk out of another male's room, staring at them both. Calming down, she thinks, I guess it is the sign of the times we live in, walking to her room and slamming the door.

While Shaun gets the disc and puts on suitable attire, Denise contacts Roger again, and he asks her to describe it. Denise tells him 'that it is circular, about thirty millimetres in diameter, with strange symbols on it, oh and the odd thing is when I picked it up a slight notch appeared on it, in the shape of a tee.'

'Thank you for that, Denise. Can I come back to you? It will be within twenty-four hours.'

'Yes, of course, bye.'

A knock on the door heralded the return of Shaun, showing signs of a temper tantrum; Roger calmed him down, then asked if he had brought his disc.'

'Yes, what is going on in your head, Rog.'

'Show me the disc, Shaun.'

Shaun took the disc out of his pocket, opened the palm of his hand and in doing so, they both saw the shape of a tee come forward from the disc. They looked at each other in astonishment; after what had gone on in the past few days, they should not have been surprised.

Roger put his hand in his pocket and retrieved his disc, again looking in amazement as an L shape notch started to appear on the disc. At the same time, they saw an L shape space appear on Shaun's disc, both knowing that they needed to be interlocked, like a jigsaw. They look at each other, smiling knowingly; they must join them together to see what happens; in doing so, a small hologram appears, mesmerised by the apparition. Not understanding it was the first part of a fusion reactor, both assumed the picture must get more apparent when they are all connected. When they went to separate them, both received a vision of the whole reactor, and unbelievably they could now understand what the hologram was. Putting the discs away, a sense that it will unfold if they can get all the discs together.

Then Roger remembers that Joanne and Kevin are getting picked up to come to the office; he contacts her, but she must bring the disc without Kevin knowing. As he makes contact, there is the sound of her doorbell in the distance; their colleagues are already there, putting undue pressure on Joanne to get the disc without anyone seeing her. Kevin answers the door; now cautious after recent events, he asks for some identification; taking a card from one of the men, he rings Shaun. It would have been quicker for Joanne to contact him mentally, but it has given her valuable time to get the disc without raising any suspicions with Kevin.

Shaun answers the phone, eases Kevin's worries, and confirms the names of the people they have sent, and this delay allows Joanne to put the disc in her handbag, which she will not let go till the disc is given to Roger. Shaun wishes them a safe journey, and they will see them in the office tomorrow morning at nine-thirty.

There is a sense of excitement between them as they can see things starting to come together, but in the back of their minds a certain amount of doubt about whether they are doing the right thing. Shaun asked Roger 'how did he know, what to do,' he should not be surprised; this thing is affecting all of us differently. Then Roger points out that we need to get the other discs from Denise, John and Raul. The last one will be difficult, especially if he is incarcerated; let us hope he can get out of his predicament for all concerned. The only problem Shaun could envisage is whether we all need to be together; if so, this will be hard to explain the need to do so. Roger points out, 'that is a problem for tomorrow; Jayne and Anne will be here shortly; where the hell is that aftershave that works so well.'

One hour later, the happy foursome is seated at a window table, taking in the nightlife of the city centre, making general comments on fashion and the cross-section of people passing by. They finished their first course and were waiting for their main meal.

The wine is flowing nicely, not too much; they will need their senses fine-tuned for the evening to come. Suddenly Shaun jumps up; moving quickly, he grabs Anne and pulls her away; Roger instinctively does the same to Jayne; he has learnt to listen to Shaun, not one for the dramatic.

Then the sound of smashing glass, as a speeding car, being chased by the police, hits a parked vehicle.

It flips into the window and lands on the table where they were sitting. Jayne and Anne scream in terror, and tears flow instantly; if Shaun and Roger had not pulled them away, they might have died. Other guests flee the restaurant as police officers pull the driver out of the car, 'probable, high on drugs,' was the comment heard from an officer. Jayne and Anne go to Shaun's room to calm their nerves, and with the help of the complimentary wine on the table, the men will find them asleep; when they finally get to the room. Police take statements from witnesses, and all say that if it were not for Shaun and Roger, two women would have died that evening. The hotel staff could not do enough for them; the rarest whiskey to calm them down was not needed, just like a day at the office. Before they head upstairs, Roger takes Shaun outside to take a deep breath of fresh air, away from prying eyes and ears; there is still a crowd over the road, the age of mobile cameras and flashing lights taking photos to go viral worldwide. They turn their faces hoping not to be seen; if Don sees this, there will be more questions to answer, silly really, he will know already. Especially as Jayne and Anne have been involved, Don seems to have a sixth sense, which they seem to be gradually acquiring.

Returning, some people want to shake hands with the two heroes, and it takes fifteen minutes to break away from their newfound fan base. They make their way to the lift hoping Jayne and Anne are awake; with the adrenalin rush, the women are in for a night of bliss, they think to themselves.

Roger opens his door, but no one is in the room; he rushes out as Shaun enters his room and follows him in.

Both do not have the heart to wake them up; they place the duvet over Anne and Jayne and return to Roger's room. Shaun tells Roger he has never slept with a man before; Roger informs him he is not tonight; there will be a pillow between them; exhausted, they fall asleep straight away. Shaun wakes up first, his body clock always at six o clock, for bodily functions and a shower; as he returns to the room, Roger sits on the edge of the bed and says, 'do you think the girls will want an early visit.' They rush to get ready; twenty minutes later, they enter Shaun's room, greeted by two happy women; last night, now gone to the back of their minds. They share the taxi back to the office; as they enter, Don greets them, 'well, well, the heroes have arrived; you do not do things by half, do you,'

'What do you mean, sir, from Roger?

Don shows them four newspapers with their faces splashed across them, 'Local heroes, save two people in restaurant crash.'

'But how did the papers get the photos, sir, from Shaun?

'The world has no secrets now, boys; if anybody should know, it is you two, the age of mobiles will be the death of some people.'

'Sorry, sir, it happened so quickly we did not have much time to react.'

'Jayne, Anne, are you both okay? Do you need to take time off?'

Both replied, 'no, sir. If it were not for Shaun and Roger, we would not be here,' this statement brought back how narrowly they missed death, and the women started to cry.

They rushed into the restroom to let out the tension, and ten minutes later, reappeared, 'it's okay, sir, we are okay,' from Anne.

Don checks again, then tells Roger and Shaun to go to the conference room, then reminds Jayne and Anne that Joanne and Kevin are due shortly, 'can you contact me when they arrive.'

Both answered, 'yes,' in sync; Don was taken aback, wondering if they were getting like Roger and Shaun; he would need to monitor them closely. Don follows his men into the conference room, 'right then, would one of you please tell me what happened last night.'

Roger pointed out that he followed Shaun's lead, it happened so fast, and in all honesty, he as not even asked Shaun how he knew it was about to happen. Shaun stood up, 'I do not think you will believe me when I tell you.'

'Get on with it, man,' from Don

'I could see it in my head, like a TV screen; it was so real, sir; what is even more strange, I heard a voice say, move now. I cannot explain it any other way.'

'It is evident to me that the people involved with this lifeform have acquired an extra sense or possibly a power they did not have before; how can I explain this one to our bosses.'

Roger jumped in again, 'plausible deniability, sir; the least they know, the better; for now, I know you disagree, but where do we go from here? 'Don holds his head in his hands in despair, already deciding that Roger was right not to tell them about their involvement in the USA incident. Nevertheless, he tells them he has taken their advice and hopes it does not come back to haunt him in the future.

Then, sarcastically, Don asks Roger 'what is your superpower? Are you about to fly? Bend metal bars, pick up cars with one hand.'

'Sorry, sir, nothing from me yet; waiting with bated breath, I will be as surprised as you when and if it happens.'

The phone rings in the conference room; Don answers,

'Joanne and Kevin are here, Don,' from a more coherent Jayne, now sufficiently calmed down to do her job.

'Thank you, Jayne, send them in.'

They all stand, handshakes all around, and Joanne makes sure she is seated next to Roger; her left hand falls to her side, and she slides the disc into Roger's right hand. He nods in appreciation and places it into his pocket, the conversation opens up, and they discuss how she is coping with everything. Surprised she is taking it all in her stride, Kevin is the only one spooked by the incident, having been the one floating down to earth from the ladder. Yet, even now, he is unable to grasp what has happened to his wife, forever beholden for this unique ability in the back of his mind. As they talk over what has happened to the Haltwhistle five, they arrange another brain scan for Joanne to see if everything is okay. Then, Joanne and Kevin left to go to the hospital, and Don asked if they had spoken to Denise and John. Roger explained they had talked to Denise, and there were no new developments, only John to find now; Don nodded his approval.

41

Lt Dicks is busy putting his case notes together and checking all the video surveillance tapes when the phone rings. It is a request from General Bright telling him to pack his bags for a couple of days; he has arranged a meeting in DC, and they are leaving in three hours. As the transport arrives to take them to the airport, the clouds darken, and a sudden lightning strike hits the mountain, where the alien craft used to be up until a few days ago. A military helicopter takes them to a cordoned-off area at Dulles Airport, where transport is waiting to take them to the Pentagon for a problematic meeting; three men's careers are on the line. The flight over has given them time to get to know each other more personally, and they find they have similar pursuits. Unusually, a father and son bond was being formed as Bright's son died in combat ten years ago, and Dicks reminded the General how he missed him. In many ways, this will be the most crucial meeting of Dicks life, as he and the General run through possible questions and answer scenarios. With this subject matter, the people in the government's higher echelons always seem unknown and wield economic power. These people have the power of life or death. If there is any inkling of this type of thing reaching media outlets, lives are at risk. Unfortunately, Bright and Dicks will open a can of worms that these people do not want anyone to hear about, regardless of whether they are a senator, General or reporter. On arrival, the two men are taken down the long corridors of power, wondering why they need so many people; good to see the people's taxes getting spent so well.

They are shown to a large room, a small table located in the centre, fifteen meters from the entrance doors. Another seven and a half metres is a raised plinth with a continuous desk in a crescent shape and six oversized leather chairs. Both men are told to sit at the table and wait and are given instructions on how to use the media system if they require it to be used. Dicks is now well versed in this procedure; having to do this at the dark site, he connects his computer to the system and turns on the computer; they wait in an eerie silence. Behind the desk is the American flag on the wall, a reminder of their oath to protect their country. A few minutes pass, and a door to the right opens; six individuals walk out and take up their positions on the six chairs. Chairperson Moreno introduces everyone, and by his tone, Bright and Dicks can already sense this will be a difficult sell. By the opening remarks thrown at both of them, Bright can tell they have no respect for his position, and this would be a battle of wills that he must win at all costs. They have no respect for his rank, which galls him; they have never fought for their country. These are the financiers who, unknown to him, finance his site for a return on the technology it brings them for exorbitant profits. Many conspiracy theorists call them a cabal that controls the world, and nothing happens without their say. Yet, strangely no representatives from the military or the president's office, Bright and Dicks confer in whispers, both annoyed and sensing a hatchet job in the making. Dicks starts his presentation by outlining the timescale of the events leading up to the incident; while he is pointing out the people involved, the six behind the desk constantly talk between themselves.

In this short time, Bright can tell they are after a scapegoat at any cost; they have lost money, and losing money is very painful for these people.

One or more people will suffer the consequences, innocent or guilty; they do not care. A kangaroo court is taking place, and Bright will not allow it; he stands up and asks Dicks to stop. Dicks turns to Bright, surprised he stopped him; with his back turned, he could not see these six people's contempt for the military.

'Gentlemen, do you want the truth, or have you decided who is guilty,' from Bright.

The surprised chairperson Moreno stuttered that the General would question their resolve, 'what is that supposed to mean,

General Bright.'

'I am not one to mince my words, gentleman, but I can see a kangaroo court when I see one; you are after someone to crucify, and it will not be any of my men.'

'What is that supposed to mean.'

'My question to all of you is, can anyone tell me what Lt Dicks has just explained.' There was silence from them, embarrassed and annoyed that the General had seen through their facade. Then, finally, they tried to gesticulate that it was unintentional, and the General misunderstood how they conducted this hearing. Bright explains, 'my code of conduct is of integrity to our flag and country, no grey areas like you have in the corridors of the pentagon, the truth is paramount to how I and my colleague Lt Dicks work.'

A muted apology is given, and Bright asks if Dicks could have the floor and prove it, and he points out again to prove the innocence of the men on my site.

They tell Dicks to carry on, and he requests them to leave their chairs and come closer to the screen, Dicks turns to Bright and whispers, 'thank you.'

Dicks points out the orb transfer between the individuals, the six gasps and look at each other; they realise if this comes out, there could be mass panic, so they ask Dicks if this is the only copy. He turns to Bright, wondering what to say; he lies and says 'yes.' It is his only copy, but he has made another copy back at the base and, unbelievably, given it to Raul for safekeeping. It was an overwhelming feeling to do so; he still did not understand why but his instincts had been good so far, and he thought it was a risk worth taking.

Chairperson Moreno requests the copy, Dicks looks to the General, who responds, 'why do you need the copy? It is our only proof that my men are innocent.' The aggression of power now comes to the fore, 'You may be the military on the site, General, but we own everything on it; nothing happens without our continued investment on your site, so we own that copy in Lt Dicks hand.'

'If we do not comply.'

'Your site closes, and we do not invest in the military; in this modern world, a lot of private investment is keeping the military going; protectionism comes at a cost you cannot imagine, General.'

'Give it to him, Lt Dicks.'

'But, sir.'

'Give it to him, now, Lt.'

'Yes, sir,' Dicks hands over the USB file; already he does not trust them; he can sense this is not over by any means, that gut feeling something is wrong.

Moreno takes the USB, and he and his five associates leave promptly without another word. Both men stand in amazement at the arrogance these men have shown.

Dicks is just about to speak, but Bright stops him, 'When we get outside,' Bright is aware that these walls have ears and does not want to compromise their position.

Once they get outside, Bright opens up his thoughts on what has just taken place, and in all honesty, he is worried he does not like how the meeting went.

He tells Dicks, 'These men have too much power; they should not interfere with our national security; anything like this should be inhouse; I was expecting a military court.'

'What do we do from here, sir.'

'Can you remember all their names? If so, write them down; we need to know more about them.'

'Sir, you seem more worried now than when we went in.'

'I am Lt; I'm perturbed; people with that amount of power are uncontrollable; they will do anything to protect their assets more than their families; I'm afraid money is a powerful drug; the more you get, the more you want.'

'I don't quite understand, sir.'

'How would you protect your assets if something like this came out? Your investment would fall like a stone, and these people do not like to lose money.'

'I do not like what you are implying, sir.'

'The wheels of power are strong, Dicks, and I think we are going into a fight for our lives; politics is a vicious game of survival; it is worse than fighting a war.'

'What do you suggest, sir.'

'Let us get to the hotel first and run through our options; who do you trust back at the base, and I mean trust 100%.'

'Why, sir.'

'We need another copy of the file, as we need bargaining power.'

'Not to worry, sir, already taken care of.'

A surprised Bright looks at Dicks, 'what have you done.'

'Let us say it is in a safe place for now; I must have your scepticism, sir.'

'I knew I could trust you, good man Dicks; let's get to the hotel.' The front desk ordered a taxi, and fifteen minutes later, it arrived; bending forward before he got in, Dicks gave the hotel name they needed to be; in doing so, he noticed a holstered gun under the driver's jacket. He gets into the taxi and whispers to Bright not to talk; not surprised anymore, Bright sits back for the ten-minute journey. On arrival Dicks pays the fare, noticing how clean-shaven the driver is and also wearing expensive attire; something is amiss, or Bright has got him paranoid. Before they enter the hotel, he mentions this to Bright, who turns to him and whispers, 'it has started already; watch everything and anything; your life will depend on it now.'

'What the hell, sir, what have we got ourselves involved in.'

'Let's get to our rooms, and I will explain my theory; we have opened something they do not want the world to know about.'

'Yes, sir.'

Bright and Dicks booked into the hotel, 'rooms 202 and 202 have been reserved,' from the hotel receptionist; Bright jumps in, 'I'm superstitious. Can we change to the third floor, please?'

The receptionist tells him, 'sorry, sir, but your office requested them for you,'

'That would be the new girl, and it was a mistake; please move us, or we will go to another, more accommodating hotel.'

'I'm sorry, sir, will rooms 304 and 305 be okay.'

'Thank you, is it, Janet? We will have dinner in my room. I will ring down the order. Is that okay?'

'Yes, sir, enjoy your stay.'

Dicks felt it was time to stay silent and is starting to understand why Bright is in the position he is, with an astute mind for seeing something that should not be there. Bright tells him not to say anything till they get to his room; within minutes, they reach their rooms, and Bright tells him to put his bag in his room. Dicks is surprised by this request but is learning quickly to listen to him. When they enter the room, Bright explains that 'he did not book the rooms, neither did his secretary, he suspects they will be bugged. He knows it sounds like paranoia, but he is sure they are in danger.'

Dicks stands silent, with his mouth open, then realises what he is doing, coughs, placing his hand over his mouth, giving him precious seconds to ask something.

'But, sir, how can you be sure, for christ's sake, you are a General.'

'To these people, all we are cannon fodder, and lives are disposable no matter the cost.'

'Why did you want me to bring my bag in here, sir.'

'We might have got away with the bugging aspect, but I suspect we will get visitors tonight; we will need to be vigilant, two-hour watch, we need to go back to military basics to survive the night.'

'You can't be serious, sir.'

'Deadly serious, Dicks.'

42

Having fallen asleep with the craft on autopilot, Xylens and Byne are woken up by the alarm on the cryo-chamber; it is time to wake Nyle from his long slumber. After ten minutes, Nyle is fully functional and just in time as the comms come to life as their home planet is now locked on them and will guide them in; more advanced than when they left, there is no need to control descent; it is automatic now. While Xylens shows outward signs of excitement, Nyle and Byne are non-plus, wondering what he is doing. They are not used to it and are worried about this change in his demeanour, and they will speak to a higher authority when they can. But by the time they land, Nyle will be changing, and an inner rage is starting to consume him; he must learn to control it, and nobody must know. Xylens planet is not known for any emotion, but as they come into land, there are vast crowds around the landing area; they have never known this type of response before; times are already changing, thinks Xylens; it may be easier than he thought to change their minds. Finally, the craft settles into the landing bay, and an automated enclosed walkway comes forward and locks around the doorway of the craft. The space travellers wait for the door to open; on leaving the craft, they are guided to a decontamination zone to rid themselves of any bacteria or viruses they may have. Little do the commissioners know the virus is within, and no form of decontamination can kill a newfound spirit. They then walk outside; in doing so, the rush of air touches their senses; the smell, the warmth, and the noise all come back to them.

Xylens had forgotten what it was like, and a single tear fell down his cheek. They step out to be greeted by silence as the other lifeforms stare in amazement at what now are three cult heroes. Then a small buzz gradually rises to a loud crescendo of sound, overwhelming the three of them. Finally, Commissioner Grohl walks forward and gives a homecoming speech, the freedom of the metropolis, and special awards that have never been offered before.

Grohl is from a long line of commissioners; this family is one of the founder members who invented the system centuries ago and knows everything about control and cohesion. He invites them to a debriefing meeting with seven more founder-member families. Xylens is now developing the will to question things but must be careful not to show them his free will. Nyle is trying to control his anger; he must get home, away from these people holding him back, he must not get too impatient, or they will most certainly detain him indefinitely.

As the meeting takes place, generalised questions are asked; these are systematically designed for particular answers, mainly to see if the length of time in space with no nutrients affects them. Xylens and Nyle pass these questions, but Byne is argumentative; that one small crisp has finally kicked in, his mind awash with differing ideas, wanting to question everything; this is against his usual character. However, the questions have found Byne to be of negative value to the system, and two controllers take him away to be re-trained till he is of value again. If unsuccessful, Byne will not be seen again, but his dust particles will grace the planet's surface for eternity.

Finally, Xylens and Nyle are sent home to rekindle their long-lost relationships. On this planet, one other being is chosen, and they are partners for life; no one-parent families to break up the unity, everything is balanced, and nothing is out of place. No love affairs; everyone fits together like a jigsaw puzzle; anything that does not match is a pariah and burnt to the ground; nothing will interfere with the planet's well-being. This planet is like a machine, but no maintenance is required, as a replacement slots into place seamlessly if a part dies. Fortunately, the commissioners watch from afar; in many cases, familiarity breeds contempt for this system that never breaks down. Xylens finally reaches his home; his family were not allowed to see him till the paperwork and de-briefing are completed; they are sent home and told to wait for his arrival. Once again, the control within the system any objections and detention is imposed until the commissioners deem sufficient penance. Finally, Xylens enters his house; it has not changed in any way since the day he left; so mundane is their life cycle; at this point, his decision is made to change this system. Their accommodation is a high-rise apartment, with no single housing; everything is commune living so they can be watched. Inside is sparse; gone are the trinkets of living a life, no pictures; they remain in their minds, just a seating area and table to communicate around, counting the days till the end of life. His mother greets him, no sign of his father, sadly passing away five years ago, coming to his end date. However, he will have the solace that his mother will be with him for the next six years, and the change in his nature will humanise her.

She will grab these human emotions she has never felt before with both hands. Then, two hours later, Xylens sister arrives with her partner and two children, a boy and a girl, the same as every family for generations, a handshake from them all, no emotion. He wants to grab hold of his sister and hug her but must hold back.

Even now, he must be cautious; any deviation from the norm will be reported to higher authorities, an obligation instilled into their mindset, irrespective of the relationship.

Nyle has finally reached home and a handshake once again, as though he had gone for a walk, not missing for twenty-five years. Even though Nyle has the benefit that his parents and his sister are still at home, he feels different inside, the need to be free and has thoughts he has never had before. So the commissioners have given Xylens and Nyle freedom of the metropolis; typically, this would be within their designated zone. But to their surprise, they have been allowed to go from zone to zone, and this freedom will be the catalyst for Nyle to vent his inner frustration. A violent time is about to change this perfect world that is not accustomed to predatory behaviour.

43

Don has asked Roger and Shaun to go with Joanne for another brain scan; by the evening, it is confirmed that Joanne's brain has stayed the same. But for his two leading men, their brains have increased yet again. So a free night for Roger and Shaun, as the trauma of the night before is still playing in the minds of Joanne and Anne, and they need a break to sort themselves out. So they decide to step away from the confines of the hotel and call into a couple of nearby bars, a change of scenery is required. The beers flow easily, but both know their limits and do not want to be chastised by Don in the morning. So they are walking to the last bar, and en route, the smell of fish and chips piques their interest; both have not had this English delicacy for some years. So they purchase this delicacy, asking for it open in the newspaper instead of those polystyrene containers, throwing ample salt and vinegar on, so their tastebuds can sample it; this was about to be spoilt by the price they have to pay in London. So they carry on with their walkabout, finish their late morsel and place the packaging into a nearby wastebin. As they walk past an alleyway, they hear a voice turning Roger sees a glint of metal as a car headlight passes by; he instinctively tries to push it away, thinking it is a knife, as it moves toward him. A shot is fired, and Roger is shot in the stomach; in the same place, as Raul was shot, Shaun grabs the assailant's arm and unintentionally breaks it. The man screams in agony and runs away while Shaun tries to save Roger's life. There seems to be blood everywhere as Shaun calmly talks to Roger; he rings for the police and an ambulance, and the next call is to Don.

The police arrive in minutes, and the ambulance pulls up shortly after; all attending are surprised by Roger's attitude, taking it in his stride as though it was a medal of honour. Roger seems to know he will be okay, but the bullet must be removed, a risky operation as the shell could be located next to vital organs. Shaun did not see this vision, so he now assumes they only come when he is in danger; Shaun gives a surprisingly detailed description to the police, even surprising him another ability has arrived. So much so that the police knew who the assailant was, an arrest warrant was issued, and he will be behind bars in less than twelve hours; at this point, Don taps Shaun's shoulder, 'Were is Roger, '

'In the ambulance, sir.'

Don opens the ambulance door, flashes a badge and requests to speak to Roger alone; the paramedic makes a call and then is told to leave and wait outside.

'Are you okay? How are you feeling? It has become an eventful few days, Roger.'

'Sir, is there any way you can get me away from here and avoid the hospital.'

'What the hell, Roger? You have been shot, and we need to get you there as soon as possible, man.'

'There will be more questions than answers, and we must avoid that, sir.'

'The pain is making you ramble, Roger.'

At this point, Roger opened the palm of his hand and showed Don the bullet.'

'Good grief, Roger, what the hell is going on with you and Shaun.'

'That's only half of it, sir,' Roger opened his shirt, 'and there was no sign of his injury.'

'What the hell, how do we explain this? Stay put till I come back.'

Don makes a few phone calls, then talks to the police and paramedics and tells them to contact their superiors, and a private ambulance will be here shortly to take the patient away for personal care. In a matter of minutes, the private vehicle arrives, and Roger is transferred to it, taking him to a special care unit at the back of their offices; Shaun and Don follow, discussing what has happened and in awe of these abilities they are getting.

When Roger got shot, only Raul felt it as it was in the exact same place as his injury; the pain subsided when Roger's bullet came out of his stomach.

The private vehicle arrived at the offices, and Roger was gently ushered in; he was placed in a wheelchair and taken to the medical unit. Everyone left, and Don and Shaun walked in; Roger stood up and greeted them, Shaun not too sure what to think; one hour ago, the man standing before him was seriously wounded, and now he was standing in front of him. They have spare clothes in their lockers, always ready for any incident; Shaun gets Roger's key, and five minutes later, he is back with a clean shirt for each of them. As there was blood transfer on his shirt, Don also asked to look at the wound along with Shaun.

'Well, it is nothing short of a miracle, Roger; another problem I cannot put up the chain of command.'

'Sorry, sir, but I am glad of our newfound skillset; otherwise, I might not be standing here right now.'

'Point taken, we had better throw these shirts in the waste bin outside, in bags. Then, hopefully, no questions will be asked.'

Shaun is still standing, staring at Roger's stomach, still amazed at what tonight has offered them, and it seems to him that these incidents show their new abilities. Don tells them to go back to the hotel and take the day off tomorrow, 'I will tell Joanne and Anne you are on a special assignment, no questions asked, and stay off the phones, do not text them either.'

Don thought, 'It's like looking after children, sometimes, but with love in the air, what can he expect.'

Both in sync, they say, 'yes, sir,' Don is trying to accept this little oddity, but it annoys the hell out of him.

'While you have the day off, try and contact Denise and John;

starting to get worried about them now.'

Both smile, muttering, 'thought we had the day off,' in sync.

44

Bright and Dicks have gone old school and tied the TV cord between two chairs, with enough space for the door to open and placed broken glasses on the floor after the cord. If someone enters the room, they hope the assailant will be badly injured, falling to the floor. Dicks hopes that Bright's paranoia is wrong, but the man has fought in many campaigns and proven to be a good decision-maker. It is the early morning hours, and two well-dressed men exit the lift on the third floor, having already checked at reception and flashing fake badges to ask what rooms Bright and Dicks are in tonight. There is a certain bravado in these two men, having killed for the cabal several times before. One of the men makes a phone call, and the power is cut off on the third floor; they put on night goggles and screw their silencers onto their guns, ready to kill. Rooms 304 and 305 are opposite each other, and each assailant enters their designated room simultaneously. They slowly walk forward into each room when one attacker trips and screams as the glass tears into his face, dropping his gun. It lands at Bright's feet, who surprises Dicks with his agility; he picks the weapon up, instantly firing into Dicks room. With a soft thud, a body hits the floor, Dicks kicks the attacker in the face, knocking him out. He was about to call the police when Bright stopped him; shaking his head, he told Dicks, 'These people have deep pockets; we cannot trust anyone now; we have to get back to base immediately.'

'But, sir, we have a prisoner; surely they must listen.'

'If we let him go, we will be dead within twelve hours, and failure is no option; anyway, he would rather die than tell us anything.'

'What are we up against, sir.'

'It's called money and greed, Dicks, and lives do not matter to these people; even with our resources back at the base, someone high up in the pentagon will be on their payroll.'

'But, that means we can't win, sir.'

'Yes, I know we need a miracle right now Dicks. Do you believe in God? If so, start praying now.' Five minutes pass and the power is returned; 'they have another accomplice; we will need to move fast,' from Bright. The accomplice was the maintenance man, and he was offered five thousand dollars for ten minutes of work; who would refuse such an offer?

They pulled the attacker up, placed him on a chair, and tied him up with the TV and kettle cords, hoping to get information from him; they waited for him to wake up. Dicks closes the door to his room; the other body is lying in the dark, gun still in hand; when he gets back to Bright's room, the other assailant starts to stir. He looks at both of them, 'how did you know.'

'Gut instinct,' from Bright

'What now, are you going to kill me.'

Bright looks to Dicks, 'no, we are going to call the police and hand you over to them,' a smile came over the attacker's face; he was thinking, 'these don't know who my bosses control; he will be out tomorrow.'

'That is if you tell us who ordered the hit on us.'

'You know I cannot do that; I would be dead in hours.'

'You are dead anyway; you have been caught; your bosses will know when your friend is found, and you are on the run without our bodies left behind.'

'I will take my chances.'

I'm afraid you have had your last chance; tell me who hired you.'

'I can't; they will kill my family.'

'Okay, goodbye.' Bright raises the gun and shoots him in the chest.'

Dicks recoils in horror, not expecting the General to commit a murder before his eyes; he is about to object when Bright explains, 'we are now at war; survival is our only option; this sends a message that we know what they are capable of and we will retaliate.'

Dicks is more composed now and agrees, 'what next, sir.'

'Untie him; we will place him on the floor, the way he came in, and leave as fast as we can. The cleaner will not access the room till eleven am; by then, I hope we are back at the base; our movements will be tracked mercilessly; we are a dangerous liability to them now.' Both men go to reception, telling them they have had urgent communication and must go to the pentagon; a taxi is ordered and arrives in minutes. Dicks automatically checks the driver over, feeling he is a regular everyday driver and requests Dulles airport and the military heliport, the taxi driver retorts, 'my information says the pentagon.'

'Change of plans,' from Dicks, the driver mumbling under his breath. Bright rings ahead for a helicopter to be ready, and the pilot is on stand-by for their arrival.

When they reach the heliport, Bright confirms, 'they will know from the manifest we have left; let us hope we can get there in one piece.'

'Sir, you don't think they will try to bring the chopper down, do you.'

'A wounded animal will do stupid things for revenge,' then Bright suddenly remembers his prisoners back at the base, 'good grief, we need to move; our four prisoners are in danger. Do you know anyone who can move them to safety?'

'But they are on the base; they will be okay, sir.'

'Money reaches all corners, and I guarantee someone will be on the take; they are in danger, believe me, Dicks.'

'I will make a call, Lt Andrews is the most reliable, and I would trust him with my life.'

'Let's hope it does not come to that; by the way, use the phone in the heliport; they might be tracking your phone if you turn it on.'

'Yes, sir,' Dicks now thinks the General has been watching too many crime series on TV, but he has been right so far. An irate Lt Andrews answers his phone, still half asleep, 'who the hell is ringing at this hour, you arsehole.'

'John, it is Dicks; I am with the General; we do not have much time to explain, but I need you to do something, and it must be done now.'

'What the hell, Justin, what's going on.'

'We will explain as soon as we get back, in four to five hours.'

'What do you need me to do.'

'Our prisoners, Rae, Lee, Compton and Rodriquez, must be moved immediately and taken to a safe place that no one knows, John.'

'But why, what is going on.'

'It is a matter of life and death, John; please do it now.'

'Okay, see you when you get here.'

'Thank you, John,' the line goes dead, and John quickly gets dressed, then rushes over to the detention centre, telling the guards he has authorisation from General Bright to take the prisoners to his office and wait. A reference code is given, which Dicks had told him to use. It changes weekly; it was a safety protocol for a situation like this. Finally, the prisoners are released into his custody, under duress, half asleep like him. Once the prisoners are outside, he tries to explain it is a request from the General for their safety; they follow him in the darkness into a building they had not been to before. The smell was unpleasant, and the site sewage works did not get very many visitors; due to this smell, many classed it as a no-go area; Andrews thought just the place. Even a staunch ex-marine like Brad Lee wanted to vomit, but he would endure the inconvenience if his life were on the line. They settle down on makeshift benches, still in handcuffs; Andrews tries to explain that he is in the dark as much as them, but when the General returns, all will become clear. He then tells them he cannot remove the cuffs till he is authorized, three military personnel know this, but a civilian is getting angry. Unintentionally this anger has tuned into Dicks thoughts, and he realises why they are in danger; this increases his agitation, and it brings forward something in the back of his mind that Xylens had planted.

If you have self-belief, anything is possible; think about it, and it will happen; this calmed him. Raul turned to his fellow prisoners, 'do not worry, all will be okay,'

Rae turned to him, 'for a civilian, you are incredibly calm, Rodriquez; what do you know.'

'Nothing, I have got a feeling it will be okay.'

Compton responds, 'if the General is spooked, something bad is about to happen; that's my feeling.'

Then Andrews hears a sound, like a short compressed air blast, but muffled, and he opens the door just enough to see four assailants in the backdrop of a descending moon. It will be daylight shortly; these men are risking everything for a big payday to break into a military installation. They already have inside information where the prisoners are being kept; such is the power this cabal hold. They must act quickly, in and out, being former seals turned mercenaries; this would be so easy for them if not for the foresight of General Bright it would have been. It will be daybreak soon, and dressed all in black, with full combat attire, Andrews can see one of his colleagues is on the floor, wounded; he is struggling to get up, and one of the men shoots him in the head; it is a kill squad. Surely they cannot be after the prisoners, and he watches as they stealthy make their way to the detention centre. Finally, Andrews turns to the prisoners, 'what is it that you know, there is a kill squad outside, and they have just entered the detention centre.'

'Rae demands that he takes the cuffs off, 'we can help, for God's sake, Andrews.

Compton and Lee agree, 'let us help before they kill more.' He has no option; he must; people's lives are in danger; Andrews releases them all, not sure why he also took them off the Raul.

Moving forward, they see two gun flashes; they are twenty metres from the entrance to the detention centre, the door flies open, and the four assailants come out. One turns and sees the five running towards them, and he shouts to his colleagues; the rest turn and open fire.

The military men fall to the ground leaving Raul standing alone, who automatically raises his left hand; the men on the ground look in amazement as bullets hit an invisible shield in front of them. The four assailants start to reload, and Raul drops his left hand and flicks his other hand.

The four men are hit with such force that they are thrown against the detention wall, knocking them out, and two break their necks on impact. Raul falls to the floor on his knees and wakes up in the medical ward; he cannot remember what he has done. The two assailants, who are still alive, are in detention, unable to talk; they are now incoherent, and all functions are lost; they will be under medical supervision for the rest of their lives. No money will compensate their families for the two vegetables sent home, and the money men do not care anyway.

Bright and Dicks have arrived at the medical centre and have been briefed by Lt Andrews, both trying to comprehend what Raul has done, but he has saved four people's lives, whose families will be forever grateful. Talking to Raul, both men are convinced that he is speaking the truth and cannot remember what he has done; Raul is getting very good at hiding the truth now. Next, Bright organises a meeting with his lower-level command structure to inform them of recent events and to pass down the chain of command.

He tells them they are under attack from within, and five people have died trying to get him and some of their colleagues.

Vigilance is the byword; anything out of the ordinary, report it up the line immediately. Bright called to speak to the General of the

Armies, Logan; as a matter of urgency, he must come back to him before eleven a.m.

45

Shaun and Roger are running through recent events back at the hotel, then a blinding vision in their heads.

The intensity of Raul's situation automatically locked into their wavelength, and they could see everything unfold in real-time, both astounded at this newfound power. Both are wondering if they will get any more outstanding abilities; only time will tell, as these unusual abilities will only surface when required, in a time of need. Roger grabs Shaun, 'we need to contact Denise and John; the discs are our priority now.'

'Why the sudden concern, Rog.'

'I don't honestly know; it's like an inner voice telling me to get them.'

'The way things are turning out, that voice better gives us a clue where they are.'

John's mathematical abilities had become so intense that in a very short time, his ability has now become so renowned he is getting phone calls from around the world. A new mathematical savant has come to the fore, and usually, these are child prodigies. Questions about why this sudden ability started so late in life are being asked. His simple answer was that he was knocked unconscious in a freak accident and could solve complex maths problems when he awoke. The consensus accepted this, especially as his ability was so unique. But there is a problem; his brain will not be able to cope with this information overload; too soon, his head will be awash with algorithms flooding his brain, but that release will soon come to him.

Shaun and Roger must contact him before it is too late, not knowing the state of his mind. It is midnight, and they decide to give it one last go.

John is exhausted, his mind does not seem to turn off, and he has just collapsed into bed at the hotel he is staying at; with his maths theories, he is invited to symposiums all over the country. But, unknown to Shaun and Roger, he is only a mile away from the office. So John's tired mind finally lets them in, and John is surprised he forgot about this foible they had all retained, classing them as friends after what they went through together. Friends are few and far between now since this cursed ability arrived, and his marriage is close to divorce; he needs to sort himself out, or life won't be worth living. He agrees to meet at ten in the morning at their hotel; Roger asks about the disc, 'did you leave it home, John,'

John replied, 'no, he carries it everywhere for some unknown reason,' this was music to Roger's ears, and he asked him to bring it with him. So the following morning, and right on time, there is a knock on Roger's door; Shaun is already waiting in the room; they greet him with handshakes all around, automatically asking how he is; he tells them of his newfound gift. Then he reciprocates by asking if they have any new skills; both spoke beforehand and agreed not to say anything other than the mind thing.

'I suppose I'm lucky; I have earned more in the past few weeks than in my last two years' salary.'

They congratulated him, genuinely pleased about his good fortune, and then Roger asked if he had brought the disc; John handed it to him, 'look, you keep it; I sense I am supposed to give it to you.'

Roger thanked him, took the rest out of his case, and then placed them on the table; Roger did not notice they were completely round; all the shapes had gone.

Shaun looked at Roger. 'what the,' his sentence broke as the discs moved on the table and created a straight line. There were gaps where Raul and Denise's discs should be, and the symbols lit up; they all looked in awe, with their mouths open. John stepped back, grabbed the hotel writing pad from the desk, he wrote down the symbols; in doing so, his brain automatically filled in the gaps between Raul's and Denise's disc should be. Roger and Shaun looked in amazement as he said, 'good grief, it is the coordinates of Xylens, planet.'

'But, how do you know that,' from Shaun

'I just do; it's in my head. I can see it all.'

The lights on the discs faded away as soon as John made this statement; all three could not believe what had happened. Roger's asked John not to tell anyone as this must be regarded as top secret; John agreed, stating, 'no one would believe him anyway.' With a sense of relief from John now, he thanked them, saying he had a talk to do at three pm and must prepare; he would keep in contact now, by mind phone, now a standing joke between them all. By the time John reached his hotel, all memory of the last few hours had been erased, the intensity of his brain had ceased, and he felt a lot better and calmer, wondering why? Once the information had been given to Shaun and Roger, another part of the puzzle was completed. John will still be a maths savant, but he will be like the old John; his family will greet him with open arms. After John left, they spoke with Don, so he was up to speed with the situation, only Denise to find now.

Don thanked them, 'contact me when you have talked to Denise, please, then hopefully we can put it all to bed.'

Both men were still chatting about the discs when Denise came into their minds, and all joked that they were saving a lot of money on phone calls.

Roger asked once again if she had the disc, 'yes, still with me, Roger,' she sighed, 'I assume you need it; I am sensing it.'

'Yes, Denise, it is a matter of urgency now.'

'Do you want me to post it, Roger?'

'No, Denise to risky if it gets lost. However, would you be willing to meet us halfway at a motorway service station? We will compensate you, above and beyond Denise.'

So they agreed to meet at a service station near Junction 25 on the M1 motorway the next day at midday. Denise is quite giddy about some undercover work, and she thinks it will spice up her day anyway; anything from the norm is a bonus smiling to herself. So Denise goes to bed that evening still with a smile on her face and subconsciously plans her route meticulously in every detail.

Being an early riser, she makes a few notes and memorises her route; she has been caught out too many times by her sat-nav, taking her down back roads to nowhere. Travel time is around three hours, so pragmatic Denise leaves thirty minutes early, always prepared for the unexpected. Her backup flask of coffee was ready, and she started on her journey. The sun behind cast a shadow in front of her, and as Denise turned the corner, the shadow moved to the side. She thinks she is not far from the motorway now.

Within another ten minutes, she drives down the slip road onto the motorway. Denise's car benefited from cruise control, so setting the required speed.

Denise settled down for a careful driving experience; she thought only two hours to go. Then a sudden downpour, so intense the road flooded, in different areas of the motorway, pooling across the motorway. The downpour only lasted for fifteen minutes, and instinctively she pulled off the motorway onto an A road, her mind acting like a sat nav to re-route her to her destination. Then over the radio, there has been a multi-car pileup where she would have been at the same time. Now thankful for this sudden insight to change her route, this will happen on many occasions in her life, helping others along the way, and she will gradually understand that this is her unique ability bestowed on her. With this situation running through her head, she could not remember how she arrived at the allotted service station. Then, as if coming out of a trance, she can see Shaun and Roger standing at the service building entrance, greeting them excitedly, then looking over her shoulders, pretending to see if anyone had followed her. She was enjoying this experience immensely, this little cloak-and-dagger escapade. It was a change from the drudgery of housework; why not enjoy the moment? The men take her for lunch and while away a couple of hours; as Denise explains her near miss, she is still struggling with it and the lost hour when she came into the service area. Shaun tells her, 'it seems that some of us are acquiring unique skills, Denise, but my advice now would be to stay quiet and go with the flow; it might take you on a new adventure without being scrutinised the rest of your life.'

Denise was surprised by these comments, but in the back of her mind, she knew Shaun was right. Denise gave Roger the disc and got up to leave, giving Shaun and Roger a hug, hoping their paths would cross again.

They depart and go their separate ways, and one hour into her journey, Denise has the urge to pull into the nearest layby, learning quickly this means something is going to happen very soon.

No sooner had she stopped than a vision in her head; she could see that Shaun and Roger were going to be involved in a crash on the M1 motorway. Thank goodness for mind phones as she makes contact with them, 'pull into the layby now, Roger.' A knee-jerk reaction by him, in doing so, a truck had lost its wheel, and it passed in front of their vehicle by millimetres. With the size of the wheel, they would have certainly sustained severe injuries to both of them. Immediately they thanked Denise for her insight, saying that she would receive an extra compensation package from them shortly.

Roger questioned why Shaun had not seen this incident as well, especially after the hotel episode; Shaun shrugged his shoulders, telling him jokingly. 'I forgot to switch it on, Rog; how the hell do I know when it will work.' Then they hear the truck screeching to a halt on the motorway; they can see the driver is safe, and other people have stopped to assist. So they decide to carry on with their journey, and on the way, they phone Don to give him an update. He is shocked to hear where they are, and the obvious question is 'why.' Then glad to hear it was to see Denise, and she is okay; they have also spoken to John, and he is also okay.

No issues with either of them; both crossed their fingers, hoping they were telling the truth. Don tells them to come to the office tomorrow, and they need to get on with some real work; enquiries are coming in thick and fast now.

Both saying, 'yes,' in sync, Don wants to shout down the phone but hopes it will gradually go away; only time will tell, he thinks.

Shaun turns to Roger, 'when do we tell him about the discs? He will go mad because we have held it back for so long.' Roger agrees, and they both decide to put their cards on the table; when they get to the office tomorrow.

Hoping he does not get too mad, they have legitimate reasons; they will use the excuse that the field incident is to blame for their inconstancies in the decision-making process. However, before they see Don, they need to contact Raul; they need his disc urgently.

46

On E2, Xylens and Nyle are getting back to everyday life, and they had enquired about Byne, but to no avail; they are banging their heads against a wall with no answers forthcoming. Deep down, they know he will not be seen again, increasing Nyle's inner anger; it is time to feel this killing. In this pure society, there is no need for security cameras or surveillance technology; everyone has a place in the wheel of life. No form of violence has been used for thousands of years since the introduction of the nutrient tablets; everything is controlled to perfection. Zonal areas are for control; if a lifeform steps into a zone that is not theirs, they are told they will die, and the coercion of fear is enough to keep everyone in their designated area. But two individuals have been given the freedom to go from zone to zone, the commissioners forgetting their coerciveness is verbal only, and they will assume the predator is within their own area.

Night time on E2 is only four hours in this world, so the window of opportunity is short for what Nyle wants to achieve, never having done anything like this before.

But this strange excitement, borne by thousands of years of control, is finally about to be broken. Nyle does not need to explain why he must leave the accommodation; just before dark, he can go anywhere, anytime. The door opens automatically, and he steps onto the moving walkways that they use to move around the metropolis, they move in all directions, and you step from one walkway to another to get to your destination. No vehicles pollute the atmosphere here, and every lifeform pays towards this crucial benefit.

As Nyle steps from walkway to walkway, it is only twenty minutes before he steps off when he sees a lone figure standing on a grassed area overlooking a river. The individual has his back to him; Nyle moves stealthy toward him, with no sound on the grass, a perfect situation. Nyle looks all around him, no sign of anyone; now behind his prey, he grabs his head with both hands, instantly twists it, and the body flops to the ground without a sound. Nyle feels a pent-up exhilaration; never has he felt such a release within; he must do this again, but not tonight; Nyle looks around again; he did not look at the poor soul on the ground, now a true sociopath. On the way home, he plans his next kill zone for the following evening, and he will never be satisfied; his family are now in danger.

Xylens is returning to family life, but his interaction with the human race has stirred his emotions; he is not violent like Nyle. After reading the papers so many times, he knows them word for word now. He realises this world of perfection needs imperfection to move it forward differently, giving people a choice to choose how they want to live. Xylens must be careful how he starts this movement of free will, and trust will be hard to come by, it will be a slow burn, but he will succeed; he has to, or this planet will only become more subversive. He will gradually introduce his thoughts to his family; they will be the most critical, and if they respond with interest, he will move forward much faster. But he did not realise that his family would be such a captive audience; he was the first of their kind to make contact with another alien race and survive.

They were mesmerised by this human race of good and evil, their conflict between war and peace, always on a fine line to disaster. Then, finally, Xylens tells them that Earth is a small insignificant planet, but it has good humans, which could teach them a different way of life. A life of achievement and fulfilment, to look to each waking day to do something different instead of their current monotonous daily routine. They must strive for a change to this system of denial, Xylens family members were amazed at these revelations, but dare they affect change?

Luckily for Nyle, his crime will not be found out; there is no witness to see his crime, as the body did not disintegrate as expected due to the untimely death. Although therefore, it was not natural causes as the body lay on the floor to be found. A crime has been committed, but what is a crime in this perfect world? Higher authorities will regard it as an unusual anomaly and unfortunate for the lifeform, and it will not happen again, just a strange oddity, the body disposed of without question.

So only a family is wondering what happened to their father, and assuming he is dead before his time, will always think, 'why.'

47

General Bright is pacing up and down in his office; it is nearly eleven a.m., and he is getting more irate by the minute. He knows once the bodies of the two assassins are discovered, there will be questions to be answered, and a certain cabal will not allow those questions to be asked. Finally, one minute to eleven, the phone rings; he picks it up, and his secretary informs him General Logan is waiting to speak to him.

'Thank you, put him through, please.'

After the usual pleasantries, a straight-talking Bright explained what as happened and hoped he was not on their payroll. Logan seems devastated by what Bright has told him, but he will have to believe him when he tells him he has no affiliation with them.

'Good grief, we came through the academy together, following each other's career paths; we cannot let this happen.'

'I'm glad to hear that, General, then the words Bright did not want to hear, 'but, without sufficient proof, his hands are tied,' and from what Bright had told him, it will be challenging to find friends to help. Everyone is a suspect; with the money hold they have on the political system and modern surveillance, it will be difficult to hide. Bright thanked him for listening, but he was not happy that he would not help and played it down; in his mind, Bright already thought Logan was working with them and was glad he did not tell them everything. He puts a call out for Dicks to come to his office urgently.

Then silently reflecting, they would usually attend fallen heroes' funerals, but due to the danger of being in public, they decided against doing so.

The three men killed in the compound trying to stop the four assailants, getting to Raul, Compton Rae and Lee, will be buried with special honours, and mentally Bright has vowed they will have retribution in some shape or form. However, he is increasingly annoyed that they are becoming prisoners in their compound; a new strategy must be found to survive. Dicks knocks on Bright's door, and he summoned him in, telling him to sit down, then explains his discussion with Logan and his worries that he is on Moreno's payroll. Dicks puts his head in his hands, and for the first time, he feels lost with nowhere to turn, 'where do we go from here, sir.'

Surprisingly Bright says, 'like any good military man, the last resort, we defend our position, and when the time is right, we attack with everything at our disposal.' A wry smile from Dicks, 'what next, sir.'

'Another phone call; we may as well go for the jugular,' with a smile on his face, Dicks looking perplexed, 'what do you mean, sir.'

'Firstly, we will try diplomacy; if all fails, then we attack.'

'I'm listening, sir.'

Bright request's the phone number for Moreno from his secretary, 'let us see what type of man he is, shall we.' A knock on the door, and his secretary provides him with the number, and Bright tells her she can have the afternoon off; he will be busy the rest of the day with no more disturbances. She thanks him and leaves with a beaming smile; a shopping spree is required anyway, sooner rather than later. Then Bright suddenly stops; he remembers his family; they are in great danger, as are all the others involved; he tells Dicks to get his family here as soon as possible.

It was the first time Dicks had seen a hint of panic from Bright and realised that Susan was home with children; she must bring her mother and father, and for the first time, thankful his parents had passed on. Bright tells him he will not ring till tomorrow once he knows all the families are safe here.

After discussions with Bright, Dicks has gone to see the now four ex-prisoners, unknown to them all, they have now become paramount to the safety of everyone. The four have been housed in a high-security section underground where the craft had been. They had been transferred one by one to avoid too much suspicion; the least anyone knows, the better for all. The men have their own canteen facilities and have built up an open dialogue over the last few days, and a certain unity has been formed between them. A scuffle of feet as the guards are disturbed, and then they hear the dulcet tones of Lt Dicks voice; calmness ensues as Dicks walks into the room. All the military men stand to attention, respecting his rank, saluting and being grateful for his help in their release. Raul stood up and shook his hand, and Dicks asked, 'if he could recall anything that had happened in the past few days.'

He tells Dicks, 'Only what the others have told him, and he can still not believe it, but he does not know how and why it happened.' Finally, everyone sits down, and Dicks updates them on the current dire situation and the urgency of contacting their families. The men cannot believe this turn of events and are shocked that they would try to kill their families, along with the General and Dicks. It is now a race against time to contact their families, and all communications will most certainly be monitored from the black site.

The sense of paranoia between them will bring them much closer than they ever imagined; with a desire to survive, this bond will last the rest of their lives. At this point, the scurry of feet again, and the door opens; General Bright enters, and the men stand to attention again.

'I assume Lt Dicks, has brought you all up to speed.'

Rae was the first to speak, 'yes, sir, but how do we contact our families? If you are right about the phones etc., what can we do.'

'Well, one thing is sure, they will know your cars and registration numbers by now, so another form of transport is required.'

'What do you suggest, sir,' from Compton

'Firstly, how far away are your families,' each one responded; they found all were within a thirty-mile zone, in a similar direction, which meant they could be picked up one after the other in a short time. Unable to contact their families, all could only hope and pray they were home and that the children could be reached quickly. Bright tells them to follow him, and as they exit the secure facility, the sunlight makes their eyes water; they are shuffled toward a military bus. They thank Bright and salute as they enter the bus, Lt Dicks gets into the driver's seat, and the four ex-prisoners board the bus; as they move down the aisle, Dicks informs them all that they have a choice of weaponry on the back seat. All the men were surprised it had come to this; three chose a weapon, Raul refusing, having not used a firearm before. With his recent ability, he may not need them anyway.

Bright contacts the front gate, telling them to allow the bus out without stopping, 'no questions asked, that is an order.'

Dicks asks for the nearest house to the black site; the first is Rae's, only twenty minutes from the site; luckily, all his family are home, explaining what is happening to his wife. It only takes ten minutes to throw some clothes into a couple of bags, his wife telling the kids they are going on a bit of an adventure. They board the bus and are kept from the rear seat; children and guns do not mix well in this environment. Rae knocks on his neighbour's door, asking if he can use their phone; in doing so, he tells his parents to go to the holiday lodge immediately and also contact Jane's parents and take them with them. With the site's sensitivity, all staff have a code for their families for an urgent response to leave until further notice. The neighbour is unaware of the code, thinking it is a regular conversation, but curious as to why he needed to use their phone. He must have a mobile phone, and he explains that he had left it at work in a rush, and their landline was dead. Then even more confused when he saw Rae and his family get on the bus, thinking these military people were strange. There was no need to go to Lee's house; being a single man, he lived his dream of going where and when he wanted, not tied down to convention. His parents were away in Norway, tracing family roots way back to the Vikings, and will be surprised how ruthless their heritage was. Another fifteen minutes and they have reached Compton's house, a shock in store, as his wife has been having an affair for the last year. He found her in bed with her lover, his subordinate on the site.

In anger and devastation, he was about to shoot him but walked out; he will let the divorce lawyers sort it out; all too regular, these trysts destroy military lives. So many wives could not cope with the loneliness; maybe if they had children, it might have been different. He storms back to the bus, his wife rushes to the door in her dressing gown, and he turns and shouts, 'I will see you in the divorce court,' the rest of the bus see corporal Harley walk up behind her. All offer their support, and new friends will get him through his torment; they now have a more significant battle to fight. Twenty minutes later, a black SUV parks on Compton's driveway; two men get out and walk to the door. A knock on the door, and they flash a badge; they enter and five minutes later, the men leave, and the two bodies will not be found for three days, the assailants thinking they had killed Compton and his wife.

Ten minutes after leaving Compton's house, they turn the corner into Dicks cul de sac; his house is located at the top, and he can see his daughter playing with a neighbour's little girl to the right. The bus stopped, and she saw her father come out; a squeal of delight, and she ran to him, he gathered her up, and she kissed his cheek. The rest of the families on the bus have older children and appreciate the true innocence of a small child. Dicks strides into his house; ten minutes pass before he returns with bags; his wife is close behind, Dicks lets his family onto the bus. Then he walks over to a neighbour's house and does the same thing as Rae, to call his parents and in-laws.

Finally, they must get to Sara, Raul's wife, with whom he had already made contact with his thoughts; she was astounded by what he was telling her.

Sara picks up the phone in her apartment to speak to her mother, and the tone is slightly different. Sara is starting to gain senses she did not have before, so acutely now the tone is not correct; she leaves the apartment and goes to use a pay phone outside the building. Sara calls her mother, saying she must bring the children urgently and pack a bag for herself and her father. Her mother starts to panic at this statement. Sara explains that it is something to do about Raul's work, and she will explain when they arrive; it will be about twenty minutes before they can get there. Sara puts the phone down and proceeds to return to her apartment, but in her peripheral vision, she notices a large black SUV pull up on the other side of the road. Then the panic, how do I tell Raul it is just another vehicle, but her senses are telling her something is wrong? So acute are these senses Raul picks up on it and contacts her, she explains what she feels, and Raul tells her they are only five minutes away.

Raul walks up the aisle of the bus, and upon reaching Dicks he tells him of his concerns, Dicks informs Rae, Lee and Compton they might be a problem ahead and to be ready for something to happen.

Sara rushed to the apartment to gather some clothes for her and the children; she was waiting in the recess of the apartment entrance, her eyes focused on the SUV. Her vision was so acute now she could see the two men in black suits sitting inside, one with binoculars and the other on his phone, all the time relaying this information to Raul. Then her parent's car pulls into the apartment carpark; Sara uses the rear entrance to meet her parents and children and explains what is going on; these accusations dumbfound her parents.

The two men in the SUV look through a list of registration numbers and pick up Sara's parent's car confirming the make and model. A phone call is made, and within thirty seconds, they screw silencers on their guns; a military bus is coming down the main street, and the occupants notice two men get out of the SUV.

Raul's anger is building up as the bus pulls up to a stop.

Dicks tell the men to stay, but Raul insists he must come; he might need him; Lee jumps forward; being a former marine, he is well qualified to help. The rest have families, so Dicks asks them to stay on the bus, and they agree if someone attempts to get to them inside the bus. The two men are out of sight, having entered the carpark, Dicks, Lee and Raul run to catch them as Raul enters, with Lee and Dicks close behind. Raul can see one of the men pointing a gun at Sara, he shouts, and the man turns round; Raul flicks his wrist, throwing the man into the air against the wall. The other man instinctively shoots at him, but Lee pushes him out of the way; Lee is shot in the chest, collapsing on the floor, Dicks returns fire, killing the other assailant. There are tears from the women and children, distraught to witness what has just happened. Dicks and Raul try to attend to Lee, who is motionless on the floor, Dicks checks for a pulse which is faint, 'we need to get him to a hospital, now.'

Raul responds, 'can you get my family to the bus? I will look after Lee; Sara will help me; please take them to the bus.' Dicks is surprised at how calm Raul is, who is coming to terms with some strange abilities he has now. As soon as they were out of sight, he placed his hand over Lee's wound; Sara was amazed to see the light emit from his hand.

Thirty seconds later, Raul put a bullet in her hand; Sara looked in awe at what had just happened. Then, as they get Lee to his feet, a black SUV enters the carpark with Compton at the wheel, shocked to see Lee standing up, especially as Dicks felt it was touch and go if he would die on the way to the hospital. Rae stays on the bus to look after everyone while Dicks assists Raul and Compton, putting the two men in the SUV. Dicks returns to the bus after a quick word with Rae, who then leaves the bus. The dead assailant is put into the boot of the SUV, and the unconscious man has his hands tied behind his back and put on the back seat; Rae will sit next to him, and Compton will follow the bus back to the compound. Raul and Sara get back on the bus, and too loud applause, the rest had been informed of their bravery, above and beyond for civilians. There is a buzz on the bus, all wishing to know what the hell is going on, the anxiety building up with not knowing.

Forty minutes later, they arrived back at the black site with an extra vehicle, Dicks had contacted Bright, who authorised the front gate to allow them straight through, as a matter of national security. The dead man is taken to the morgue, and the other is in the medical ward, handcuffed to a bed. The families are in the secure unit underground, ready to be informed what and why they have been brought to the facility. Before everyone had returned, Bright instructed one of his staff to pick his wife up; on arrival; he gave her a letter from Bright. Without hesitation, she packs her bag and returns to the compound with the driver.

48

After their close call, they endured and leaving Denise at the service station, Roger and Shaun headed back to their hotel in London. They arrive at the hotel, and the smiling receptionist greets them, now known as incidental heroes, regarding the restaurant incident; currently, the window is being replaced behind a wooden hoarding. They request two meals and a bottle of red wine to be sent up to Roger's room in one hour. The meal arrives on time, and Shaun follows the waiter into the room, dressed in a more casual dress. They would have a different dress code if they went to the restaurant; the waiter opened the wine and asked Roger to try it; Roger nodded in appreciation that he was happy with their choice. In truth, he would have nodded anyway, more a lager drinker; wine was not his normal tiple. The waiter leaves with a ten-pound tip; Roger says, 'I hate this spiral of inflation we are in; last year, it would have been five pounds.' Shaun laughed, 'that's the first time I have heard you talk like that,' Roger looked amused, shrugging his shoulders. Then, halfway through their meal, they discuss the discs and how they can get the last one from Raul without creating suspicion. But that inner voice tells Roger they must contact Raul later in the evening and get answers quickly. As the wine flows, the evening passes quickly, and the advantage of a local derby match on TV, with some aggression, helps the banter flow. Three hour's pass, next thing they know, it is one a.m. time for a mind call to Raul; they both concentrate, hoping to make contact with him.

Finding great difficulty in contacting him takes a stressful twenty minutes; they are about to give in when they hear Raul's American accent, and they both smile at each other. Shaun explains about the different discs and the urgent need to have all six together, but how can we get it? Raul tells them it is buried in his garden, never thinking he would need it so soon. Next, Raul informs them of their current situation, their battle against a cabal, and the attempts on their lives. The obvious question from them is whether there is any way they can help him. But being so far away, it is impossible; he tells them it is a problem that he and his new friends will resolve, and he is confident they will; Raul does not tell them about his newfound abilities. They say their goodbyes and wish each other good fortune; Raul tells them he will contact them soon regarding the disc. Shaun and Roger finally go to bed, and both will only get a couple of hours of sleep; their recent conversation with Raul has opened up a situation they never expected. Before leaving his room, Roger collected the five discs and placed them in his jacket pocket, and they decided to walk to the office. The traffic was heavy due to another rail strike; Shaun commented, 'they were holding the public to ransom again. If he were Prime Minister, he would make the strikers pay the wages for the people not getting to work and losing money.'

'That's a bit radical,' from Roger

'There's only so much the public can take, Rog.'

'Agreed, but that does not help us in our situation.'

Shaun's comments seemed justified when some members of the public blasphemed at a picket line outside a train station.' Roger held his hands up in defeat, saying, 'smart arse.'

Turning the corner, they can see Anne and Janye about to enter; Shaun cannot help himself and calls Anne. Both women turned and ran to the men, happy as ever to see them; they kissed. Finally, they all link arms and walk toward the office as though they were walking down the yellow brick road, a scene from an old movie long gone. As they enter, the ever-present Don stands at reception, waiting patiently. The women immediately take up the positions behind the two separate desks, each working for different departments within the company. Roger jumps in first, 'conference room, sir.' Even Don smiled at his cheeky sarcasm, and they walked to the conference room, the women watching the men, and Roger and Shaun gave a thumbs up simultaneity behind their backs. The women now notice these quirky foibles and will need an open conversation when they have their next meal together.

The men sit down, and Don asks about John and Denise, amazed at the abilities that the Haltwhistle five have acquired but wondering why they have different skills, all unaware these will change depending on the priority and urgency of the situation. Then Roger tentatively approaches the issue of the discs, and he can see the change on Don's face. They have only seen him like this twice before; as his anger builds, they are on a fine line, and their jobs are in jeopardy now. Shaun interjects witnessing this change, trying to explain why they had to take this decision, telling him, 'outside forces have dictated how everything will happen for the good of the planet.'

Roger is taken aback by what Shaun has just said but lets him proceed; tuning in mentally, he realises why.

Don is more annoyed that they have not said anything; he does not like that they seem to be intermittently controlled; if they could give him some insight, it would help their cause. Back in the black site, Raul is talking to Bright and is requesting to leave the site for an important task; if he allows Dicks to come with him as a chaperone, they will be back in three hours. The General is reticent; their lives are in danger, and the risk is far too significant; Raul enters his mind, learning the benefits of his new skill sets fast. Within two minutes, Bright informs the gate to allow Raul to leave alone, and Bright is unaware he has done this.

Raul thought through his statement if Dicks had come, there would be far too many questions; he must get home quickly. As he drives to his house, his mind is buzzing, running scenarios through his head, finding solutions to problems far more accessible than before; his self-confidence is coming through now. He turns the corner into his road, passing pristine gardens tendered with love and care. People are just trying to be better than their neighbours, a curse of modern life, everyone trying to be better than the other, people wanting to know your business. Privacy is a rare commodity now with the introduction of the internet in modern society. As Raul reaches his home, his senses are at an all-time high; he has already noticed an out-of-place vehicle two-hundred metres ahead of his house. He parks on his drive, and with his acute peripheral vision, he can see the two men in dark suits move when he drives up to his house; it seems a common remit now, trying to blend into everyday life, not realising they are highly paid assassins.

He does not enter the house but goes to the rear garden; Raul goes to the right-hand side of the garden and removes loose soil with his hands.

With his finely tuned hearing, he hears the car doors slam shut, instantly forming an invisible shield around him; before he locates the disc, he hears his assailants behind him. Turning around, the two men fired two shots, and the shield absorbed the bullets; Raul flicked his left hand, and a ball of light hit one man; he disintegrates before their eyes. He does not need to think now; his brain is in protection mode. The other man tried to run, but to no avail; another ball of light hits the man, and all evidence is gone. Raul's mindset has changed; they are attacking them, and survival is paramount now; he will not say anything to Bright. Leaving the shield around him, Raul returns to digging up the disc, brushing away the soil; he stares in amazement as the symbols light up. Then that feeling he must contact Roger and Shaun; he concentrates, and within seconds he makes contact.

After an intense discussion, Don has calmed down and understands their reasoning, but he does not like that they did not follow protocol. They have finally told Don about the discs, and Roger has placed them on the table; Don stares at them, unable to comprehend what they are. He was about to touch one when Roger stopped him; he was receiving communication from Raul; Shaun was also in on the conversation. Simultaneously, they spoke; Don was annoyed at this, but he listened, quickly explaining they were in contact with Raul. Finally, Don threw his arms in the air, 'don't do this with me, guys; what are you playing at.'

Shaun explains that their boss is with them; Raul responds, 'I know I can see through your eyes,' this shocked both men, 'good grief, what else can you do, Raul,' from Roger.

Shaun tells Don, 'Raul needs all of us to hold our hands over the discs, sir.'

'My head says no, but after what has happened lately, I suppose I have got nothing to lose.'

As soon as he touches their hands, they tingle, and he hears Raul for the first time; he should be concerned, but surprisingly he wants to hear more. Raul explains he is holding his disc and felt compelled to contact them immediately, and his mind is giving him instructions they must follow.

'They must hold hands over the discs in a star formation, about six millimetres above them, do not break this formation or all is lost., The closer they got to the discs, the warmer their hands felt, and then a glow of intense light for ten seconds, the light disappeared, and the heat stopped. Raul tells them to break formation, and when they look, the sixth disc is there; the three men look at each other in awe, 'what the hell has just happened,' from a rarely shocked Don. Then Don suddenly realised he was talking to his men via his mind; he was taken aback, yet pleased in a way he now feels Roger and Shaun will confide in him more. Forgetting about Raul, who interjected at this point, telling them, 'to save the planet, otherwise, Xylens and Asku's visit was in vain.

Raul says his goodbyes and wishes them well and to keep in contact with him in the future, jokingly saying, 'my mind is always open, you know that.'

Don now wondered what this statement meant; there was still a lot to find out, but he was now glad he had become part of this inner sanctum.

The three men are standing up, still looking at the discs, then looking at each other; Don was the first to speak, 'now what the hell do we do.'

Roger responded, 'believe it or not, sir, we will get a sign when we need to do something.' Shaun nodded his approval.'

'I need a coffee, and I still do not understand what we have got involved in,' Don sits back on his chair, staring at the discs.

49

On Xylens world, there are no class systems; only rulers called commissioners and the populists, pre-ordained, programmed via the nutrients given from birth. No pay structure to fight over, everybody is at the same level, and no jealousy trying to beat your neighbour for the next new material thing. If it was not for the apartment number, anyone could walk into it, and it would be the same as thousands of others. Everything is in its place, a particular frequency humming in the background, which changes pitch at a specific time to tell them to go to bed. This frequency changes the next morning when it is time to get up to start another day of a mundane life of little choice.

Back in his apartment of mediocrity, Xylens once again starts to read the papers he was gifted, and a sense of humour appears in his demeanour as he notices the writing on the side of the bag. Underneath the roadside café's name, in smaller writing, were the words, 'America, the land of the free,' ironically, these words will be his motto to change this world. His family are mesmerised by what he has told them, that the small planet he visited is thousands of years behind them, but in a social context, they are years ahead of his own race. But, during the furore of Xylens and the arrival of the others back to E2, a vital question was missed, and there will be a request to come to the tower from Grohl, the head commissioner. All his relatives and friends would walk in without a knock on his door, so he automatically knows it is someone he does not know, as three loud bangs reign down on his door.

Xylens opens the door; commissioners eleven and twelve are standing there; they do not enter but request him to come with them to the tower. Xylens does not make a fuss; he does not want to create any suspicion; they guide him across the walkway to a flying vehicle hoovering ahead. These vehicles are for the elite only, and the populist ignores them, programmed so that they have no form of jealousy, and in many ways, it does not register with them. Xylens was different; he was always programmed to do his job to leave his planet and visit Earth, to watch and report, but not to make verbal contact. His fateful last flight was his third; with no return, he was classed as (LIN) 'lost in space,' forever, after two years. New candidates were chosen to take his place, those being Byne and Nyle; when they went missing, they considered abandoning the project. But even on this planet, the commissioners have a conscience, and their involvement in Earth's evolution has made them responsible for its growth; they must keep an eye on the planet. Xylens journey will take thirty minutes, with no conversation, a sure sign something is a miss; he will need all his senses on high alert for this interview.

Nyle has waited a few days to see if there are any reports of the dead body he left behind. The silence only builds his confidence, and he is eager for his next kill; he has run through every move he made to kill the innocent bystander. The thrill of that kill has kept him on a high; he has never known, and this feeling of raw emotion, he must do it again tonight. He wonders will the feeling be different if he kills the next innocent victim in another way; he searches the apartment for a utensil.

He finds a knife at the back of a drawer, something they rarely use now due to how the nutrients work. So picking up the knife and realising what he will do with it excites him even more. His mother has noticed a change in Nyle but puts it down to his space trip, and she will give him time to adjust; it will take time, she tells herself.

Xylens transport lands on the landing zone, two floors from the commissioner's office, he is shown to the main elevator, located near another four elevators, but these go down to the lower levels. Only the elite can use this lift that Xylens has been told to enter; the glass doors open; even in this utopia, the commissioners like to see who is coming to see them; self-preservation is always high on their agenda. The doors close, and in an instant, they open again; Commissioner Grohl waves him forward and guides him to a chair. He explains that the arrival interview was not completed due to the length of time he was away; they felt it was inappropriate at the time. But now they wanted more information regarding his contact with the human form, if any, Xylens explained that he was behind a glass screen for 99% of his time on Earth. Grohl asked how he escaped, knowing he could not achieve this without some help; Grohl was trying to trick Xylens, knowing he could not lie. But Xylens is learning the art of deception himself, and he will only tell Grohl what he wants to hear. He speaks only about his contact with Raul, and he took over his body when he sensed that Raul had the strongest genetic marker all the time he was there. Xylens told him how he took over his mind and guided him to the craft of Nyle and Byne, which was in a barren, desolate place, then erased any form of memory that Raul may have had.

Grohl thanked him; satisfied that Xylens was telling the truth, he called for commissioners eleven and twelve to take him home. Then, having been released, a sign to his two guides that all is well, there is an open conversation among all three on the way home. But, when they arrive, there are no good wishes or thanks for his cooperation, just a solemn gaze lost in their eyes. Finally, Xylens gets out of his elite travel and walks to his apartment; with a sense of joy, he has beaten the system, and he smiles, something his mother has not seen in many years.

As that short window of darkness approaches, Nyle knows what zone he will go to tonight; he has left home early, not wanting to create suspicion within his household. The predatory instinct lost for thousands of years is coming back with a vengence, planning every detail of his crime until that final thrust of the blade. He moves from walkway to walkway, and as darkness falls, he has reached his destination; the only thing that can spoil this rush is if nobody is there. As he searches, frustration is taken over, as no one is there; his calmness taking over by his anger; he must have that buzz of killing. Two hours have passed, and it will be daylight soon; the frustration is showing; he does not want to rush his next kill, and then he sees a lonely figure ahead. His body stiffens; the excitement has returned; he wants to see the face of the lifeform he will kill tonight. Nyle gets closer and closer, and the lifeform looks at him; his face changes as he is struck twice, one in each heart; for the first time, the feel of another lifeform's blood runs down his hand. The body falls to the floor, carried away by the moving walkway; Nyle looks at the blade and smiles.

Nyle should be asleep, but his lust for killing has broken the frequency hum, his brain not registering the sound. He must get home and clean up before his family wakes up; the rest of the family is so in tune with the frequency that they are unaware he is not there. As he enters his apartment, the thrill he feels is beyond description; he cleans the knife and puts it in a safe place; Nyle will need it soon, already planning his next attack; soon, it will become a daily occurrence, but how long before he is caught?

As daylight comes, a lone body is found on a moving walkway, and two lifeforms look down at the body with no emotion, no screams for attention; they do not know what to do; this has never happened before. They walk away; it is not their problem; unfortunately, the body will stay on the walkway till a commissioner is summoned. Quick discomposure will occur, so they cannot determine what has happened, and it will take several more kills before it comes to the attention of Grohl.

Nyle is one lifeform grateful for visiting a small planet called Earth.

50

With all the families safe within the black site, Bright and Dicks have gone to the medical centre to interview the sole survivor of the attack on Raul's wife and family. He had been sedated and handcuffed to the bed but was wide awake when they entered the bedroom. Unfortunately, there was no ID on him, so he already knew this interview could be a waste of time; similar to the hotel incident, Dicks was concerned that Bright might take the same action. As soon as they entered, the man questioned where he was, 'a place your people cannot get to you,' from Bright.

The man who would only refer to himself as Alan responded, 'they can get to me anytime they want. I am a dead man walking; we failed our task.'

'Why were you sent to kill that family,' Dicks did not want to give him Raul's name.

'We were given photos and addresses, our remit to kill all, no questions asked.'

'Who gave you the instructions.'

'That is all I can say; if I say more, my family are dead.'

'Good grief, they are acting like a drug cartel,' from Dicks.

'Well, they can be destroyed, these bastards will be destroyed, or I will die trying; time to take the battle to them Dicks.' The man on the bed recoiled at this unexpected statement; he said to them, 'you can't win; they are too powerful; they have too much power and money.'

'We will see about that, Dicks; let's go and fight a war.'

Dicks could see that the General was right, but how could they fight a war within their own country.

So they left the handcuffed Alan and walked over to Bright's office. His secretary greets them both with a list of callers who have rung him; strangely, the most persistent is a name he did not expect to see. 'It seems Mr Moreno is eager to talk; this should be an interesting conversation,' from Bright.

Dicks asked if he wanted him to leave the room; Bright beckoned him to sit while he dialled the number. Bright was expecting Moreno to ask for a truce to save any more bloodshed, but life is cheap; it is not what Moreno cares about, money being his drug of desire. Instant aggression towards Bright, he starts complaining that the technology they had received from the black site is starting to fail. Lawsuits are piling up against him, and his fellow investors, Bright, howls in laughter, and tears begin to fall down his cheeks, Dicks can hear Moreno bellowing down the phone. Dicks takes the phone from Bright, 'hello, General Bight is busy at the moment. Can I help?'

'Who the shit is that.'

'Lt Dicks, you know your men tried and failed to kill us if I remember correctly.'

'You are dead men walking; do you hear me.'

'I believe it could be the other way round, Mr Moreno.'

'What? You dare to threaten me; I can buy and sell your pathetic little army.'

'Not with the lawsuits tying you down, Mr Moreno.'

'Who the hell do you think you are talking to.'

'A distraught man, gasping at straws, remember there are two sides to every story.'

'You will not be alive to tell it, you moron.'

'Possibly not, but several newspapers will have this recording if you try to attack us again.'

Thank you, Mr Moreno, everything you have said will be used in a court of law.'

'You will not get the chance, you idiot; we own everybody.'

Dicks looks to Bright, who nods for him to put the phone down, Dicks puts the phone down while a still-irate Moreno is rambling, then silence. Then, with a wry smile from an old campaigner, Bright is over the moon about the way in which Dicks handled Moreno.

'What now, sir.'

'A plan of attack; they are not going to stop till we are out of the way.'

'Why do you think some of the technology is failing.'

'I wish I knew, but these men hurt more when they lose money rather than being shot after the vitriol we have just received.'

Unknown to them, it was a slow process that when the spacecraft was destroyed, any sensory connection to it was lost, and it will gradually degrade to nothing. Xylens did not want another world to develop weapons of destruction, hence the reason for the gradual decay of the weapons. When men like Moreno start to lose money, they attempt dangerous and foolish ways to seek revenge, and they have contacts that even Generals cannot reach. So it will be difficult for Bright and Dicks, and they will need every bit of guile to beat him and his associates. Dicks asks Bright, 'Surely there must be someone we can call on for help, sir.'

'Our backs are against the wall, and we do not know who we can trust now; it will be a battle of wills now. We are supposed to be the land of the free, a democratic society, but the super-rich runs it, and nobody knows who they are.'

The short silence is broken when Bright's secretary knocks on the door, and pops her head around the door, 'Sorry to bother you, General, there is a problem in the medical centre regarding the recent prisoner.'

'Okay, we are on our way.'

As they enter the centre, the doctor stops them telling them that

Alan, their guest is dead, courtesy of poison from a tooth. 'Good grief, it's like the old Russian spy days; these men are afraid of this bastard Moreno.' They go to the room where Alan is located, surprised that he would take his own life; Moreno certainly knows how to control and coerce; they will have a battle on their hands to survive. However, they still do not realise that they have a secret weapon in Raul; they have threatened his family; it may be wise to reciprocate and take the battle to them.

51

Three men have just witnessed something amazing and are still trying to get their heads around it; then a knock on the door; Jayne enters with two coffees and one tea; she knows it is too early for Don to have coffee. Seeing the discs, she was about to ask when Roger stopped her and took her outside, explaining they would talk about them tonight. Jayne was taken aback by Roger's intervention, but after five years, she should be used to some of its employees' strange behaviour, still raw over the hotel incident. Fifteen minutes later, the men have finished their drinks, and Roger offers to take the cups away, an excuse, all he wants to do is apologise to Jayne, feeling it may have seemed he was aggressive when he took her out of the room. However, love is blind, it seems, as Jayne did not take offence, and she and Anne are looking forward to the night ahead. Roger returns with a laptop, and both men look perplexed; there is no need for one at the moment. Roger tells them the voice in his head has told him to bring it in, and both men are now learning to go with the flow regarding Roger's inner voice. The discs are on the table in random order; as Roger came into the room, Don was about to touch one, but in doing so, the disc created a shield around itself; the more he tried, the stronger it became. Don and Shaun looked shocked, but Roger smiled; he seemed to be in tune with them; he placed the laptop next to them. As soon as he did so, the discs lit up and started to move into a straight line and then interlocked into each other. Then, all lit up brighter than before, a hologram appeared, showing the complete form of a fusion-integrated generator.

Then the laptop automatically switches on, to their surprise, and a drawing appears on the screen; different languages start to scroll down the screen, languages they had never seen before, they assumed could be alien in form. After a few minutes, they can see Chinese, Japanese, and Italian, and then it stops on English, and instructions appear on the screen for the construction of the generator. It gives all the materials required to make the generator from sustainable materials on planet Earth. They look in astonishment as it indicates that they can vary in size, dependent on power requirements from an individual house to a city, all clean air products with no waste, total efficiency at its best. But what are they supposed to do with this technology?

Questions will undoubtedly be asked about how they came by it. They now have a conundrum of epic proportions; who do they talk to? It will disappear forever if they pass it over to the wrong people.

Then the reality of Raul's statement about the cabal in the USA, how big is this cabal, are there different ones in each country, and does their power reach everywhere in society, or could it be one singular unit that controls everything financially?

Don advises Roger and Shaun to keep quiet for now, and they have a lot of soul-searching to do. However, they have a solution to climate change if they can get the right people to help. At times, the world's climate activists sound more like they have been drip-fed information in a dark room. But, rightly or wrongly, they are desperate to save their children's future if the information is accurate. After all, there are two sides to a story, and forming factions trying to create disorder in society, could create a backlash from the public.

But people can be easily motivated if fear is the key; if their leaders are strong enough, many followers do not ask questions but blindly follow over the abyss, as in any cult, commonsense is long gone. Most people who are questioned about their cause deliver the same monotone rhetoric, as though they have all been taught in the same room or radicalised by the same video online. These people mean well, but when they try to force their ideology upon other individuals who do not believe, they will not listen to the other person's point of view. The rhetoric they deliver will inevitably create panic in the oil and gas industries, driving up prices and the money men get large-scale profits. These people have not done anything, but they sit back in their ivory towers and wait for the money to come into their pockets. The obvious question is, who started the rhetoric? Nobody knows, but a well-paid think tank subsidised by unknown benefactors might be a starting point.

But the revelation that Don, Shaun and Roger have uncovered might be enough to bring the world order back in line if they can reach the right people. But, unfortunately, there will be dark forces who will stop at nothing to control the world and stop the world from getting free and clean electricity.

Don tells Shaun and Roger 'that another two days won't matter,' giving him time to think things through and hopefully find a solution. They agree and get up to leave, thinking they will have a couple of days free; how wrong they could be; Don tells them to sit down, and both look at each other, surprised, as Don passes over a file they have a job to do, it is back to normality it seems.

Don smiled when he gave them the file, as our intrepid investigators were going to check out a sighting of an unknown creature. Don rang the front desk, and Anne answered, 'hello, P.H. Enomenon can I help,' forgetting it was an internal phone, embarrassed when Don spoke. Then Jayne saw the disappointment on her face when Don asked her to arrange three bookings for Shaun, Roger and himself on a flight to Edinburgh on the company jet, 'Also, please arrange for a hire vehicle, preferably an SUV, where we are going; we will need one.' Jayne and Anne were devastated; they had made arrangements for a special anniversary meal, a surprise because they had been going out for four weeks. When the three men came out of the conference room ten minutes later, Roger and Shaun could see something was wrong with Jayne and Anne. Apologising but telling them they will make it up to them when they get back, telling them to book a table for four at Fortunelli, the upmarket Italian restaurant, the women appeased they left on a brighter note. The file given to Shaun and Roger was only thirty minutes old, which was the best indicator that an urgent response was needed. Roger glanced briefly at it, knowing Don was coming with them; it must be important to him. They only have two hours before they board the plane; Don decides he will drive them to the airport, and Shaun asks to look at the file, wanting to see what it was that had put a stop to their current situation. They were going to a farm on the outskirts of Edinburgh, and reports of livestock disappearing and mutilation; local police have ruled out poachers and think it could be devil worshippers, but with no witnesses, they need specialist help.

After reading it out to Don and Roger, he saw that it was different with Don. With their newfound abilities, Shaun and Roger have already picked up; there is something personal with this case.

As they arrive at the airport, Don drives into the lower ground parking area, strangely a personal space for the company vehicle; Roger and Shaun keep silent; they do not know about this company perk. They then went straight through customs, a high-level phone call can do that for you, and they board the small twenty-seater jet; now Roger and Shaun know this is important for Don; they are the only passengers on the plane. The pilot tells them to fasten their seat belts and that they will be in Edinburgh in two hours. As soon as they level off, cruising at twenty-five thousand feet, Don turns to them, tells the story of his son Bob and his colleague Pam Little, and shows them the Devil's Hole incident video.

Both were shocked at what they saw and now realise that Don needs closure for the loss of his son and Pam Little. Landing at the airport, they are rushed through baggage reclaim and are directed to the car hire company; only a signature is required, and they are given the keys to the hire car. Don was silent up to this point, but as soon as they got in the vehicle, he discussed what could happen if this creature was what he thought it was. Shaun was the designated driver and had been given the address, and the sat nav indicated a thirty-five-minute journey time. Don explained that he hoped their new abilities would help solve this riddle once and for all. Inside Roger and Shaun's minds, they hoped so as well; after a short while, they pulled off the motorway onto an (A) road and five minutes later, they turned onto a farm track.

A sense of excitement more intense than usual, the hairs on the back of their necks stand up, a sure sign they are close to something out of the ordinary.

A phone call to the farmer who owned the property they were coming and asked if he could give them access to the barn, all so similar for Don, pictures in his head of that fateful day, anger now building inside him. The farmer informed them that he dared not go near the barn; the way his animals were butchered frightened him; it was inhumane they were torn apart. They can see the farmhouse half a mile ahead and to the left, a large barn, dating back several years, an uncanny resemblance to the barn his son was killed. Memories of that day are getting clearer now, and Roger and Shaun can sense it; this is out of character for Don; in many ways, this could jeopardise their chances of resolving this problem. As they get nearer, Don takes a gun out of his briefcase, surprising the intrepid investigators; never in all their previous enquiries had there been the requirement for a weapon. Then on reflection, what they saw in the video was no ordinary creature; both talking in their minds, they thought a gun would not bring this creature down. The sun is setting behind the barn, casting a long shadow across the farmhouse; the temperature is a warm twenty-six degrees as they drive up to the barn. They all take a deep sigh just before they get out of the SUV; even with the sun's warmth, all feel a cold chill, and the hairs rise on their arms; they are about to enter the unknown, but now is not the time for any faint hearts. They move toward the barn, and Don, with weapon in hand, opens the right-hand door, stiff due to lack of maintenance over the years.

It creaks loudly, the main reason the farmer did not oil the hinges; it was his alarm that someone was going inside. On entering, they see one mutilated cow.

The animal was torn apart for a feeding frenzy, and blood was everywhere. As they enter the barn, the lighting is dim; without saying anything, Shaun can hear Roger in his head, 'why the hell are these adventures in dimly lit places, for God's sake.' Shaun nods over to him, and this could be a waste of time, both thinking, 'whatever it is, it won't wait for an invite; it could be gone by now.'

Don finally speaks, 'if this thing is true to form, he will come back again; it tends to stay for twenty-four hours, then moves on.'

'How do you know that, sir.' from Shaun.

'I have documentation from all over Europe, several cases, always twenty-four hours; that is why we needed to be here now, or it will be gone again.'

Roger asks, 'What do you think it is, sir.'

'I don't think you would believe me, and it is only conjecture on my part.'

Simultaneously, both men said, 'carry on, sir.'

Don, for once, ignored the annoyance of them talking together but carried on, 'sightings started in Russia around 1992 and gradually spread across Europe, where most attacks happened, but unsure how it got into the United Kingdom. But through logical reasoning, I think it is a mutation from the Chernobyl radiation fallout.'

'Good grief, what do we do with it if it comes, sir,' from both men.

'There is always a fear that if it cannot find livestock, it will attack more people; unfortunately, my son and Pam were its first human victims that I know of, in the wrong place at the wrong time, so we must destroy it.

The feeding frenzy seems to last twenty-four hours, and then it goes quiet for weeks, it seems to hibernate then moves on, so it is not tracked.'

'What do you suggest in the meantime,' from Shaun

'Sit in the shadows and wait, eyes open; this creature is fast and with minimal sound.' The sun is setting outside, and the long shadows have disappeared. Two hours have passed, and the heat has started to dissipate from the building. All hope this is not a waste of time, and the lighting seems to be dimmer by the minute. It is dark outside as Don opens the barn door; looking out, he can see a clear night sky, no clouds; it is a full moon, ominous, to say the least; another deep sigh from him. When the barn door opened, a sensor switched on, an outside floodlight shining brightly into the barn just as the floor opened up. Then to their shock and awe, three creatures emerged from the hole, one heading directly for Don, he fired his weapon, but the creature was still coming at him. Roger instinctively puts his hand up, and the creature stops, unable to move; Roger has created a force shield around it, and it screams in pain as Roger closes his hand; when he closes his hand, the creature is slowly being crushed by the shield. Don, now grateful he had brought them along, Shaun had copied Roger's lead, and the screams were so high pitched it was hurting their ears, but they all knew they had to kill them for everyone's safety. The men look at the bodies; they can see that these were human beings once in their lives through their deformities.

Still staring, they hear a noise behind them as the first creature turns over, and in his dying breath, he says 'thank you.' They all look at each other and, with a tinge of sadness, realise that they have released them from their torment. They cannot let anybody see them; more questions will be asked; Don suggests that they bury them in the hole they came from, all evidence is gone, and they take pictures for their files, hoping no one will see them. It is a moment in time they will never forget, etched in their minds for a lifetime. Two hours later, Don tells the farmer that all is well and there should be no more incidents, the farmer wants answers, but Don explains he could not give him that information, 'let's just say it is over.' As they are about to get into the car to leave, staring at the full moon, Roger comments, 'eerie, isn't it,' they all agree this is a night to forget. Shaun drives to the hotel Anne had booked; it was only fifteen minutes away, but no time for a meal, so curry for all before they get to the hotel.

When Don gets into his room, he collapses on the bed, 'We got them, Bob, rest in peace,' not questioning Shaun and Rogers's abilities, happy they had them; fate is a strange thing, as he drifts to sleep, years of emotion finally released.

52

As time passes on E2, Xylens underground movement is gaining an unprecedented following, word of mouth spreading quickly, while the commissioners in the tower look down on the populist. Unfortunately, they are unaware of how things are about to change, not necessarily for the better. A certain amount of free speech can create derision between different thought groups. Surprisingly the commissioners have not given any thought to the situation; if the populist stopped taking the nutrients, years of this repetition broken in an instant, what the effect would be. Zone by zone, the populists are throwing their tablets away; they feel different, invigorated by a new thought process they have never felt before. Conversations are changing, and arguments they have never had but feel it is the right to state their point of view. The commissioners do not have an army to quell such dissent and have never needed them; the nutrients were their army of choice, complete control. So the anarchy will come slowly hidden behind walls, secret meetings to decide who will lead the new world movement, and as always, it will be a quiet lifeform they did not expect. It will be a slow-burn situation until the right fuel ignites the fire of resentment. But Xylens will find a problem with this new world, his race, like the human race, will start to argue and fight, and a second Earth of constant descent will be formed. Many will change their personalities, some good, some bad; Nyle will have many new allies, and he will become the leader of a terrorist organisation. Like on Earth, the constant struggle between good and evil will begin, and E2 will change forever.

Nyle's euphoria is reaching new highs as his killing spree is escalating; no one has raised any questions about these regular deaths, and even the commissioners are inexperienced in such matters. They do not know how to respond to this unprecedented situation. Yet, strangely through this euphoria,

Nyle has realised that his transition started on the spacecraft and has put two and two together, that Earth food was his saviour. However, even though he has registered that it might not be the same for all, he decides to experiment with his two neighbours, remembering the transition was short indeed. First, a visit to Xylens, hoping he still has some remnants left; a couple of hours later, he is in deep discussions with Xylens, asking if he has expanded on the talks they had while in space. Feeling what they went through together has formed an unbroken bond, and they open up feeling free in themselves and looking forward to a different future ahead. However, even though the conversation was enlighting, both held back on their true feelings, not realising that they would become bitter enemies in the future; amazing what free thought can give you. It is getting dark when he leaves Xylens, both happy with the outcome of their discussions; Nyle says his goodbye, glad he has left with the last bag of salt and vinegar crisps, looking forward to his new task. With the night falling, Nyle should be eager for his next kill, but his mind is elsewhere, looking forward to seeing the change in his neighbours or was it just him who was affected?

Nyle has now found that if his mind is distracted, the urge to kill is suppressed; he is unsure if he likes this situation.

When he arrives home, he looks in the bag of crisps, remembering how tiny the morsel was that changed his life. Nyle can see the potential of hundreds of new colleagues and the fight against the authoritarian rulers holding them back. He waits for his neighbours to arrive home from their mundane jobs and invites them into his apartment. Offering them some drinks, he sits them down, and they talk about his adventure in space and his visit to another planet and how brave he was; they could not do that; nutrients can do that to you, he thought. Then Nyle explains about the food from planet Earth, which he enjoyed. Would they like to try some? The neighbours look at each other, their eyes widen, 'why not,' and they take a tiny piece of the crisp each; both wince at the taste, as did Nyle and fall asleep. Not long later, they both awake seconds apart and agree it was incredible, but they feel different as their brains start to open up and years of regressed information come through. Finally, they look at Nyle, who explains what has happened, and they must tell him as soon as possible; if their emotions change, he can help because it has happened to him. His neighbours leave still on a high, their feelings changing constantly; these two will not hear the frequency hum tonight. They will be awake all night, their minds seeing things they have never seen before but are they fact or fiction? They will need to speak to Nyle urgently tomorrow. The rest of Nyle's family have gone to work; they have done the same tedious routine for so many years; they do not think anymore; everything is like the cog of a machine, nothing out of place. Then, lost in his thoughts, Nyle is brought back to reality by loud banging on his door.

Opening the door, his two neighbours, who are showing signs of anxiety, rush past him; both tell him they have feelings they have never had before, and they do not know what to do. So Nyle sits them down, telling them to calm down and speak one at a time; he must understand what troubles them.

Tyle was the first to speak, explaining all this information in his head; he could not get his head around it, but worst of all, the feeling he wanted to harm someone, a feeling he had never felt before, it is so intense. Lyne, the other neighbour, confirms he has violent thoughts and expresses the same feelings. Deep inside, Nyle is elated, he now has two new subjects to nurture and control, but his control is different to the commissioners or is it a narcissistic sociopath that thinks like that?

Nyle confidently confides in them, telling them that thousands of years of repressed anger is coming out in them, and what they now feel is natural; this was how their forebearers were. It was like a rallying call to bear arms to his two new followers; what do they do next?

Nyle explains that they must kill someone; he looks for any hesitation, but there is none; in the back of his mind, it is already telling him he will enjoy the next few months recruiting his new followers. Tyle and Lyne are now feeling that rush, and like wild animals baying for blood, they want to go now in daylight; Nyle now must teach them the art of control, 'saying the rush is better if you wait.' They are agitated, and self-control will be difficult as the urge is unbelievable; they ask Nyle how long before they can leave. He tells them they will go as soon as night starts to fall, and the window to kill is small; this accelerates the feeling, and the buzz is exhilarating.

A few minutes later, his two new followers are asleep, and soon they will be fresh for a killing frenzy.

53

With all that has gone on in the last few days, Raul and Sara have finally found time to talk about what she witnessed in the carpark and whether she should be frightened. Raul finally tells her about their encounter with Xylens; she does not act surprised, already having recurring dreams which confirm what Raul has told her. But Sara has more news for Raul; she takes him through to the kitchen and sits him down, and this behaviour worries Raul. Sara tells him not to worry, but she can feel her body strangely telling her that her pregnancy will be shorter than nine months, and she feels it could be six months. Raul stares, trying to make sense of this statement. Should he laugh or cry, then the sudden realisation that Sara could be carrying an alien lifeform, she must get scans, but they cannot leave due to the cabals vendetta against them. Sara gently holds Raul's hand, placing a finger on his lips, 'shush, I am not worried; honestly, everything will be okay; we do not need scans believe me.'

Raul already knows that when Sara's mind is made up, she will not back down, and he admires her for that; she is his backbone. So he accepts her decision, but the thought of a life of running from the cabal is deep in his thoughts; they must find a way to end this nightmare. Nobody has the right to decide who lives and dies; Raul's anger is building; he needs to talk to the General; Raul has an idea and hopes he will agree to his suggestion. He talks to her in her mind so no one can hear; Raul is finding another benefit of his skillset, and he explains that he must face this problem head-on, or more people will die.

Raul leaves Sara and walks across the compound, heading toward General Bright's office, and on the way, he sees Lt Dicks; he runs to him, more spritely than Raul used to be, taken aback at how quick he is; he can sense danger. He was never a true athlete in the sense of the word; he liked to watch rather than participate.

But another surprise is that his fitness levels are improving without training, and his body is gradually changing within. Lt Dicks, looked astonished at the speed as he approached; many men twenty years younger could not do it, 'he must be in peak condition,' he thought. They started to talk, and after a few seconds, Raul suddenly pushed him away, a sniper bullet passed the point that Dicks was standing, and a fellow soldier fell to the floor twenty metres away. Luckily the soldier was only wounded, but Dicks would have been killed. Dicks picked himself up and went to grab Raul, waiting for the next shot; then Raul told him, 'it will be okay; I have dealt with it.'With a half-hearted laugh, Dicks exasperated, 'what the hell does that mean, Raul? What are you saying? What Dicks did not see was that Raul's reflexes were instantaneous; as Dicks fell to the floor when in danger, his senses become fine-tuned, his hearing, peripheral vision, and whatever was needed at the time to help him. Even to the point, he could see the bullet coming as if in slow motion. Then with the flick of his wrist, a power surge followed the bullet's trajectory back to the sniper's rifle; it exploded in his face; Raul heard the screams half a mile away. Raul tells Dicks he cannot explain, but he will find the sniper at these coordinates, Dicks is taken aback at how precise the location is, but Raul is not so surprised now.

Raul has finally accepted the gifts that Xylens has given him, and it is time to help everybody else.

As a medic tends to the wounded soldier, Raul and Dicks head toward Bright's office and before reaching it, Dicks sends two military police officers to locate the unfortunate sniper. They will return in under an hour, but the sniper is unrecognisable, his face destroyed by the rifle explosion, another life lost to rich men's folly, and wanting to control the world.

In Bright's office, three men agree that enough is enough, and they must act now; Bright and Dicks are astonished at what Raul is offering, but they feel the risk is too great. Raul reminds them that a dead sniper will be here shortly; these people are trying to kill us one by one, and we will not be able to live a normal life.

They have changed my life forever; a few weeks ago, I had a quiet, uneventful life, and now I have killed people I do not know. Finally, they agree to Raul's plan, and Bright makes the call to Moreno for a temporary truce; Moreno can see by the number on his mobile phone that it is Bright. Still annoyed after the last conversation, he hesitated to answer, but curiosity can kill you, even for a wealthy man in a stately manor.

'What the hell do you want, Bright.'

'A truce; too many people are dying, Moreno, mostly your men.'

'No.'

'Not even if I can give you the man in the video.'

A pause and Bright could virtually hear the cogs in Moreno's head turning, 'why would you give him to me.'

'Self-preservation, one man's life against hundreds, do the maths, man.'

'Will you deliver him to me?'

'No, he will come voluntarily.'

'What's the catch, Bright.'

'He wants to explain what happened to all of you, for you to understand how and why it happened, to stop this madness, that is all; he will meet all of you anywhere you want.'

'I will ring you back, and I have calls to make; my colleagues have empires to run; it will be tomorrow,' abruptly ending the conversation.

Bright issues a half smile, 'he will try to take you out into the countryside, no witnesses; I am confident he will try to kill you.'

Raul shakes his head, 'no, it will be where he feels safe, his own home, with plenty of security.'

'Why are you so sure about that,' from Dicks

'Let us say; I got inside his head.'

Bright and Dicks shake their heads in disbelief, now happy this unusual man is on their side, hoping this personality change will not get out of hand. But in many ways, their hands will be clean if an investigation occurs from any judicial system. Raul senses their concerns and tells them he wants a quiet life to raise his family without fear. Three hours later, Bright receives a text from Moreno; they will meet tomorrow at eleven p.m. at his home. While Bright and Dicks are pleased it could be over soon, they are worried for Raul's welfare, and the security will be intense. He will be watched all the way to the door, and a full body search will occur. Then Raul tells them they cannot strip search his mind, his weapon of varying abilities, which he does not fully understand. Then Raul explains he does not want them anywhere near Moreno's home.

The least contact, the better; there should be no dots to connect to anyone else, Raul's confidence is growing by the day, and for the first time in his life, he is looking forward to his fight for freedom.

54

The paranormal investigators have just woken from a restless night for two, finding the day before a memorable event for all the wrong reasons. While in separate rooms, Shaun and Roger had a mind call during the night, still trying to come to terms with these abilities they had been blessed with or could it become a curse in the future?

They drift asleep; Don has had the best night's sleep for many years, refreshed; they meet in the restaurant for breakfast; as Don enters, the two men stare at him; he immediately checks his zip fly, not that he usually leaves them open. Roger and Shaun start to laugh; Don strolls toward them, and he asks, 'what is it.'

Both in unison, 'Your hair, boss.' Don is taken aback,

'My hair, what's wrong.'

In unison again, Don was about to shout in the crowded restaurant, 'what about my hair, you pair of idiots.'

'The grey hair has gone; your trade mark as gone, boss.'

'Is that all,' now calmed down, Don realised that his constant reminder of Bob was gone; sad and happy at the same time, he told them to 'eat up; we have a plane to catch.' So Shaun drives to the airport; there is no conversation between them; the plane is waiting for them, and they are in the air for ten minutes when Don breaks his silence about the evening before. Firstly, he asked how they could do these impossible things, how do your bodies feel, are you in pain, 'and for God's sake, do not talk together.' Both men look at him, unaware that they talk in unison at times; Roger speaks first, 'when we were in Haltwhistle, Xylens said we would each have a gift, but we did not realise as to what extent.'

Shaun tells Don, 'we do not feel anything; everything is reactionary; all I can say is our brains seem to go into autopilot and adjusts our body to meet the problem. Roger and I think our bodies go into protection mode to help others; that's the only way we can describe this gift, sir.'

'Okay, when we get back, we will need to get on with our regular duties and a unique problem to solve, our predicament with the discs; if you have any ideas, I will listen to your proposals.' Before they land, Roger is busy making notes; Don assumes he is finalising the report for yesterday's event, so he does not ask any questions.

Landing in London, the three men go to the underground carpark to pick up the company vehicle and head back to the office; the paperwork must be finished in this computer world. Shaun always smirked when they did this, wondering how many trees in the amazon had fallen for this mountain of paper. However, two young women were delighted when the men walked through the front door, a bunch of flowers laid on their desks, sent by two admirers. Don tries to think, when did they find the time during the day to do that, memories of his youth and the good times he and his wife had. He will give them a few minutes to re-acquaint themselves before he joyfully bellows from the conference room, 'time for work, boys.'

With their love lives back on track, Shaun and Roger enter the conference room and sit opposite Don; a knock on the door and afternoon tea arrives, courtesy of Jayne and Anne. The men had forgotten time was passing, and they must find an answer to their dilemma, and in frustration, Don says, 'we don't go home till we have a solution.'

Roger and Shaun looked at each other, wondering when they would see Jayne and Anne; another disappointment would ruin everything. But, once again, raging hormones trigger the thought process; Roger takes the discs from the drawer of the side table, left there for safety reasons; anything could have happened in Edinburgh. He placed the discs on the table; Don and Shaun looked at Roger, knowing he was zoned into the discs, an ability he only seemed to have. They did not say anything, entranced by Roger as he placed the discs randomly on the table. Then smiling, he looked up from the discs and explained the most straightforward answer was staring us in the face. Don and Shaun look with open mouths, 'what's so funny,' from Don.

'It was said in the field in Haltwhistle, and I cannot remember who, Joanne, I think.'

'For God's sake, spit it out, man,' Don started to get annoyed at Roger.

'We e-mail every newspaper worldwide with all the plans and information to build the generator.'

'What the hell are you mad, Roger? It's insane, if not impossible.'

'We have these discs, and they will do it for us, sir.'

'But how? They will trace it back to us.'

'Believe me, sir; they won't if we trust the discs.'

'Good grief, man, you sound like a delusional cult leader.'

'If we can look at the bigger picture, sir.'

'What do you mean? I want to believe you.' Shaun jumped in, 'so do I, Rog; what is it you see that we cannot.'

'In all honesty, it is trust; we have been given an opportunity to help save our planet, and with the gifts that Xylens has given us, it is as though the discs are telling me what to do.'

'I'm sceptical, but at a loss to another solution, carry on Roger,' from Don

'Yes, sir,' Roger gave him the broadest smile, then strangely, after Don gave him permission, the discs re-aligned and locked together. The computer automatically turns on again, as if the discs were listening, and to everyone's surprise, there is a prompt on the screen. Again different languages scroll down the screen till it stops at English; Don and Shaun look at Roger, perplexed that he is just staring blankly at the screen. Don was about to speak, and Roger raised his hand for him to stop; a few seconds later, he apologised to him; he was listening to the discs. Both men stare at Roger in disbelief, thinking now he must be going mad; Don thinks, 'no change there, then, but I must trust him after all they have gone through recently.'

Roger starts to type at a speed both men had not seen before; within seconds, he has described the generator to its full extent and cost benefits to the planet. Again, a knowledge he did not have, it flowed without him thinking; the discs took over his thoughts, telling him what to write. The two men look in astonishment yet again; Roger has surprised them with his belief in these discs; they both ask to read his transcript. They were taken aback by its detail and the truth that it was from an alien planet, worried by our decline into oblivion. It was their last resort to help the human race survive, begging us to try this new energy source.

It could save the planet by reducing the requirement of fossil fuels, which they realise is still required, but in minimum amounts. Also, this would stop the monetisation of their energy source if everyone knew about the availability. Then Roger told Don that it would speed up production worldwide, reducing the need for fossil fuels; it was a win-win situation either way. Then Roger asked them to hold hands; Don and Shaun stared in surprise, 'we need to contact Raul; he needs to know now what the discs were all about,' both men agreed.

Raul is preparing himself for a task he would never have thought he was capable of; he and Sara are having breakfast in the room the General kindly provided. Sara could see a change in Raul's face, and he raised his hand so she did not interrupt him. Sara could tell by the changes on his face Raul was talking by thought to someone but who, just a little oddity that he forgot to tell her about his transatlantic friends. Ten minutes pass, and like any woman, she needs to know what he is talking about and to whom. The mind conversation ends, and Raul returns to the breakfast table; astounded at the revelation of an alien fusion generator, he speaks to Sara through his mind; nobody must hear what he has to say. Sara and Raul are excited by this; should they tell anybody else? Raul has asked Roger to hold back till tomorrow, he has something to do first, and the information could affect the outcome with dire consequences.

The three men break hands, wondering what Raul needs to do that requires a twenty-four-hour reprieve.

55

Nyle wakes his two new apprentices, two disciples that will obey his every word, and he will control them by fear; after all, a message to the tower and they will die. All information is hidden, only to be found if something happens to him; Nyle learnt the art of coercion, picked up from reading the papers Xylens had given him, and he liked this thing called control.

Tyle and Lyne are instantly awake, their emotions all too clear to see, both more aggressive and worrying for Nyle; they are like wild animals. So dangerously, he assumes it is the rush for that first kill, and he will watch, always ready in case he needs to retaliate, now realising being in the same bed as others can be both good and menacing. He calms them down and needs to show he is their mentor and controller, not to question anything he says, a challenge he will excel in. Nyle tells them to breathe slowly, slowing their heart rates until they need the strength to kill. Looking out of the window, daylight is falling; Nyle is already starting to feel the rush, and his two apprentices get to their feet; they want to run, but Nyle holds them back. He tells them 'time is on their side and; controlling their emotions will give them the biggest high they will ever feel.'

They leave Nyle's apartment, and he has decided to keep it close to home for their first kill; he is going to take them to zone two; Tyle and Lyne suddenly stop as they reach the borderline between zone's one and two. Nyle looks at his disciples in shock. Has he lost control already but still dormant in their minds?

They are not allowed to move between zones, a problem Nyle did not foresee.

He now realises that his movement could be short-lived. Moreover, it will most likely draw attention to zone one, something he does not want. Then his baying hounds see a lone figure who had stepped out to see the beauty of the night sky, one moon directly ahead and the other slightly smaller one behind him. The figure silhouetted against the backdrop of the moon, Nyle instructs Tyle what to do; to kill the unsuspecting being. It was over in an instant, Tyle snapping his neck just like Nyle had done before him. He turns to Lyne, wanting to shout; the exhilaration is indescribable, this making Lyne agitated; he must have that feeling. Nyle realises he must find another victim quickly, feeling Lyne will get out of control; then, as if fate was on his side, another victim came into view, the other body lying on the ground.

Lyne will kill him with a knife, just as Nyle had done; Lyne explains to all that he has found a new vocation and meaning to live life to the fullest extent. Nyle now realises he can get the same buzz watching a kill and not doing the deed. Finally, the triumphant trio head home, the disciples asking why Nyle had not killed anyone; it is called control, to know when and when not to kill. But Nyle must find a way to increase his fold; in many ways, he is now learning to become a problem solver. His brain now has to work; differently, he looks for inspiration in his new bibles, the newspapers from Earth. There before him a solution, he will become the first lower-level being to start a lucrative business; as the free new world grows, there will be beings who need a solution to a problem to remove a political opponent, for example. He will recruit individuals with the same mindset and oversee them as a silent leader.

He will get reimbursement for their work, and a new social order is starting. Nyle will form a new business model, a (franchise to kill.) It only takes a small virus to cause a pandemic, as more lifeforms are infected in different ways, some good, some bad. They could never lie; the truth was their bi-word until they tried the crisps. The political structure will move fast as Nyle goes from zone to zone, gaining believers in the new world and grasping this new freedom with both hands.

Further afield, Xylens congregation finds new believers quickly, and in the large tower, Commissioner Grohl is still oblivious to the tidal of discourse heading his way. They have not had any disruption in thousands of years, and there was never a need to look at the lower-level subordinates. The nutrients are their saviour, and why should anyone stop taking them? The fallout was due to the self-righteous commissioners living above the populist, not knowing what was happening below their feet. They cannot think for themselves; everyone is in their place, and nothing is wrong. The hardest part of a growing movement is secrecy. With other beings realising they have a voice, suddenly, new politics started on E2; these new politics will rip out the heart of E2 with constant derision, splinter factions constantly springing up as the youth finds a voice. The once-perfect planet will change forever, and more urgently, they will need the introduction of policing to control the violence, E2 now becoming a second Earth. They will be overthrown, and a new political era will be born, and in the distant future, that visit to that insignificant planet Earth will be their demise.

As the political structure evolves, Xylens will become the Prime Minister of E2, but he will be in a constant battle to find Nyle's hideout, who is bringing new brutality to E2. Xylens will need to learn quickly to be dogmatic in his belief, as complacency will be his downfall. He will find that this freewill he has learnt on Earth will be his biggest burden of all

56

After his mind call with his allies in the United Kingdom, Raul goes to see the General and Lt Dicks before he leaves to go to Moreno's abode. Both think he wants to run over any possible scenarios that might happen at Moreno's property. They cannot believe what Raul has been told, what this chaos is all about and why Xylens destroyed his craft. Both being military, they can understand, but on the other hand, they need to be one step ahead of their enemy. Always in hindsight now, wishing they could have communicated with the lifeform, giving it a personal name did not seem right to them. But when Raul told them that the fusion generator would be known worldwide and the main reason Xylens came to Earth was to save us seventy-five years ago. Raul told them that his new transatlantic friends were doing this to try and break the cabals' power, controlling the world's money. Bright is now apologetic about what they might have done to Xylens, this constant suspicious nature of the human race, as they let them down again and again. To shoot before you ask questions, always the aggressor, never wanting solutions, wanting to be the winner at all costs. Bright sits back in his chair, hoping Raul will come out of this alive; in that instant, he decides it is time to retire and give his family the quality time they deserve. Finally, Bright gives him the address of Moreno's home, only ninety minutes away; it will give him time to compose himself; Raul has a self-confidence he has not known before. Moreno's fellow board members live far and wide; three have flown in the night before, and the final two are within a four-hour radius.

To be in this select group, dedication to power and money is uppermost in your mindset; nothing else matters. All their wives have a similar mentality, and few marry for love; money is their husband with no right of reply. However, with this extraordinary board meeting, their wives are willing travellers; there will be an after-party to celebrate, and food and drink so expensive that to ordinary working people, it is repulsive. The servants have set two tables for breakfast in separate rooms, one for the women and the other for the men to make crucial decisions, mainly how to dispose of Raul and his colleagues. They have a sniper in the woods surrounding the house; all it will take is a call as he leaves the house, and once again, life is cheap, not as valuable as money. Thirty minutes away, Raul is aware he is going into danger; his senses are starting to tingle; what he is about to do, Raul will have to bear for the rest of his life. Can he carry that burden? Only time will tell.

Raul finally reaches the end of the driveway, his sat-nav still indicating one mile to go. He turns to the left, and the driveway is pristine. The lawns are picture perfect, not a blade of grass out of place, and he can see two gardeners tending to flower beds; then he thought, 'I hope they are real gardeners.'

Half a mile to go, he could see a building, not a house; it was so big it could have been a hotel. Thinking, 'this is what money can give you, unbelievable,' trying not to be jealous. But this has been handed down through generations of greed, taught from childhood what wealth can give you, but best of all, the power you have to keep it all if you have no conscious. Strangely a similarity to the commissioners on a far-distant planet.

Raul can see an abundance of expensive limousines, a central water feature in a roundabout, with jets firing water into the air; Raul pulls up, four security guards come from hidden spaces and his vehicle is surrounded. Staring at several guns, he smiles; shaking his head, Raul opens his car door, stepping out with his hands in the air. Two men robustly search him for weapons, thinking to himself, 'if they only knew what he was capable of.'

In his acute peripheral vision, Raul noticed a movement in a tree to his right, a picture instantly in his mind, a sniper positioned in a tree; he flicks his wrist, and the sniper floors to the ground dead.

Two guards guide him to the house while the others search his car for a bomb, inside and out. Then, walking up the six steps, one security guard speaks into his collar, and the large front door glides open; another guard greets him, no words spoken. As he walks in, he can see a large central staircase; on the first floor; it runs left to right to separate wings. The foyer has solid marble floors, which looked unbroken; an Italian master tiler was brought in from Milan for the installation costing thousands of dollars. Finally, the guard taps him on the shoulder and invites him to a large dining room that could have been a dance hall; Moreno signals the guard to shut the door on the way out. Six arrogant men stare down at him, one exclaiming, 'this is the imbecile that has caused our problem.'

'Raul Rodriquez at your service, gentlemen,' smiling after this statement, annoying all six men.

Moreno jumped from his chair, 'why have you come here, Rodriquez? What do you hope to achieve.'

'To tell you what happened and to stop these crazy attempts on innocent people's lives is that too much to ask.'

'You must be a fool to come here alone.'

'I have nothing to hide. Would you like to hear what happened to me that has got you so mad?'

'You have cost us billions of dollars in lost revenue.'

'Is that what this is all about? Money lives lost because you lost a few dollars, anyway, it was not me technically.'

Moreno looks at his colleagues, 'what the hell is that supposed to mean.'

'Do you want to know or not.'

'I cannot believe your arrogance. Do you know how powerful we are? We can snuff you out like a candle in the wind.'

'Arrogance can be a two-way street Moreno; nine lives lost because of your lust for money and power.'

'Who the hell do you think you are.'

'By the look of it, a simple physicist is getting under your skin,' Raul's actions have surprised even him. Moreno's face was now red with anger when one of his colleagues came over to calm him down. Eli Johnson, the owner of two large oil companies and one high-tech silicon valley start-up company, turned to Raul, 'the floor is yours; tell us what happened then.'

Raul tells them his story, knowing it will not go any further when this day is over; the six look at him already he can tell they do not believe him. Then the wanton sarcasm about little green men started to irritate him, as there were still remnants of Xylens brain inside Raul. Then the accusation was that he was the man to blame for everything and would pay for his actions.

'So you would kill an innocent man because you lost money without proof.'

'Oh, we have proof, you idiot.'

'That would be.' Raul knew about the USB and needed to destroy it before he could carry on with his plan. Then stupidly, with bravado, Moreno pulls the USB from his pocket, condescendingly waving it in front of Raul.

'That could be any rubbish; prove it; let me see what you think you have on me.'

Moreno and his colleagues are annoyed at what they can see as delaying tactics before the inevitable, knowing once he leaves, he will be a dead man.

'You are accusing me based on what you think you have seen on that USB, and in my defence, I would like to see it, so humour me, please.'

Moreno shouted to one of his staff to bring his computer, returning moments later with it. Moreno places the USB in the computer, and the staff member leaves. Then, turning the computer on, he selects the file he requires, turning the laptop to face Raul and sighs in disbelief, thinking this is a waste of time.

As soon as the USB was installed, Raul automatically deleted the file, now liking these abilities even more. But, surprising him, once again, his brain is scanning the computer and has found damning information, which Bright could use for the benefit of all.

'I don't see anything, so you are looking for a scapegoat, no matter who.'

'What the hell are you talking about, arsehole,' turning the laptop around, he sees a blank screen; he howls obscenities at Raul, more annoyed at him, laughing at them. 'that is impossible; what have you done?

'I'm over here; how could I do anything? I came to prove my innocence.'

'I don't understand it; how? Then he automatically blames Lt Dicks; he must have done something to it.'

'Before I go, please invite your wives in.'

'What the hell are you playing at, Rodriquez.'

'I would like to show them something; believe me, it will be worth your while.'

Johnson jumps into the conversation, 'let's get it over with, Moreno; the sooner he leaves, the better for all.'

Moreno calls his servant, and three minutes later, six women enter the room, surprised to be summoned by their husbands. They look at Raul, wondering why their husbands would entertain somebody obviously not of their money status, looking at his attire. Moreno's wife is as obnoxious as he is Jolene, demanding to know who the low life is in front of them. A wry smile from Raul,

'I am probably your worse nightmare.'

'What is that supposed to mean,' looking over to her husband, he shrugs his shoulders, more interested in Raul's boldness, standing in front of the most powerful men in America.

Raul turns to Jolene, 'I came here to prove my innocence, but your better halves have decided that I must die when I leave, but the sniper is already dead,' turning to Moreno, 'try ringing him if you like he won't answer.' He fumbles with his phone; it finally rings; straight to answerphone, he throws the phone across the room.

'How did you know? You could not know.'

'Firstly, it seems your wives are not blind to how your fortunes are made, living off your wealth, covered in blood.'

'Who do you think you are, you moron? No one speaks to our wives like that.'

Raul shouts at Moreno to be quiet and listen, 'I have told you the truth, but you laughed in my face and came after all our families; you do not have the right to pick and choose if someone lives or dies.' Johnson and the rest tried to attack him; Raul raised his hand they could not move. With the other hand, he freezes the wives; all cannot speak; he goes to the top of the table and turns to them.

'You laughed at me when I told you what happened; you ridiculed me about little green men, but in all of us, there is a little bit of alien, a genetic marker installed thousands of years ago, some stronger than others. But the point I am trying to make is you must lose something to appreciate it, and you are willing to kill for greed; it is time to lose something now.' Raul closes his left hand, and the six women die instantly; the men scream silently, no sound from them, tears falling down their faces.

'Now you know what it is like to lose someone you care for, and you are not God; I will leave here alive, and all of you will make a substantial donation to the Roswell Military Foundation for all their work for humankind. General Bright will be most thankful for your kind and unexpected generosity. Then, with the others still motionless, he releases Moreno, who falls to his knees, and the once arrogant man begs for mercy for him and his colleagues.

'Too little too late, Moreno; I am not a fool; our lives would be in constant danger, better to remove the cancer now.

Then, your bodies will disappear, no evidence will be found, and your house will fall around you.'

The fear in their faces is self-evident; knowing they will die, Raul decided it would be best to put them out of their misery now, and with one swift movement of his hand, all were gone, vapourised with no physical evidence. He picks up the computer and heads toward his car; opening the door, he shouts to the security people that Moreno needs to speak to them urgently. When they enter, they are surprised that all the men and women cannot be seen, assuming they are upstairs and courteously wait downstairs. Suddenly the house starts to shake, and the front doors twist; they cannot get out all will perish who are inside. It will take months to find the people inside, and it will be one mystery that people will speculate on, but no answers will be found.

Raul drives away down the pristine drive, the sun shining above in his rearview mirror, a lone cloud in a clear blue sky. Then suddenly, a lightning strike hits the falling house; Raul smiles and lowers the driver's window for some cooling air. His hand dangles outside the window, and then he sees the gardeners rush to a bush. Turning, Raul could see their weapons; with a flick of the hand, both men disappeared. Raul is not proud of what he has done, but when your back is against the wall, the best form of defence is to attack; he looks at the computer, knowing already there will be financial houses worldwide that will collapse when the information is shared.

Raul drives back to the black site hoping never to use these gifts he has been given again, feeling that a significant burden has been released from his shoulders.

57

Jayne and Anne have had a blissful night with their true loves and are thankful that there were no unexpected interruptions; everything is back on track. So much so that there are talks of meeting their parents. To both men, it is monumental in their relationships, and all four decide to walk to the office; nonstop chatter for fifteen minutes, and then they realise they have nearly walked past the office. The ever-present stalwart Don is standing at reception waiting, wanting to get their task over and done with but still waiting for that call from Raul. Then Roger tells everybody that they must get into the conference room; a call is imminent; Don and Shaun should be surprised but are now taking these oddities in their stride. Roger and Shaun kiss the women on their cheeks and walk to the conference room; Roger takes the discs from his safe place and then places them in a line; they automatically connect to each other. The computer turns on, and all the information is on the screen; as they re-read to check it is okay to send, Roger hears Raul's voice in his head; he indicates for all to hold hands, and they listen to Raul. He did not give full details but told them the problem in the USA had been finalised, and all was well to proceed with their project. They thanked him and wished him well, hoping their paths would cross in the future; they bid him farewell. As they disconnected hands, Roger could sense that Don was hesitant, 'what is wrong, sir,' Shaun looked at Roger, taken aback by his remark to Don.

'It's a big decision, and I was thinking last night, are we doing the right thing.'

'Of course, we are, sir.'

'I'm usually good at making these decisions, and it is the first time I'm truly hesitant.'

Shaun interjects, 'sir, after what has happened, the gifts he has given us, I can only see a win-win situation.'

'In the back of my mind, all I can think of is beware of gifts from false prophets, and we know nothing about this alien race.' Don was starting to raise his voice. But, with Don's hesitancy, even Roger is beginning to question himself, looking to Shaun for moral support.

'Sir, this is our last chance; we have an opportunity to help the world survive.'

After a short pause, 'I know what you are saying, and I hope this is one decision I will never regret; press the button, Roger.'

Instantly, Roger pressed the button, and the lights changed from white to blue, then a sense of panic from Don and Shaun; as they were about to speak, Roger raised his hand to stop them. Then, instantly tuning into them again, he told them to wait for two minutes, explaining that more information was coming. While waiting for the information, news outlets receive an epic e-mail. Some will regard it as a hoax, but by the end of the day, TV outlets will be broadcasting a new turning point to a worldwide energy crisis. As usual, there will be scepticism from some, but a space agency will be annoyed that this technology has reached the populist and, more importantly, how did it happen. Only a finite group of people will be happy that all the things they have been through cumulated in this success, deep down now a sense of pride. But greed will try to take over once again; companies will race to patent the engineering, but because it is in the public domain, who was the inventor?

A legal minefield will ensue, and governments will decide to take it over with minimal profit, contracting it out to ethical engineering companies and fast track it out to the populist. A race against time to be the first country to build one, to be logged in the history books for eternity, but the intervention of an alien race will be forgotten.

Two minutes pass, and the blue light gets stronger; then a hologram appears, and to their surprise, an alien apparition introduces himself as Xylens. For the first time in their lives, they have seen the form of an alien lifeform. However, the hologram would only follow after they committed to the fusion generator, and Xylens informs them that four more discs are to be found. They will need the help of a mathematician, and an algorithm will come on the screen, write it down it will disappear in thirty seconds. Xylens carries on and tells them they have five years to solve the algorithm; it will be the locations of the four discs spread around the world. These discs will give them the drawings for a worldwide filtration system that will purify the ozone layer. But if they fail to find them, the ozone layer could reach unrepairable levels. The fusion generators will slow down the pollution, but they must clean the ozone layer to stabilise a new world. Then Xylens explains the other discs were a safety backup, as the fusion generators should have come to fruition seventy-five years ago, but due to the crash, it never happened. The hologram disappears, and the lights return to white and fade away.

The three men look at each other and are shocked at what they have just seen and been told. They will need every ounce of mental and physical strength to achieve this monumental task.

No one knows what the future has to hold for this team to help save the world, but no doubt it will be eventful.

Raul has finally returned to the black site and is immediately requested to go to General Bright's office. As he enters the office, he is fast-tracked to Bright's office, and Dicks is in attendance; Raul explains the difficult decision he had to make so that they could have a normal life. They accept his reasoning, happy they do not need to look over their shoulders anymore and have now made a pact never to talk about it again. However, Bright surprised Dicks, informing him he had requested a retirement package; life is too short after recent events; also, he has put Dicks forward for a substantial promotion. Dicks thanks the General, but in two years, he will retire; drawn into a race against time, he will join up with Bright, Raul and three Englishmen to find some alien artefacts to help save the world.

Raul thanks both men; he and Sara are now free to go home, and all charges against Lee, Compton and Rae have been dropped, and all privileges returned.

Sara will give birth to a boy six months into her pregnancy, his eyes will be slightly bigger than normal, and his brain will be two millimetres bigger, and as he grows, he will tell his parents about visions of a faraway planet with two moons. He will father four more brothers, and a new generation will be formed, and they will form a system of control called the commissioners.

While back on E2, the once stable landscape is constantly changing, with uprisings creating more and more discourse, with the commissioners gradually being overthrown by an unknown virus called humankind.

Discover what happens next…

A Time For Hope

will be available in 2023

* * *

Feel free to contact the author:

dswest62@gmail.com

Available worldwide from Amazon

Michael Terence Publishing

www.mtp.agency

www.facebook.com/mtp.agency

@mtp_agency

Printed in Great Britain
by Amazon

16218114R00161